AN OCEAN OF TIME

KENNEDY KERR

Storm

PUBLISHING

Ebook ISBN: 978-1-83700-377-8
Paperback ISBN: 978-1-83700-379-2

Cover design: Debbie Clement
Cover images: Trevillion

Published by Storm Publishing.
For further information, visit:
www.stormpublishing.co

ALSO BY KENNEDY KERR

Echoes of Cornwall

An Ocean of Longing

Loch Cameron

The Cottage by the Loch

A Secret at the Cottage by the Loch

The Diary from the Cottage by the Loch

A Gift from the Cottage by the Loch

An Invitation to the Cottage by the Loch

Keepsakes from the Cottage by the Loch

Lost Memories of the Cottage by the Loch

Inheriting the Cottage by the Loch

Magpie Cove

The House at Magpie Cove

Secrets of Magpie Cove

Daughters of Magpie Cove

Dreams of Magpie Cove

Mistress of Magic

A Dance with the Fae

A Kiss from the Fae

Standalones

A Spell of Murder

For Matt, with love. Time waited for just the right moment to bring us together.

PROLOGUE

The dream was always the same.

I stood on a cliff looking out to sea. The black rock outcropping under my feet was a natural dais, high above the waves below. Under me, the cliffs cleaved away steeply; their once jagged edges softened only slightly by thousands of years of the relentless power of water.

The breeze ruffled my hair gently and pulled at my long skirts. In the dream, I was always wearing a long skirt and a corset; I could feel the restrictive boning against my ribcage. It wasn't painful; instead, I had the feeling of being poised and graceful. I felt like a figure in a painting. A queen, watching for her returning king across the sea; a lady waiting for her lost love.

I could smell the salt spray from the crashing waves settle on my skin. Behind me, bordering the winding path that led to the headland, I knew that I could glance back to a profusion of cerise heather and yellow gorse.

The dream was so real, so visceral, that whenever I woke from it, it was as though I could still smell the sea at the edge of my perception.

The sun was setting, and the wide sky was a confection of glorious pinks and oranges, tinged with gold. The sun itself, a glowing crimson ball, lowered gradually towards the sea. I knew, in the dream, that I had stood there and watched hundreds of other sunsets.

But I also knew that I had not watched them alone.

There was a man next to me. He was always there. I didn't know his name, and I could never see his face clearly; his features were always a silhouette against the setting sun.

I knew that I – we – had stood here, our hands entwined, countless times.

I knew that he was mine, and that he had been mine – and I had been his – forever.

I knew him in the way that one soul knows another. I knew him in the way that one soul calls to another across time. I knew that he had been devoted to me, and I to him, for so long that though our bodies might have been separate from each other, one couldn't live without the other. As I stood there with him, in the dream, on the clifftop, I knew that was where I belonged.

And when I woke from this dream, whenever I had it, I felt the crushing loss of my disconnection from this man. Whoever he was, I knew that he was the king of my heart. He was home to me, and every moment I spent away from him was a moment I was only half-alive.

ONE

PRESENT DAY

The gates of Trevarron House had always fascinated me.

There was a tale told about them, in the village of St Nantes where my aunt lived. If you walked past, or drove to where the end of the drive met the village road, then you would swear that there were two griffins perched atop the two stone pillars that bookended the gate to the large but derelict manor house that sat somewhere behind acres of woodland.

Everyone knew about the stone griffins. If you'd asked me when I was a kid, I would have been able to draw them for you: tall, with fierce, gaping mouths and claws that clutched at the pillar beneath. Carved of the same sandy stone as Trevarron House itself and sprinkled with a greenish-grey moss. They were a local feature, a part of the scenery.

The gates were a good mile from the house. A long, winding drive divided Trevarron House from the village, set back off the road and secure in its capacious grounds. You couldn't see the house from the gates, but my aunt Bill had snuck me in to see it. Six-year-old me had been asking about the house; since I'd found out that it was there, I was fascinated with it. Who lived in it? Why was it all tumbling down? Was it haunted?

Aunt Bill – Wilhemina, really, but she hated it, she was much too brisk for such a floaty name – had been the one who had showed me the gap in the fence; the same gap that I continued to use to break into the grounds of Trevarron House when I was older. She had held my hand and tiptoed with me through the lush undergrowth, the bugles and bluebells tickling our ankles, placing a finger on her lips and whispering *shhhh* with the same impish glee with which she did so many things. *We don't want the fairies to know we're here.*

We had snaked our way through the ash, beech and oak trees, their leaves whispering quiet shushing songs to welcome us as we made our way towards the meadow in front of the house. It had probably been a beautifully manicured garden once, but then it was wild and filled with knee-length grass. Red poppies and yellow toadflax dotted the green.

The house had been just as derelict then as it was now. I remembered staring up at it with a mix of horror and fascination as Aunt Bill held my hand and told me tales about ladies in long dresses, dancing at balls with gentlemen, and the days of carriages and butlers and lady's maids. I stared at the broken windows, imagining that I could see through them, into another world.

When we left, what I do vividly remember was Aunt Bill telling me about the griffins.

The thing about the griffins on the gate of Trevarron House is, she said, *they ain't been there for years, my love. Not in the livin' memory of most folks in the village. Eighty years afore I was born, there was a picture taken of the gate, an' it showed the griffins standin' proudly there. But then, the next year, a wild storm blew them griffins off the top of the pillars, and they was never replaced. Yet, everyone in the village swears they still see 'em.*

But I've seen them too! I remember insisting, knowing that I had. I felt the truth of it in my six-year-old bones.

I know you think you 'ave, Tegan Penrose, Aunt Bill said, *but you ain't. 'Tis a strange mass 'allucination, is all I can think.*

I didn't know what a mass hallucination was at the time – I was six – but it was true that while the griffins had never stood atop the pillars in my lifetime, I definitely remembered seeing them. It was like a strange slippage between the present and the past, a blurred photograph or the space between two old-fashioned slides in a projector. It was an echo.

A local legend that becomes so real, we all sees it, even though it's not there, she had explained, to my confused little face.

And she was right, because when Aunt Bill and I walked up to the gates that summer day when I was just a child and looked squarely at the pillars, we saw that they were empty.

I *had* seen the griffins. They *had* been there, I would have sworn to it, then, at six, and now, at twenty-five.

As I got older, I accepted it. It was as Aunt Bill described it: a mass hallucination, though I was at a loss to explain how that worked.

Somehow, the gate of Trevarron House was the site of an echo through time, strong enough for multiple people to witness it.

I had no idea until later that the strange phenomenon of the stone griffins was just the beginning of Trevarron House's echoes in time, and its strange ability to be more than one thing at once. Like everyone in my aunt's tiny village, I thought nothing of it. It was a local amusement; an old wives' tale, and yet also an experience we had all had, like the fact that many people had heard the ghost that haunted the local pub, the Old Crown, laughing in a certain corridor. In Cornwall, old wives' tales, hauntings and legends are as common as tourists in the summer and storms in the winter.

But I was wrong to think nothing of it. And I was about to find out what other secrets the house held; a mysterious place, flickering with the unquiet ghosts of the past.

TWO

I'd snuck into the grounds of Trevarron House that afternoon to read.

Trespassing was forbidden, or at least, that was what it said on a couple of rusty old signs at the perimeter of the house grounds. But everyone local – not least my aunt, who had showed me in the first place – knew that there were places in the thinning hedges and in the broken fences at the edge of the property where a person could slip through unnoticed.

Aunt Bill was too old to come with me now – she was a lot older than my mother – and, in fact, I didn't know if she had any idea that I had continued to come here when I came to St Nantes.

She was my mother's sister, and I had been coming to stay for the summer pretty much as long as I could remember. My mother worked as a jazz singer, mostly at night in hotels, and in the summer, she'd generally get a job on a cruise ship that would take her away for the whole of the school holidays. The hotels didn't pay that well, but cruises did: hence my trips to see Aunt Bill.

St Nantes was a tiny village on the North Cornwall coast, just along from Tintagel, King Arthur's supposed birthplace. I liked visiting there. You could take a bus to the coast and walk along the dramatic clifftops, being whipped by the wind even in the summer and watching the waves crash on the slick, black and craggy rocks below. The smell of the sea air was like breathing in diamonds: sharp and pure.

You got to Tintagel Head by a bridge across a deep crevasse between the mainland and the island. It was a popular tourist attraction: the site of castle ruins dated from the Dark Ages and were supposedly the birthplace of the mythical King Arthur. From the top of the cliff, buffeted by wind and sun, you could look down into a deep cave that cut through the headland: Merlin's Cave, supposedly where the magician had spun his magic, though Aunt Bill told me that it was more likely to have been used by smugglers, once upon a time.

A few miles in from the coast, St Nantes comprised about twenty cottages arranged higgledy-piggledy along a narrow road, with some placed along muddy tracks which made them almost inaccessible in the bad weather. A dairy farm, Cullen's, sat at the end of the village, usually downwind, which Aunt Bill said was a blessing. I was often sent down there to get eggs from the honesty box at the farm entrance, and to see what else Mrs Cullen had put out for the villagers: in the summer there would be strawberries, courgettes and tomatoes.

When I was staying with Aunt Bill, we ate local and fresh. She baked her own bread, grew her own vegetables and had milk and cheese delivered from the dairy. She rarely ate meat – we ate a lot of salads, sandwiches, tarts and quiches – but sometimes she'd send me to the little grocer's a few doors down, a tiny, stone-built cottage which was also a post office, if she'd heard that the 'meat man' was visiting, and we'd get a couple of steaks and a pack of pork sausages, or some rashers of thick bacon, all from a farm in the next village over. The meat man was, in fact, that farmer's son, who would load up a few cool boxes with whatever was fresh and bring it over to sell.

Aunt Bill often said, *'Ere, maid, these celebrities wi' more money than sense'd pay a dragon's 'oard for mine or Mrs Cullen's tomatoes, or some o' those sausages,* and I had to admit that she had a point. Staying at St Nantes felt as if you were going back in time – everything was slow, everything was local, and everyone knew everyone else – but I liked it.

Even though I was at university now, I still spent my summers with Aunt Bill. My mother was hardly home nowadays, and we'd never really been that close. Whereas, Aunt Bill and I had a special connection. She had never exactly felt like a mother to me – she was a fun aunt, often chaotic and unpredictable, but she cared about me, and I knew that she liked having me around.

I liked staying at her cosy little cottage. It sat at the end of a dirt track, optimistically called a lane – Pellar's Lane, named, so Aunt Bill said, for a wise woman that lived there once. *Pellar* was the old Cornish word for wise woman or witch, though I knew that it could apply to men or women. Sometimes I would tease Aunt Bill about being a witch, and she would laugh and say, *If I knew how to cast a spell, my love, I wouldn't be 'ere, I'd be on a yacht somewhere, sippin' champagne.* However, I knew she would never want to be anywhere except her cosy little cottage in St Nantes, which was where she had always lived.

The cottage – called Yew Tree Cottage – was exactly the same, each time I visited. The wooden gate which led into the garden was set into an old stone wall, which was head height and ran around the whole cottage and yard, protecting it from view. I didn't exactly know why the wall was so high, because no one ever came up the lane, unless it was to see Aunt Bill, and the lane was definitely more of a muddy track than anything.

It was impossible to get a car up there, in fact. The cottage and the lane had clearly been built at a time well before cars – there was a stone laid into the wall around the doorframe that said 1678, the date that the cottage was built.

Inside, the cottage was surprisingly capacious, which was because it had been extended a couple of times from its original 'one up, one down' structure. Now, it had an indoor bathroom, where originally, all cottages like this would have had an outdoor privy. The cottage had also been extended to include a bigger kitchen and utility room with a washer-dryer, though Aunt Bill had stacked the utility room with bookshelves. There were three bedrooms, and Aunt Bill's even had a cute little Victorian-style en-suite bathroom which she'd had put in so she didn't have to *risk fallin' down those narrow stairs in the middle of the night when nature calls*, as she put it.

When you walked in the front door, you came immediately into to the lounge. An impressively large inglenook fireplace sat in the centre of the back wall. You could have sat on one of the two benches built into its sides, though Aunt Bill had filled them with dry wood on one side and pottery on the other. There used to be a working fireplace when Aunt Bill was a child, so she said, but in the intervening years she had put in a modern log burner which gave off more than enough heat to warm the room.

The lounge was cosy, featuring two ancient burgundy sofas covered in cushions. It was usually lit with two floor lamps that gave off a warm glow, and the wood-panelled floor was covered with a floral-patterned rug.

I liked staying in the same tiny bedroom under the eaves that had always been mine, with its narrow twin beds that hugged opposite walls and a small space between them that held a bedside table where Aunt Bill would leave books – mostly her own well-thumbed historical romances – that she thought might interest me, and an ancient reading lamp.

I tried not to imagine Aunt Bill having any sort of romantic urges, but I had to remind myself that she was human, just like anyone else. And, in a way, I wished that she had found someone to share her life with, especially as she'd got older. I didn't like to think of her alone in the cottage when I was away, even though she assured me that she was *as right as rain, my love,* and that she was too old to have a man around.

It would be nice to have a bit of company, wouldn't it? I'd asked her, the day before. *Not just me when I'm here for the holidays.*

Pah. I'm not washin' anyone's socks, she'd replied, rolling her eyes theatrically.

You could get someone who would wash their own socks, I'd argued, good-naturedly. *I hear men do that now.*

Maybe one o' your younger ones, she said, pulling a face. *But let me tell you that no man my age don't expect his dinner on the table at five an' his laundry done, an' he's off to the pub of an evenin', an' that's all for the pleasure of me bein' able to say I've got a man in the 'ouse. I think not, my maid. Plus, I owns this 'ouse. An' it'll go to you when I die, no' some no-'oper*, she'd added, fiercely.

The rhythm of our days when I came for the summer had changed as I'd got older, and now she was content to let me drift in and out as she pottered around the garden, took a nap or made dinner. She was proud that I was studying history; she'd told everyone in the village when I'd started, the year before. *Always the bookish one*, she'd say to her neighbours, as I stood there, blushing. *Clever. Gets it from me, ha ha. Not her looks, though. That's her mother – she was always the looker, I was the brains. Clever girl got the best o' both worlds.*

I didn't think I was a *looker*, in Aunt Bill's parlance, but I'd never paid much attention to my appearance. I wore my hair long – it was a dark blond, with some natural highlights – but mostly because I could never be bothered to get it cut. I didn't wear makeup much, and I favoured jeans and T-shirts.

Aunt Bill was quite striking, in fact. She downplayed her looks, but I didn't know why. Perhaps it was because she was so keen not to get a boyfriend and wash his socks for eternity, as she would have put it. She had started giving herself an undercut in recent years after *seeing it on that internet* and leaving the top and back long. She had curly blonde hair streaked with grey, as opposed to my straight locks, and the same hazel eyes as me and my mother. She was taller than average, with a frankly Amazonian figure, if she'd chosen to show it off, but she preferred a mixture of long, loose patchwork dresses that she found at outdoor markets and leggings and cardigans for when it got cold.

Anyway, when I said I had to go somewhere to study, she never questioned me, even though most of the time I wasn't studying, but sneaking into the grounds of Trevarron House to read Aunt Bill's tatty old romance novels.

That day, the house seemed even more sorry for itself than usual. No one seemed to be taking care of the old place, which I thought was a shame. I knew that there had been a fire there once, long ago. I had sometimes heard people talk about in the village – you could see that the house was damaged. The stone was blackened so badly that the fire must have raged for days; stone doesn't burn, but it cracks and fractures, given enough heat.

I didn't remember the details about how the fire started. I doubt anybody knew for sure.

However, I did remember Aunt Bill telling me the story of one of the lords of Trevarron who had apparently been a criminal, but had disappeared when the local sheriff had come to arrest him. I remembered being curious as to what crimes this lord had committed, but Aunt Bill was vague on the details. *All's I know is that he was a wrong'un*, she'd said, *an' the powers that be came to take him away an' he'd disappeared into the woods an' never came back. Likely threw himself off the cliff or somethin' with the shame, I shouldn't wonder.*

I remembered this little snippet, and when I had snuck into the grounds of Trevarron House, I'd often idly wondered what had happened to the disappearing lord. Like the griffins, it seemed to be a part of the strange mythology of the place. How could a man disappear and never be seen again, unless he had done what Aunt Bill suggested and ended things in such a dramatic fashion? I didn't like to think about that; I hoped that, whoever he was, he hadn't resorted to anything so tragic.

Regardless, whatever had once happened, it was peaceful now in the grounds of the old house. Enough time had passed, enough rain had fallen and enough sun had shone to wash any bad things away.

I liked to come here. Some people might have been put off by the grim history, but I always felt a connection with the place; maybe it was that memory of Aunt Bill bringing me here, maybe it was just a vibe.

Maybe though, it was something else.

At the back of the house, if you made your way through the overgrown gardens and through the weeds, you would find yourself at the edge of the cliffs, looking down onto the sea below. There was a black rock outcropping there, raised a few inches from the land behind it like a step or a platform, and the view out across the sea to Tintagel was breathtaking.

I'd found it a couple of years ago when I'd decided to go exploring around the property. The gardens at the back of Trevarron House were of considerable size; there were old stone steps cut into a sloping lawn and what looked like a sunken lawn beyond that. I'd made my way out as far as I could with the house behind me, striding through the tall weeds and brambles, brushing them away when they tore at my clothes. I knew that the house backed onto the coastline, and I wanted to see if I could get to the sea.

I don't really know what had possessed me to push my way through all of the brambles, but when I eventually stood on that black rock and looked out to the ocean, I realised that I was standing in the same spot I had dreamed about, on and off, since I was a child.

There was no mistaking that this was the same place as in my dreams; I had known the heft of the rock under my feet, the smell of the salt in the air and the feel of the breeze on my face. I knew the view, down to the details of the slick, black cliff face below; its crevices and contours, the places where gulls and cormorants nested. I knew it all.

It had occurred to me before that my special place on the cliff might also be near the spot where the lord of Trevarron had plummeted to his death. I hadn't ever forgotten that story; Aunt Bill still mentioned it from time to time. It was part of her repertoire of stories, a chorus of tales she recited every time I saw her.

I didn't know whether I had found the spot on the cliffs when I was a child, and forgotten being there, only to be reminded in dreams, or whether it held some kind of deeper significance. All I knew was that it was a strange thing, part of the collection of strange things I associated with St Nantes, and Trevarron.

Had Aunt Bill brought me to the edge here once, to see the view? Or, far more strangely, had I somehow known about this spot for another reason? And, if so, why did I continue to dream about it – and who was the man that was always there with me?

THREE

Now that I was in St Nantes for the summer, I was taking a book to the overgrown lawn at Trevarron most days, with a few snacks and a bottle of water, to enjoy the quiet. I felt at home there. Sometimes I walked, exploring the grounds. Sometimes I imagined what it would have been like to live there, at the house, before it had fallen into ruin.

I was studying history at Falmouth University, down on the south coast. I was a bit older than most of the students on my course, but it didn't bother me – I'd had to live at home for some years and save up before I went. I still had to take out loans to cover my fees and some of my living costs, but at least I had saved up a decent amount to cover accommodation by not having to pay rent. My mother had suggested that I live with her while I studied, but at best it was an hour and a half from her house to Falmouth, and that was without traffic.

And I had wanted to leave home. I had worked so hard to get some independence and to follow my dreams. I wanted to be free.

Never could be persuaded, she'd said, when I insisted on moving into university accommodation. *Stubborn as a goat, that one, when she's got the bit between her teeth.* My mother was fond of mixed metaphors. I didn't bother pointing out to her that horses were the ones with bits.

I'd seen on one of the accounts I followed on social media that there would be a solar eclipse that day, so as well as enjoying the peace and quiet at Trevarron, I'd brought my sunglasses with me so that I could watch the shadow pass over the sun.

I remembered watching a solar eclipse through my mother's dark sunglasses when I was a kid: being scared stiff to watch it without them, because she'd told me it would burn my retinas. I knew that lunar eclipses were more frequent and, on the whole, less sensational to view.

Cornwall was a great place to view natural phenomena like eclipses and meteor showers. The skies were wide and the views were long; at night, the stars over the sea were so bright that you felt as though you were looking up into the inky blackness of heaven, dotted with a million diamond angels.

You could still see the features that had made Trevarron House so notable: wide stone steps edged with stone balustrades led up to its wide, arched entrance. The steps were broken now – no longer the clean, smooth surfaces they had once been – and a profusion of weeds and long grasses had grown in the cracks. Griffins – like the ones missing from the gates at the end of the drive – sat on stone plinths at the bottom of the steps, chipped and weathered, but still exuding grandeur.

The frames of the old sash windows were still in place, but the glass in many of them was broken. The plaster façade of the building, once a gleaming white, was now a dark grey, most of it desiccated and missing, exposing the Cornish stone underneath.

On one side of the main building, one wing had been almost completely ruined by the fire: someone had tried to protect the interior by hanging protective plastic over the windows, but now it was in tatters, and fluttered in the wind like widows' weeds. I wasn't sure when the fire had occurred, or whether it was in any way connected to the story about the disappearing lord, but Trevarron seemed like a place that held many secrets.

The owners – the Trevarron family – had been well-known in this part of north Cornwall for generations. As far as I knew, there were none of them left now, but once they had been powerful landowners. The house would once have stood among the other grand Cornish manor houses, belonging to powerful families: Cothele, Lanhydrock, Trerice, Pencarrow. Once, it would have been just as beautiful as those places still were, but those houses had been preserved and cared for.

Trevarron House had been left to rot.

That afternoon, I was flicking through one of Aunt Bill's books on period dress. She had quite the variety of books in her little cottage, as well as her historical romances, and I'd picked this one up because I'd always been interested in fashion, and especially – being a history student – what people wore in the past.

I had many favourite periods for fashion, but I really loved the full-skirted, tightly laced bodice dresses popular in the 1700s. I loved the opulence of the rococo period – the art and architecture, full of gold, curves and colour. I particularly loved Marie Antoinette's dresses of that time with their spectacularly low necklines, bright fabrics, bows and pleats, underskirts and frills.

It was such a sexy and yet elegant look. Clothes nowadays were so practical and drab, though I knew that Marie Antoinette's dresses must have been incredibly uncomfortable to wear, not least in the blinding hot summers. I myself wasn't one for glamour, particularly, but my mother had to wear glamorous evening dresses on the cruise ships and sometimes I thought it must be nice to make a bit of an effort. Mostly, it was a confidence thing for me. I was comfortable in my intellect and my studies, but I'd always been quite shy about 'girly' things like clothes, makeup and how to do my hair.

I thought about how sweaty I would've been in that moment if I was wearing something similar, and how I definitely wouldn't have been able to sit down on the grass in it, or slip through a gap in a fence. *Glamour, ten; practicality, nil,* I thought. Still, maybe we all had a little hankering for glamour and romance inside us somewhere – even Aunt Bill with her well-thumbed historical romances.

The book also contained a whole series of chapters about corsets and undergarments, and I was fascinated to learn about how they shaped a dress. It was so interesting, how the different layers of a ball dress were put on, in the 1700s: it was a meticulous process with many steps. A woman needed at least one maid to help her assemble the undergarments, lace them tightly and then arrange the dress in many parts over the top, frequently pinning pieces in place.

I thought again about my recurring dream. In it, I was always wearing a corset with a long skirt. It was an oddly specific detail for a dream.

As I flicked through the pages, I daydreamed about what it would have been like to live as a member of the nobility back then. I'd never really felt that I belonged in the modern world; like a dream, the past called to me, as if I belonged there and not here. I loved the idea of the costume balls, the dancing, the etiquette. I knew that was only how the rich lived; the vast majority of people were poor, in service or living hand-to-mouth in farming or other manual trades. But that wasn't the history that I thought about. I was romantic about the past. I was a romantic, full stop, really. Clearly, Aunt Bill knew that about me, otherwise she wouldn't have left me out the romance novels.

I was so caught up in my reverie that I didn't notice the dog racing towards me; too late, I looked around to see its wagging tail and spittle-covered open jaws. It went straight for my bag, which contained a sandwich and a bottle of water. I swore and shooed it away, but it dodged me, thinking I was playing.

There was no owner to be seen, which wasn't that surprising; dog walkers weren't likely to break into the grounds of a manor house. The dog was probably a stray, and had found its own way in. I shooed it away again, but it kept coming for my bag.

Realising that it wasn't going to leave me alone, I picked up my book and slung my bag over my shoulder. Feeling a little uneasy, I thought about where I could go to get the dog to leave me alone.

I decided to walk around to the back of the house where I knew there was an enclosed, overgrown rose garden. It had rusted cast-iron gates at both ends of the walkway that cut through its middle. I had peered through the gates before and seen that the walkway featured a large stone trough at its centre, though it was overgrown with ivy and vines as well as the roses.

The gates were finely constructed, though battered with age: each featured an ornate *T* in the centre of a circle, and lines of iron emanating from the circle as if it was the sun. *T* for Trevarron; perhaps, once, the owners of Trevarron House had felt as though they were at the centre of all things. *Must have been a nice feeling,* I thought, wryly.

I rarely came to the back of the house; the meadow at the front was my favourite part, and though I could see that the back would once have been grand, with the rose garden and a sunken lawn, now it was so overgrown that there were few places to sit.

I approached the rusted iron gate at one side of the rose garden, reached for the latch and pushed.

It didn't give. I wasn't overly surprised; I'd tried it in the past, curious to see what lay within the garden, and it hadn't budged then.

The dog had followed me. I shooed it away again, but it continued to bark and dart at me. It wasn't aggressive, but it was bloody annoying, and I wanted to get away from it and back to my reading.

Also, I suppose I had always been a bit of a quiet rebel, since childhood; maybe I followed in Aunt Bill's footsteps. I wasn't ever naughty, but I'd always known my own mind, and I could be outspoken if I felt something was unfair. Not everyone would have made the grounds of Trevarron House their sanctuary, but I was willing to trespass to be there, because it felt right.

I looked at the ornate wrought-iron fencing that surrounded the garden. Like the gate, it featured an intricate design, but of roses: petals and blooms curled and curved in its aged, rusted design.

I peered up at the fence, measuring the footholds in my mind's eye. If I climbed it, the dog wouldn't be able to bother me anymore. I wanted to get into the rose garden; in that moment, I couldn't say exactly why, as there would probably have been other ways to escape the dog. But I knew that I was going to climb up that wrought-iron railing, and I was going to get in that damned rose garden.

I put my foot into a gap in the ironwork and carefully pulled myself up, praying that the rusted metal would hold my weight.

When I reached the top, I felt a shudder go through the iron fence. The ridiculousness of what I was doing struck me: what if I fell? What if the iron gave way and drove a rusty spike through my leg? Even a scratch from the rusty metal would mean a trip to the hospital for antibiotics.

The dog appeared at the edge of the fence, below me, now snarling and barking, clearly thinking that a hunt was in progress. It jumped, trying to catch the skin of my bare shin with its teeth. On its second attempt, its nose met my ankle, and I pulled my leg away in fright. The dog began to snarl.

'OK, now I don't feel like this is a game,' I muttered, feeling panic flower under my skin. The dog was now barking and throwing itself against the railings. I jumped from the top of the fence onto the overgrown pathway below.

And, as I leaped, everything around me changed.

FOUR

I took a moment to catch my breath, and then stood up painfully. I'd landed on my right knee, and when I looked down at it, I saw that I'd grazed it quite badly. I was wearing a yellow sundress that day because it was hot, and it had been no protection against the iron gates and the hard ground. In fact, it had got caught on the ironwork as I had climbed over, and now there was a long rip in the skirt.

'Damn,' I muttered, and bent over to look at the wound, which was pouring blood. The last time I'd grazed my knee this badly, I had been a child in the school playground. I swore again.

As my dress was ripped anyway, I gripped the fabric that was still hanging half loose in the skirt and pulled it, taking off a longish piece of cotton that could act as a bandage until I got home and cleaned up. I tied the fabric around my bloody knee as best I could, though the blood started seeping through almost immediately, and stood up carefully, trying not to put my weight on that leg.

'Ouch,' I gasped.

I had landed in the rose garden. Yet, everything was completely different to how it had been when I looked in from the outside.

The roses were now orderly; they climbed delicately up the

wooden posts that lined the long, impeccably neat walkway ahead of me and spread across the top of a long pergola. Profusions of wide, deep pink roses and blowsy, peach blooms, their sunset hue deepening at the edge of their thick, velvet petals.

I looked around me in confusion. To the left I could see a lavender garden surrounding a stone statue of a goddess figure pouring water from a shell; to the right, a wildflower garden boasting creamy white stocks, tall violet foxgloves, blood-red poppies and rosy-pink hollyhocks.

Slowly, I limped to the central point of the garden, where, I realised, two walkways converged. Before, when I had looked in, I hadn't seen this meeting of the ways, assuming that there was just one path through the rose garden. Now I realised that it was a square garden, separated into four quarters. I looked down again at my leg: the blood was starting to roll down my shin.

I breathed in the cloyingly sweet smell of the roses, but there was something else under the familiar sweet top note of rose. I was reminded of picking rose petals as a child and infusing them in water to make 'perfume' for Aunt Bill, who had dutifully dabbed it on her wrists. In the same way as my home-made rosewater had begun to stink after a few days, under the sweet smell here, something rotted. It was a high, warm smell of decay. I wrinkled my nose.

I walked along, trailing my fingers on the top of the large stone trough that sat at the point where the walkways crossed. Now that I was close to it, I could see that in fact it was a water feature, with a fountain in the shape of a mermaid at its centre. I held my fingers under the stream of water, half wondering whether it would be acceptable to bathe my bloody knee in it, and half wondering how the garden had changed so much in a matter of seconds.

Before I had a chance to explore further, there was a loud creak as the iron gate at the other end of the garden opened, and a tall man stood there, staring at me aggressively.

As soon as I met his eyes, I felt like I was falling.

There was a sudden buzzing noise in my ears and my vision

blurred. I flung out my hand to find something – anything – I could hold on to. My fingers found the stone trough, and I steadied myself, staring up at him.

I estimated that he was perhaps in his late thirties, even forty. He was tall, wide across the shoulders, solid and muscular. He was even a little intimidating, physically, with a kind of barely suppressed power about him: something animalistic.

This man had such a presence that it took my breath away. It was both comforting and strangely unnerving.

The unnerving thing was that I felt happy to see him, as if I had missed him terribly. I wanted to run to him. And that made no sense at all. I'd literally never seen the man before.

But when I saw how he was looking at me, I knew that I couldn't run to him.

His expression was part confusion and part horror. He seemed terrified of me, and that reaction stopped me in my tracks.

'You, girl!' he called out gruffly. 'What are you doing here?'

When he spoke, the illusion that he was a dream evaporated. It was a silly thought on my part. He was clearly real, not a fantasy.

He was dressed in clothes that, because of studying history, I recognised as belonging to the eighteenth century: dark brown breeches which covered his muscular legs to the knee, and cream-coloured socks – they were called hose then, I remembered – below. He wore leather shoes which looked as if they had been either painstakingly handmade or, at the least, not made in a factory.

On the top half, he wore what I thought was a yellow silk waistcoat in a kind of brocade fabric, and, under that, a white shirt with a kind of ruffle at the neck and voluminous sleeves. He had dark, curling brown hair, which was longish and caught at the back in a ponytail. The whole outfit reminded me of a pirate, without the hat or eyepatch.

He frowned imperiously at me, taking in my sundress and bare arms. 'You seem to be wearing... your nightgown?' He raised an eyebrow. 'It is torn. You are bleeding,' he grunted, a statement rather than a question.

'I climbed over the fence and jumped, and fell on my knee,' I explained, feeling as though I was caught in some kind of surreal movie. I wondered then whether he was involved in some kind of period drama – perhaps I'd stumbled into the filming of a historical TV series, or there was a local group running an elaborate murder mystery costume dinner party?

Why was he dressed so oddly? Why did the rose garden look so different?

And, most of all, when I looked up at the manor house, why did it look so new and no more derelict than if it had just been built? I marvelled at the smooth white render of the façade, the sparkling whole windows, and the manicured gardens that I could see even from within the rose garden. *Wow. That's weird*, I thought.

'Why were you climbing over the fence?' He strode up to me and, without asking permission, picked up the hem of my dress and pulled it up to get a better look at my knee.

If I had thought that there was some kind of ethereal connection between us, that idea seemed even more ridiculous, given his aggressive gesture. Dream men didn't grab women.

'Hey!' I protested. Instinctively, I slapped his hand away. 'Don't touch me.'

'I will touch what I like. I own everything here, including you,' he replied, evenly.

What? What sort of person would say, clear-eyed and without an inkling of irony, that they *owned* another person?

'I don't even know where to start with that. You absolutely do *not* own me. And you can't just go up to women you don't know and pull up their skirts. We aren't in medieval times. I'm not some...' I searched for the words, annoyance rising in my throat. 'Some... *peasant*.'

'Hm,' he grunted, again; his manner was gruff and rude. I

couldn't tell whether his response was a question or an agreement. 'I must admit that you are more well-spoken than I would expect.'

What did you expect? I thought, wildly. My heart was pounding; I felt untethered from reality.

What on earth was going on?

At that moment, a dog barked, and I looked behind me to see the same dog that had chased me up to the rose garden run down the path. It whined excitedly at me and started jumping up.

I swore and backed away, but it seemed friendly enough now. Not like before, when it had thrown itself at the railings like it was possessed.

'Jasper! Heel!' the man ordered, and the dog went instantly to him. The man put a firm hand on its collar.

'Is that your dog?' I asked, now more confused than ever. It was definitely the same one. Which meant that the man must have been in the meadow, earlier, walking the dog, perhaps, and it had got off its lead.

'Yes.' He rubbed the dog's ears for a moment. 'That looks bad,' the man said, nodding at my knee.

'It's all right,' I said, defensively.

'You have not answered me about why you were climbing over in the first place,' he continued. 'I can see no reason why you should be out here at all, never mind climbing things that are not supposed to be climbed,' he scolded me as if I was a child. 'There is a perfectly good gate at that end, as there is at the other,'

'It wasn't... I couldn't open it, before,' I said, not quite knowing what to say. I knew that I was trespassing; the signs, even though they were rusted and old, said to keep out. I guessed that I could get into trouble for being here, after all.

'Hm. I assume that you are a scullery maid? I don't recognise you,' he stated. He had a slightly odd way of talking, formal and clipped.

'I'm not a *maid*.' I couldn't help but laugh at the sheer ridiculousness of what he'd said – after the strange assertion that he *owned* me, which I hoped was some sort of unfunny joke. 'Who're you? Why are you wearing all that?' I gestured to his outfit, and he gave me an odd look.

'All of what?'

'Your clothes. Your costume,' I added, impatiently.

'My *costume*?' He looked at his wrists, and down at his legs. He was acting as if I was speaking in another language, and it was annoying as well as discomfiting.

'You do not know who I am?' he asked, disbelievingly.

'Should I?' I frowned at him again, thinking what a weird interaction this was. He still hadn't explained why he was dressed the way he was.

'I am William De Vere Trevarron,' he said, slowly. 'This is my house, these are my gardens, and this is my estate. Do you not know where you are, girl? Are you distracted? Injured?' He looked me up and down disparagingly.

'Trevarron?' I repeated, disbelievingly. 'Like the house?'

'Yes... like the house. I am the lord here.'

FIVE

'The lord of Trevarron House?' I echoed, staring at him.

'I do not repeat myself,' he retorted. His gaze took in my torn dress again. 'I think your fall has made you confused. I will take you back to the kitchens.'

He took my arm, gently but firmly, and propelled me towards the end of the walkway. I followed for a few steps, and then realised what I was doing. Following a strange man, just because he said so? *Oh, hell no.*

'Stop it! You can't just grab me. I'm leaving.' I pulled my arm away, my heart starting to pound. But he pulled me closer towards him and into his arms, so that my chest was pressed against his, and I was suddenly looking up, into his eyes.

A flicker of sudden heat passed between us, which took my breath away. His eyes were a deep brown, long lashed, and his cheekbones were high, lending a regal grandeur to his face. He was clean-shaven, although he had what Aunt Bill would have called a *swarthy* complexion: a man that looked like he might have needed to shave twice a day.

He was about a head taller than me, and very well-built. I could feel the hard muscle of his chest under his waistcoat, and he held me tightly in his strong arms that strained under his shirt.

There was that sense of the animal about him, like a bear or a bull.

He smelt lightly of sweat, but not in an unpleasant way. There was a musky, woody scent about him, something that made me want to nestle my head into his neck and breathe him in. He smelt of *man*, pure and simple.

I wasn't exactly *used* to being held by a man, but in that moment I just wanted to melt into him. It was absolutely primal; I'd never experienced anything like it before, and never with the boys I had gone for the occasional drink with at university. That was one thing. This... this was something else.

As I looked up into those eyes, I had a strange feeling of familiarity: that I *knew* this man. It felt as though, just for a moment, I saw into the past and knew him, like family. I saw one static picture, like a photo: an image of the two of us embracing on a Cornish clifftop, silhouetted against a vivid orange and pink summer sunset. It wasn't just a picture, though. I also had the sudden conviction that there was a deep bond between us, and I felt a furiously hot glow of sexual attraction. I *knew* this man. I knew him intimately, like a wife knows a husband.

My lips parted involuntarily and I gasped, taken by the insight that was almost a vision.

It was my dream. The cliff, the sunset. Somehow, I was getting this man mixed up with that recurring image. Perhaps it was wish fulfilment...

As I gazed up into his eyes, I saw fire ignite in his. I could see that he too felt something between us: something unusual, a spark of desire that he didn't expect to feel. He released his grip on me, looking as if he was about to say something, but he stopped himself.

I looked down at his hands, and realised that his knuckles were bruised and cut. He had obviously cleaned them, but there were still traces of blood in the rough cracks of his skin.

I turned away and started to walk quickly in the other direction. It was a panic response. I didn't know what to do; the whole situation was a little scary. As attracted as I felt to this man – chemically, physically, whatever it was – I also didn't feel safe being held in a stranger's arms – a stranger that, for all I knew, might have set his dog on me and was trying to kidnap me or something worse.

I looked behind me, panic filling my chest, but the man just stood where I had left him, holding the dog's collar in his hand and watching me.

'Now, then. What's all this?' A woman had appeared at the end of the rose garden I had originally entered. 'Who're you?' She stared at me with a hostile expression. 'I don't welcome beggars, an' I ain't buyin' anything. Not from a ripped-apart baggage like you,' she said, meeting my stare with hers.

Well, that was inappropriate. I started at the old-fashioned insult; I knew what *baggage* had once meant, because it had been a comment that one of my history tutors had made about old-fash-ioned slurs and insults. In the eighteenth century and for a long time before and after that, *baggage* had meant *hussy* or *slut*.

She was a large woman, dressed in a long brown dress with a high collar which was made of what I estimated was some kind of rough-spun cotton. Over that, she wore a clean white apron with a large pocket in it, and her hair was covered with a white cotton cap. Was this another historical re-enactor, or someone involved in whatever TV project was being filmed here? I was sure that there hadn't been any word of it in the village, and certainly no sign of it outside the house – no vans, catering trucks, no traffic at all, in fact, apart from the usual occasional car along the quiet, twisty road outside Trevarron House.

'I beg your pardon?' I retorted, but the man – William Trevar-ron, so he said – stepped forward and nodded briskly at the woman.

'Cook. Good day.' His tone was businesslike and direct and I was amazed to watch the transformation in the woman before me. She went from solid and obstreperous to meek and mild in about three seconds. *Quite a feat*, I thought.

'Good day, milord.' The woman even curtseyed. I looked from one to the other, waiting for them both to start laughing at the obvious joke they were pulling on me – *Ah, we had you there, it's all a role play game, it's a Renaissance fayre, it's a BBC drama* – but neither of them did. 'My deepest apologies. I didn't see you there. I was rather taken aback at the vision of this...' She stopped for a moment, considering her words more carefully. 'This... young lady with so much flesh on display, in such an indecent fashion. Why, she is almost naked, I—'

'Indeed, Cook, as was I.' He nodded curtly, cutting the woman off before she could wax lyrical any further on my nudity, which was a complete lie. I wasn't naked at all. I was wearing a sundress, and though I had come out without a bra because the bodice was elasticated and shirred, I was otherwise decent enough, apart from the tear in my skirt and the bloody knee. 'I assumed that she was one of your staff.' He looked from me to her.

'Indeed not, milord. I've never seen this young lady before,' Cook replied, looking me up and down with so much derision, I felt as though I might fall through a hole in the ground. 'My staff would not wander around the grounds for no reason, and they are always dressed smartly.'

'Hm. Are you aware of Mrs Cottingley awaiting any new staff for the house? A lady's maid, perhaps?' William continued. Cook shrugged. I looked from Cook to William and back again in disbelief, expecting the pretence to slip at any moment. But it didn't.

'Mayhap she is, milord. I will take the young lady and investigate.' Cook reached for my arm and gripped it tightly; I squirmed under her touch. I could feel her fingers digging into my flesh.

'Ow. Let me go!' I protested, but apparently no one was listening to me anymore because they both acted as if I hadn't said anything. A coil of genuine fear began to unroll in my stomach.

'I wonder whether you would be kind enough to take her back to the kitchens to dress her wounds and put her in something more appropriate before you do so,' the lord of the manor continued, in a tone that assumed that his will would be carried out without objection.

'Of course, sir.' Cook curtseyed again and steered me out of the gate with my arm bent behind my back. 'I am sorry for the interruption.'

'Hm,' William De Vere Trevarron grunted in response. I was now seriously freaked out. 'As you were.'

I felt Cook's wide palm shift quickly and expertly downwards, where it easily encircled my wrist and pushed me forward roughly. The way that she had my arm held against my back, I couldn't move it, and so I followed where she guided me.

'No funny business, whore,' she leaned forward and muttered in my ear as we travelled out of William's earshot, 'or I'll whip you black and blue.'

That made me angry. I stopped walking and wrestled my arm back from her, breaking free of her grip.

'I don't know who you are, but I'm going to have you charged with assault,' I said, in a low voice. I was still scared, but I was damned if I wasn't going to stand my ground. 'How dare you attack me!'

The woman – Cook – stared at me as if I was crazy.

'Get in that kitchen,' she hissed.

'Make me.' I stood with my hands on my hips and stared her out. She was a heavyset woman, but I was ready to fight. Not that I had ever had a fight before, but the fight-or-flight instincts had well and truly set in, and I was not going to just go along with whatever was happening here.

However, when a door behind Cook opened and I saw inside, I was dumbfounded. My hands, which had tensed into fists, fell to my sides.

On the other side of the door, I could see a bevy of women, all dressed the same as she was. They clustered around a long table, clattering pans and talking loudly. One of them stuck her head out of the door and hailed us.

'Oi. Cook! Get some carrots from the garden while yer out there. Mistress wants that soup again,' the woman called out, giving me a harsh look.

I looked around at the large vegetable garden that spread

around me. Root vegetables nestled neatly in rows – I spotted beet-root, carrots, potatoes and onions, being used to helping Aunt Bill in her garden. Lettuces and tomatoes flourished under glass-topped raised beds. Bees buzzed around the fragrant leaves and delicate flowers of an herb garden, and the pleasant smell of rosemary and lemon balm scented the breeze.

None of this had been here before. I was a thousand per cent sure of that.

Trevarron House was very definitely not derelict anymore, and if I thought William and Cook were part of a filming project, then I was clearly in the wrong, because what TV show went as far as sowing a whole vegetable garden at least a season in advance before they got there?

Cook grabbed my arm again and led me into the kitchen.

I started to wonder where – and when – I was.

SIX

'Well, well. What do we 'ave 'ere, then?' Cook propelled me into the large kitchen and stood back to look me over, her arms once more crossed over her chest.

I was still freaked out, but I was also temporarily distracted by the scene around me. We had walked into a hub of activity. A team of women, all dressed in the same way as Cook – which was odd in itself – were working at different stations along a long wooden table, chopping vegetables, preparing meat and, in the case of one woman, making what looked like pastry. The women's bare hands were filthy, and they seemed to regularly wipe them on their cotton aprons, making me instantly concerned about the hygiene of the food being prepared.

They were working industriously in dim light and smoky air from a hearth at one end of the room. I realised that there were no lights in the kitchen, and even though it was a bright day outside, the one small window that looked out onto the kitchen garden outside wasn't enough to bring natural light into the room. It was, therefore, dingy, compared to what I would expect for a professional kitchen in a large house.

The second thing I noticed was that there were no electrical devices whatsoever. No fridge, washing machine, dishwasher, electric kettle, air fryer... none of that was in evidence. Aunt Bill's kitchen was basic and old-fashioned, but even she had an electric fridge and a gas stove.

There was a large white porcelain sink at one side of the kitchen where one skinny, pale teenage girl was washing a mountain of dirty plates, and a table next to that where another girl stood, drying them up and stacking them in piles. A number of copper pans hung from the ceiling from a rack, along with bundles of drying herbs.

'The master seemed quite curious about you, missy, but I can see you're little more than a common slut. So, the question is, how did 'ee get 'ere, and what're you after?' I returned my attention to Cook, who narrowed her eyes at me. 'I've a mind to drive 'ee up the road with a whip, an' tan that behind for botherin' me at all. As if I don't 'ave enough to do,' she tutted.

'My name is Tegan Penrose. I am not a... prostitute.' I tried to keep my voice steady and calm. 'I think I'll be going now.' I turned to leave, still no clearer on what was going on. It *must* be some kind of historical re-enactment society, I thought. That was sort of slightly believable – maybe they'd hired the house for some kind of dinner, hence all the preparation? But the thing that was really throwing me up against a mental brick wall was how Trevarron House had been revived in such a spectacular way. I hadn't imagined how derelict it had been; how fire damaged it was, how it had been left to rot for decades, even centuries. It had been a ruin for as long as I could remember.

How was it possible that I was standing in its kitchen, having a conversation with this woman, as a legion of other women prepared food around me? *How?*

'Oh, you're a fine lady, I'm sure,' Cook sneered. 'Walkin' around in your underclothes like baggage. Aye, *baggage*.' She saw the reaction flare in my eyes and squared up to me, as if she was dying for an excuse to wrestle me to the floor. 'I said it before, an'

I'll say it again, now that the master's out o' earshot. No decent girl would ever walk around in that get-up.' She hooked her finger around the strap of my dress and snapped it.

I flinched and pulled away. Whoever these people were, they had zero respect for personal space or physical boundaries. 'Yellow, indeed. Whorish. No stays; no stockin's; no petticoat. I wonder 'ow you dared leave whatever establishment of sin you woke up in.' She shook her head disdainfully. A couple of the other women had turned around to watch us, no doubt feeling the tension in the air, but Cook made a gesture with her hand and glared at them.

'Back to work, girls. Nothing to see 'ere except for some cheap strumpet come to try her luck,' she added. My temper flared up again; this was unacceptable and completely unfair. Not only that, I found it amazing that this woman seemed committed to staying in the character of the cook in a historical manor house as she insulted me. She didn't even use modern phrases to do it. She could have called me a *dumb bitch* or worse, but she called me a *cheap strumpet*. Who even said that?

'This is just a sundress! What are you, some kind of abuser for hire?' I just couldn't make sense of it. What was happening?

The woman looked confused, as if I'd said something she didn't understand. We faced each other like two gunfighters, each waiting for the other to take another shot.

At that moment, the door at the other end of the kitchen, next to the hearth, opened, and a neatly dressed woman walked through it. Her steps were calm and precise, but the way she held herself indicated a sense of purposefulness.

Unlike Cook, this woman didn't wear an apron, but a dark blue cotton jacquard dress – I was quite good at recognising fabrics as well as styles – in the style of the eighteenth century. The man outside who had called himself William De Vere Trevarron had also been dressed in the same period style.

'Cook. Good afternoon. I understand that you may have taken custody of my new lady's maid,' the woman said, in a clipped and no-nonsense tone.

'Good afternoon, Mrs Cottingley,' Cook replied in a mulish and yet subservient tone. 'I dunno about that. I found this...' She moderated her language as she had before, in front of William Trevarron, or whatever historical re-enactment actor was playing William Trevarron. 'This *young lady* outside, wanderin' through the gardens an' waylayin' the lord. I was about to get one of the footmen to escort 'er off the premises.'

Oh, please, I thought. *I'll be gone as soon as I can, believe me.* I was eager to leave this bizarre role play party, yet something in me was still curious about what was going on, and who this woman was.

'Hm. Lord Trevarron informed me that he thought this young lady might be one of my staff. He didn't recognise her, so he asked me if I was expecting a new maid, which I am. I was expecting a lady's maid to arrive today. Did something happen to you, child?' Mrs Cottingley walked up to me and inspected me far more kindly than Cook had. 'She's been hurt. It looks like she was in an accident.' She turned to me. 'Come with me, dear. Cook is not well-known for her kindness, or her social graces.' She gave Cook a withering glare and beckoned me towards the door she had come through. 'We will tidy you up, and you can tell me what happened.'

I didn't want to stay in the kitchen to be insulted by Cook any further, so I followed Mrs Cottingley. I wanted to see what was beyond the kitchen, and how far this strange fantasy extended. The idea occurred to me that I might have fallen asleep in the grounds of Trevarron House and all of this might be a very detailed dream. *If so, I want to wake up,* I thought, looking down at my knee to see if it was still bleeding. If it was a dream, the wound might have disappeared, but it was still there.

The fact that I was not the lady's maid that Mrs Cottingley was apparently waiting for, or in any way involved with this elaborate role play, would surely soon become obvious. I'd make my excuses and leave.

But as I followed Mrs Cottingley out into a narrow hallway

and then, at the end of it, up a narrow staircase, I caught my breath. Because I saw that Mrs Cottingley was holding a newspaper – not one I recognised, but I could see it was one, despite its differences: the print text, the size and shape and thickness.

And the date on the front of the newspaper was 20 June 1755.

SEVEN

I swore under my breath and stopped dead on the stairs, staring at the paper in Mrs Cottingley's hand.

She stopped at the top of the stairwell and frowned down at me.

'Come along, dear. Just up these stairs and we will get you to your new quarters, and get you cleaned up. Then you can tell me what happened. Highwaymen, no doubt, attacking a young lady in her carriage. It has become all too frequent these days, I am afraid.' She tapped the newspaper with the fingers of her opposite hand. 'Why, just two days ago, there was an awful attack on the stage-coach from Plymouth. You weren't on that, were you?' she queried.

'No...' I still didn't know how to respond to her, or anyone here. Yet, I got the sense that, unlike Cook, Mrs Cottingley was a kind person and she might explain things to me more than anyone else had so far. I pointed to the newspaper in her hand.

'The date. 1755?' I turned my eyes towards her in a kind of mute appeal, as if she must understand the ridiculousness of the situation, but she merely nodded.

'Indeed,' she replied. 'Do you keep up with current affairs? Can you read?' Her eyebrows knitted. I climbed the last few stairs and followed her into the room at the top: a luxurious bedroom, with a smallish double bed, a gleaming dark wood dressing table with an upholstered stool in front of it and a tall room divider screen – a wooden frame covered in floral fabric. To the left stood a wide wardrobe made of the same dark, gleaming wood.

'Of course I can read.'

'Well, not all lady's maids can.' Mrs Cottingley looked vaguely offended. 'Lady Trevarron will be delighted to have someone so educated waiting on her. She's a poet, as you might know, very literary.'

'Lady Trevarron?' I echoed.

'Edith Beresford Trevarron. You have come to be her lady's maid,' the woman said slowly, as if I was some kind of forgetful old bird.

'It's not 1755,' I protested, feeling as if I was going insane. 'You can stop the pretence. Whatever it is. A performance. I'm not... *in* this, whatever it is.'

Mrs Cottingley frowned. 'You do seem rather out of sorts, dear. Were you attacked? Should I get the doctor to make a visit?' she asked.

'No... that's not necessary.' I sat down on the end of the bed, feeling overwhelmed. 'Maybe I just need a moment.'

Mrs Cottingley pointed to the screen. 'Hm. If you pop behind there, we can get you changed into something more fitting, and you can tell me about your previous house.' She pointed to the screen and turned away towards the wardrobe, opening it and taking out a light green dress. 'I think that once you've got changed into something more decent, had a good meal and a glass of beer, you'll be much more yourself. Of course, you'll have to have some new gowns made, for the balls and suchlike, and a few daily dresses. Lady Trevarron has a good mantua maker and draper in Exeter. We will take a trip there, once you've settled in.' She continued drawing items from the wardrobe: some stockings and what looked like a corset.

'Honestly, if you were waylaid by the highwayman, then it's no wonder you've arrived in such a state. Quite why your mistress would send you alone, I don't know,' Mrs Cottingley tutted, her back turned to me. 'I was not familiar with Miss Boyd, but Lady Trevarron heard by word of mouth that she had passed and that her lady's maid was available. I usually appoint the maids, but she requested you herself.' She sounded as if she disapproved. 'Still, you're here now. I would have sent you with a chaperone, but everyone does things differently, I suppose. Lady Trevarron never even told me your name, now that I come to think about it. I'm not even sure if she was aware of it.'

I didn't know what to do, so I hid behind the screen for a moment, appalled that this woman evidently thought that I was going to take my dress off in front of her.

'My name is Tegan Penrose,' I said.

'Very Cornish,' Mrs Cottingley said. 'Are you from Cornwall, originally? Before you worked in London?'

'Yes,' I replied. 'I'm from Cornwall.' That wasn't a lie, but I didn't comment about the working in London part. I was bewildered by what was going on and had slipped into survival mode.

I had to get out of here. This was now all too strange, and the date on the newspaper – a prop, no doubt, the attention to detail in this historical TV show or whatever it was, was impressive – had freaked me out. I kept asking people to be normal, to just drop their damned roles for a moment, but they didn't seem to want to.

It was like I was trapped in a nightmare, and – even though Mrs Cottingley seemed the friendliest of the people I'd met – the longer it went on, the stranger it got. The fact that nobody was willing to break cover was really creepy.

I can't do this, I realised. *I have to get out of here.*

I realised that my curiosity wasn't enough to keep me there. For all I knew, these people wanted to do awful things to me – though, I admit, it seemed like on overly elaborate way to kidnap or murder someone – and I shouldn't stay a minute longer.

Panic overtook me, and, as Mrs Cottingley had her back turned, I tiptoed towards the door through which I had entered and down the stairs. Once I was in the corridor at the bottom, I ran.

I didn't know where the long corridor went, but I turned in the opposite direction to the kitchens. I had no desire to run into Cook again, and so I made a dash for a grand entrance hall which loomed ahead of me, at the end of it.

Voices echoed in the rooms I passed, but I didn't see anyone. Panic propelled me forward. A man emerged from one of the rooms, dressed smartly in a powdered wig, waistcoat and jacket and breeches and tried to grab me, but I dodged him.

'You! Girl!' he cried out, but I kept running.

Without stopping, I sprinted into the wide entrance hall, pushed the heavy wooden door open and ran down the stone steps outside. The steps that I only ever remembered as cracked and broken, with weeds growing in them. Now, they were perfect: smooth and clean, as if they had just been swept.

Once I was outside of the house, I ran into the meadow and to the broken part of the fence where I usually entered and exited the grounds of the house.

It made no sense that, when I looked over my shoulder, the house was perfect and undamaged. I had never seen it as anything other than derelict, and it had been derelict when I had climbed up the side of the rose garden fence. But I was spooked by it all, and I ran and ran, feeling a soft horror in the soles of my feet and a nervous tingling in my stomach.

But when I got to the entry spot I remembered, everything was different. The fence wasn't there. The trees that I remembered nearby – oak, ash and beech – weren't in the right places, either. In the distance, a dog barked.

I stood, out of breath, in front of where the gap in the fence should have been. Was I in the right place? Maybe I had got it wrong? But when I looked behind me, I knew I hadn't. I was at the right angle in relation to the house. So, why wasn't it here?

I pushed forward, looking desperately for a way out, but I couldn't find one. Instead of the old chain link fence that used to surround Trevarron House, the perimeter was marked by a tall privet hedge that didn't appear to have any gaps in it whatsoever –

and, for good measure, there was a row of closely planted dark pine trees behind that.

There had to be a way out. I jogged along the drive; it was longer than I expected, but when I finally got to the gates at the end, I stood there in disbelief.

The gates were open. I could run through and leave this odd day behind me. Only, the gates weren't as I remembered at all.

The last time I had seen them, the gates of Trevarron House had been covered in moss, and the tops of each gate post had been empty – despite the memories I knew I had of them being there.

Now, the stone posts of the gate were clean and new, and the fabled griffins sat atop them, looking down at me sternly. I thought of that day with Aunt Bill, when she had taken me into the overgrown grounds of Trevarron House and explained the odd mystery of St Nantes to me. I stared at the griffins. They were *there*.

They hadn't been there, before. Not when I had gone in. Not for years. We all knew it. So, how was it that they had come back?

How were they *actually there*?

As I stared, an old-fashioned horse and carriage arrived outside the gate, the horses clip-clopping along the country lane, the carriage's wheels huge, round, gilded spheres slowing to a halt as I stood there.

I stared up at the carriage dumbly, not believing what I was seeing.

On top of the carriage sat a man in smart navy blue livery with white piping on the shoulders and around the buttonholes, holding the reins to the horses. He glared, and rudely gestured for me to get out of the way. I stepped to one side, instinctively, and the carriage passed me by, just like one I would have seen in a historical drama.

As it passed, one of its windows wound down, and a woman's face looked out. She wore her dark brown hair in a series of elaborate curls and ringlets, and on her pretty face was a perplexed expression. I could see that she was in a light blue dress with a low neck and a bodice, matching the eighteenth-century clothes that everyone else I had met in the last hour was wearing.

Her eyes met mine, and I saw a question in them. That question stopped me in my tracks, because I knew it was the same question that I had been asking myself for the past hour or so. And that was the question of my belonging here, because I very definitely didn't.

There was something about the honesty of the woman's expression that frightened me to my core. It was clear that she was genuinely surprised to see me, and that I looked odd to her. I was wearing the wrong clothes and I was in the wrong place, and I could see that she knew it.

And, the vision of the carriage, the man in livery driving the horses, the horses themselves, who had clearly been pulling the carriage for some time, because they were flecked with mud and wore a moist sheen on their glossy flanks; all of it stopped my breath in my chest with a sudden sense of shock.

This woman was coming from the *outside* of Trevarron House. It looked as though she had come from a reasonable distance.

How was that possible? I had assumed that whatever was happening at Trevarron House was some kind of historical re-enactment, a bizarre makeover, which I had no way of really explaining, but I'd been hanging on to that idea because there had been no other feasible explanation.

But the arrival of the carriage, and the sight of the gates, had made me consider a radical possibility that I did not want to face. I stood there, my heart pounding, still out of breath, with the weight of the only other possible explanation crushing my heart and threatening to drag me into a deep spiral of panic.

What if I was no longer in the twenty-first century, and I had somehow been transported to the past?

EIGHT

'You, there!'

The carriage had passed me, and I was watching it approach the house in a kind of dumb fascination.

I was in shock. Was this a dream? Was I hallucinating? Had I been in some kind of terrible accident, and I was currently unconscious somewhere?

It had to be one of those things, because the other truth was too incredible: that I had somehow found myself in the eighteenth century.

'You! Girl!' It was a command: loud, deep and sonorous. A voice that was used to being obeyed.

I heard hoofbeats behind me and started to run again, through the gates and along the lane, veering off the hard-pressed ground of the drive and onto the grass at the side of the road.

'Leave me alone!' I cried out, my voice jagged from lack of breath and fear. But before I knew it, a man's strong hand gripped the back of my dress, and before I could even cry out, had lifted me onto the horse in front of him. A strong arm wrapped around my waist, and he pulled me into his lap.

'Stop struggling,' he ordered. 'I've got you.'

I ignored him and pulled away from his grasp. I wanted to get off and run, get back to Aunt Bill's cottage, where I would be safe, but the horse reared and I was afraid that I'd fall. I'd never been on a horse before, and the feel of it moving under me was disconcerting. It was all muscle, and it whinnied loudly at my presence.

I turned around in my seat, furious at being manhandled.

William De Vere Trevarron regarded me coolly, one hand controlling the reins of the horse, and the other arm pressing me tight against him.

'Keep still,' he said in a low voice that, despite everything, sent a thrill of electricity through me. He twisted the leather reins and drew me closer to him at the same time. 'Or you will fall and be trampled.'

I looked down at his hands again, once again noticing their roughness and the broken skin on the knuckles. I wondered what the hell he could have been doing to leave them so injured.

'Let me go!' I pulled his arm away, but the movement made me lose my balance, and for a moment, I felt my centre of gravity displaced on the back of the horse; William swore under his breath and replaced a steadying hand on my waist, pulling me back into place.

'For God's sake, girl!' he remonstrated, his tone harsh. 'When I say keep still, I mean it,' he hissed. His hand gripped my waist harder, his fingertips digging into my flesh.

I stopped struggling for a moment, afraid of falling. Even though his tone was harsh, something in the timbre of his voice – deep and well-spoken – resonated deep inside me like a bell. I was chagrined to realise that, when he replaced his arm around my waist, I leaned back into him, instinctively, wanting to be near him. It was the same feeling as before: primal and unmistakeable. He smelt *right*. That was ridiculous, I knew that, but all my instincts wanted to melt into him.

This is no time to go silly over a man, Tegan, Aunt Bill's voice warned in my mind. But there was nowhere to go. I was trapped in his arms, pressed against William's hard, muscular body.

For a few moments, neither of us said anything. He had turned the horse back towards the house and we were cantering along the drive. The rhythm of the horse under us repeatedly threw my body against William's, and the steady reverberations of the hooves pounding against the ground, as William held me tight, gave me a sweet and hot feeling in my abdomen.

My body felt right next to his, and – I wasn't proud to note the feeling, and yet it was there – I was aroused by his voice, his presence. I could feel a sudden heat and wetness between my thighs.

I was appalled at myself. What was *wrong* with me?

His jawline grazed my neck, and he made a low noise in the back of his throat. His touch, and the sound he made, aroused me even further. It was as though he found the feel of my body next to his almost unbearable; I had the sudden impression that it was torturing him.

'I need to leave. I don't belong here,' I panted, trying to maintain focus.

'I thought Mrs Cottingley would have taken care of you. I have better things to do than to chase after some servant girl,' he snarled.

'Listen. You can drop all the pretence.' Why had he ridden out on a *horse* to get me? Why was everyone so concerned that I stay at the house? Surely, it couldn't be... I roused myself from the erotic torpor that had overtaken me. 'I'm going home. Let me off.'

'Where is home?' He slowed the horse down.

'I live locally. I come here sometimes to read. That's it. All this' – I gestured to the house, his horse, and him – 'all of this is crazy. I don't know what's going on.'

We were riding back towards the house. I craned my neck back in the direction I'd been running. All I could see now was the long, snaking drive, bordered by gleaming, dark green rhododendron bushes. It was beautiful, and much better-kept than it had ever been before. But the sight also gave me a very unsettled feeling. There was something about the thick greenery that was oppressive. I remembered the high, sweet smell of decay in the rose garden, and shivered.

As the drive receded behind me, part of me wanted to leap off the horse and run away. But there was also a part of me that wanted to be next to William, or whatever his name was. I had felt it when we'd first met: an attraction that was undeniable. Despite the ridiculous situation, despite whatever was going on here, my body knew the truth.

'Please. Let me go,' I begged, but, as he slowed the horse at the side of the house, next to a stable, William merely shot me a strange look. He dismounted neatly, and then offered me his hand.

'Get off,' he said, abruptly. I had no choice but to climb down, out of the saddle. 'You're going back where you belong.'

NINE

I awoke in the dark.

The dim orange light of dawn glowed gently through the heavy curtains at the window, and, somewhere outside, a cock crowed.

I groaned and rolled over, my neck sore from the hard pillow and the lumpy mattress. I closed my eyes again, thinking that I'd try to go back to sleep. Whatever had happened, it must have been a dream, and I was safe in my little room at Aunt Bill's.

I felt a sense of extreme relief.

I had dreamed the same dream again: of the rock, and the sunset, and the man in silhouette. But, this time, he had had something very important to tell me, only I couldn't hear him over the crash of the waves beneath us.

In the dream, I was looking over the edge of the cliff at the waves, wondering why they were so loud, and he had been shouting at me, trying to pull me back from the edge.

I woke up the moment my foot slipped off the slick, wet rock and I felt myself fall.

Before I could close my eyes again, the door to the room opened, and I heard footsteps moving across the wooden floorboards. Then a young woman appeared by the window, opening the curtains briskly.

I sat up in bed, startled.

'Who are you?' I asked. The woman – though *girl* would be a better description, now that my eyes had adjusted to the light – blinked at me, and dropped into a semi-curtsey.

'Mornin', miss. I'm Elowen, one o' the maids. I'll be lookin' after you. But in this 'ouse, you can call me Betty. That's what's all the lower maids gets called,' she said, in a thick Cornish accent. I pulled the floral coverlet up over myself, noticing that I seemed to be wearing a high-necked cotton nightdress.

One of the maids? I looked around me, panic rising in my throat, realising that I wasn't in my little room at Aunt Bill's house. Now that the orange dawn light was streaming through the window, I could see it was the room that Mrs Cottingley had led me up to the day before: the small bed, the wardrobe, the dressing table.

I was still there. I was still at Trevarron House.

I don't remember putting this on, I thought, feeling sick with the realisation that I was still stuck inside whatever nightmare this was. *Or getting in bed. Have I been drugged?*

I estimated that Elowen – or Betty – was at most thirteen years old. She had auburn hair, pulled back in a neat bun, and wore a simple long brown dress with a white apron.

'How did I get here?' I demanded.

The last thing I remembered was William bringing me back to the house on his horse. I dimly recalled getting off the horse outside the stables, but after that, nothing.

'You passed out in Lord Trevarron's arms,' Betty said, with more than a tinge of envy in her voice. ''Ee brought ye up 'ere 'imself, an' told me to bathe ye and change ye. Ye were out of all sense. Kept ravin' about goin' 'ome. Like ye 'ad a bump on the 'ead or something,' Betty came to stand next to the bed and peered at me suspiciously. ''Ow you feelin' now?'

Oh, no.

I couldn't believe it. I felt dread wrap me up like a spider in its web.

'Can I have some water?' I croaked, realising that I was thirsty.

Betty nodded and went to a jug on the dressing table, filled a glass and brought it to me. 'Breakfast's in the kitchens fer the lower staff, but as you're the lady's maid, you 'ave the servants' dining room with the upstairs maids, the footmen an' the butlers, an' Mrs Cottingley. We'll get ye up an' dressed an' I'll take ye down,' she added.

'Sorry. Did you say that you would be... looking after me?' I caught on to what she'd said earlier.

'Aye. I'll make up the fire in the winter months, make yer bed, take yer laundry, bring water for your ablutions, take the chamber pot,' the girl said, patiently. 'Lady's maids usually are at the disposal of the lady, which in this 'ouse is Lady Trevarron. Mrs Cottingley wanted you up an' about today so that she could give ye the tour and instruct ye before ye go in an see the mistress,' Betty continued.

I was overwhelmed by everything, and the fact that I had awoken in Trevarron House, apparently still in the eighteenth century, remained inexplicable.

Come on, come on, I willed myself to some kind of focus. *You've got to cope. You can't just crumble. Whatever this is, you have to find a way out of it.*

I decided that the only course of action was for me to play along and try to find out what was going on, and then form a plan.

'All right. Thank you, Betty,' I said, a little stiffly.

'I bathed you a little last night, miss, as you were dusty from bein' outside, and tended to your knee,' she added, shyly. 'But I'll bring up a basin of water for ye now an' you can freshen up yourself.' She nodded, and left me for a moment. I heard her walking down a corridor, and went to the door to see where it led.

Outside the room, a narrow, dark corridor led towards a stairwell. I could hear the sound of running water, and in a moment, Betty emerged from behind another door along the hall, carrying a large jug of water.

'That's the bathroom. You have your own up here, bein' the

lady's maid, an' there's three outhouses off the kitchen, an' a public bathhouse in the village. Course, there's the river, in the warmer months.' Betty set the jug of water down on the wide dressing table. One side of the table seemed dedicated to washing, with the jug, bowl and a few folded towels, and the other half displayed a neat set of hairbrushes, a mirror and a comb.

'You'll see that the Master an' Lady Trevarron, an' Lord Charles, all have their own private bathrooms. Tubs, even 'ot water, fired by wood. 'Tis remarkable, what we 'ave at Trevarron.' Betty sounded proud, as if unbothered by the fact that she didn't have access to a working bathroom herself.

'Thank you...' I wasn't sure what to reply; the fact that I considered hot running water a basic requirement – and was used to getting it by turning on a tap – seemed on one hand an obvious thing to say, but to Betty, it appeared that it was a thing of wonder.

She turned away discreetly as I poured some of the water into a deep porcelain bowl next to it and picked up a square of muslin, wetting it and wiping my face with it and then my underarms and as much of my body as I could reach under the nightgown. I dried myself with a cloth that was more like a tablecloth than a towel.

I saw that someone – presumably Betty – had tended to the deep graze on my knee and applied a bandage. However, the covering seemed quite lumpy.

'Thank you for dressing my knee,' I said, to break the silence. In the distance, I could hear sounds of the house getting ready; voices raised, pots clanging, people moving around.

'Most welcome, miss. I put a herbal dressin' on to 'elp heal it. My mother is a pellar,' she added, in an undertone.

I nodded. I recognised the term, but I couldn't quite remember what it was.

'A pellar?' I asked, politely, as she carried the same dress towards me from the wardrobe that Mrs Cottingley had yesterday.

'Aye. Cunning folk. Those wi' knowledge of herbs and remedies,' Betty replied. 'She lives in the village.'

'You mean St Nantes?'

'Yes, miss. Do ye know the village?' Betty's expression brightened.

'I have passed through it a few times,' I replied, noncommittally. I was supposed to be a Cornish lady's maid who had worked in London: it probably wouldn't do to let slip that I'd all but grown up in St Nantes.

I flexed my leg, but it felt fine: not hot or tight, as it would if it was infected. 'Thank you, Betty. It feels much better.'

'No' a bit of it,' the girl replied, looking pleased. 'Honey, marigold an' garlic, in a paste. 'Tis all. Now. Let us dress you.'

She began by pulling off my nightdress, even though I protested, and then handed me a clean cotton shift. I pulled it on, embarrassed at being naked in front of a stranger, but Betty seemed unbothered.

She placed a cream-coloured corset-type garment around me and began lacing it up at the back. I yelped as she pulled the ribbons tight, but she continued with her work, coming to stand in front of me to adjust my breasts and push them up so that the corset helped to keep them firmly upraised.

It was hardly what I was used to: my interest in fashion was more academic than anything and no one wore corsets like this anymore. Thankfully, underwear was all about comfort now. As soon as Betty finished the lacing, I took a few careful steps and felt as though I could hardly breathe.

'Could you loosen it a bit?' I asked, indignant. She frowned at me.

''Ardly, miss. The dress won't fit if I do. 'Appen you've got a more generous figure than Lady Edith's last girl.'

Charming. I couldn't think of anything to say to that, so I let her carry on. Breathing was obviously overrated in the eighteenth century.

The next task was to step into a wide underskirt that Betty tied around my waist. I was surprised that I would be naked from the waist down under the shift, but didn't ask her about it – it wasn't the kind of question you could ask a stranger very easily. The underskirt was huge. Over the top of that went a skirt in a cream-coloured jacquard material and then a matching jacket with a long skirt attached that draped over the skirt, open at the front. The sides of the top were pinned to the bodice she had laced me into, and then a separate panel front was pinned over the corset. The panel was embroidered with pink roses, and the jacket had pink bows at the elbows where the sleeves ended.

I looked at myself in wonder in the full-length mirror that stood to one side of the bed. I still had no idea what was going on, but I was now apparently dressed for a costume ball.

'Now, then. Hair and then face. Would you like to do your powder and such, miss? Or I can do it for you?' Betty asked solicitously. I cast a glance at the dressing table and some suspicious-looking powder in a glass bowl. If this really was the eighteenth century, God only knew what sort of harmful mix of lead and whatever else might be in there, so I shook my head.

'I don't wear makeup,' I replied. In fact, I did usually wear a little, but there was no way that I was going to let her know that. Bare-faced was probably safer.

She nodded.

'As you say, miss,' she said, and began attempting to style my hair.

When my hair had been set in curls with some heated metal tongs – I shied away from them at first, seeing that Betty had heated them in the hearth, but she insisted – Betty looked pleased.

'Now, then.' She nodded again. 'That's much better,'

I followed Betty to the servants' dining room, which was down two flights of stairs and along another cream-painted corridor. It was plain, but clean and tidy, and when I walked in, the people who were already sitting at the table stood up. Instinctively, I curtseyed, wondering if it was the right thing to do, but Mrs Cottingley smiled thinly.

'Thank you, Betty.' She dismissed my maid with a subtle nod, and I felt a sadness at having to say goodbye to the one person I had felt safe with so far. Still, I supposed I'd see Betty again later.

'Good morning, Miss Penrose.' She extended a hand and gestured that I should sit down at the table. 'I trust you feel refreshed after a good night's sleep?'

'Umm... yes, thank you,' I replied. I wondered what would happen when or if the real lady's maid turned up? But, hopefully, I'd be gone by then.

'We tend to remain formal with names at Trevarron, for the senior staff,' Mrs Cottingley continued. 'I am Mrs Cottingley, this is Mr Brown, the head butler—' She indicated the man to her right, who was probably in his mid-fifties, clean-shaven with long grey hair tied at the back in a black ribbon as seemed customary for men here. He possessed a stocky frame that suggested he was strong when he needed to be. He was very smartly dressed in a black waistcoat and jacket with brass buttons, a white shirt underneath and the same knee-length breeches all the men seemed to wear.

'Welcome to Trevarron.' Mr Brown nodded kindly at me. 'This is Mr Cooper, my second-in-command and butler to Lord Charles. I tend to look after Lord William, and keep an oversight of the house. You will, of course, be looking after Lady Trevarron, who is Lord William and Lord Charles's younger sister.' He spoke in quite a proper way, but he still had hint of a Cornish accent at the edges. Ah, so the lords and ladies of Trevarron were brothers and sisters. None of them were married, it seemed.

'Yes, indeed. Hello.' I nodded to Mr Cooper, who was a little younger than Mr Brown, with sandy hair that was receding a little at the top, and was also tied at the back with a black ribbon. 'Pleased to meet you.'

'And you, miss.' Mr Cooper nodded formally and returned to his breakfast: two poached eggs and a couple of sausages. My stomach rumbled.

'And these are Letty and Molly, parlour maids,' Mrs Cottingley introduced two girls who looked to be in their teens, like Betty. I noticed that they were apparently not senior enough to be called by their surnames, but not so lowly as to be called the catch-all name of Betty. I smiled at them, and they smiled back shyly. 'And then we have Eric, our footman, and Richard, our driver. Richard also helps in the house.' I recognised Richard as the man who had been sitting on top of the carriage, the day before. I nodded, shyly, wondering what he thought of me. He had probably seen William carry me off on the horse, and I knew that they all thought I had been dressed oddly.

'Do help yourself to breakfast, dear.' Mrs Cottingley indicated a number of silver trays and tureens laid out behind the table on a sideboard. I stood up, took my plate from where it was set in front of me and looked down at the selection.

The plate was white and monogrammed with an ornate black *T* at the centre. It made me think of the cast-iron gates outside the rose garden that also featured a *T* in their design. *T* for Trevarron. I had to get back out to the rose garden and see if there was something in there that would... what? Enable me to time travel back to normal life, I supposed. The thought that I really was in another time was still so ridiculous I couldn't believe it, and yet here I was, taking a poached egg from a silver tureen also monogrammed with a T, and a couple of sausages and a piece of bread.

The door opened and Cook walked in. I shrank away from her, instantly on my guard, but she merely gave me the once-over and nodded, placing a large teapot on the table.

'Don't you brush up well,' she said, in a dull tone. 'I 'ear you're Lady Trevarron's new maid. Apologies for the mix-up.'

'That's... umm. Thank you.' I wasn't sure what to say. The day before, Cook had seemed ready to fight me, and she'd threatened to give me a whipping twice. Now, her attitude was sulky but respectful. I wondered at the change in her, then realised that I outranked her, so she had to be polite to me.

'Thank you, Cook. That will be all.' Mrs Cottingley gave her a brisk nod, and Cook left the room. It was obvious that, as housekeeper, Mrs Cottingley was superior in rank to Cook. I knew from my studies that in large houses belonging to the gentry, the servants had different ranks, and the most senior were the head butler and the housekeeper. So, I had at least managed to enter this weird little world at a relatively high level, which would mean that my life here – or my hallucination, whatever it was, as long or as short as that might be – would be easier than it would be if I was a scullery maid.

'So. After you have breakfasted, we will take a tour of the house and I will show you all of Lady Trevarron's clothes, her accessories, hats and coats, and show you her quarters, and, of course, introduce you,' Mrs Cottingley continued. 'I understand that you worked for Miss Boyd for three years? So, you will be aware of the requirements of a lady engaged in the arts. Lady Trevarron possesses a kind heart and an eager mind, but I fear she is all too often frustrated at the restrictions laid upon her in her role as lady of the manor,' the housekeeper explained.

'I see,' I replied. I didn't really know what she meant, and of course I had no idea who Miss Boyd was. Mrs Cottingley looked at me expectantly. I cleared my throat. 'Err. Yes. The arts.'

'Lady Trevarron enjoys poetry and the arts,' Mrs Cottingley prompted me. 'She thought that you would be a suitable lady's maid, considering that you assisted Miss Boyd, who she thought very highly of. It is a terrible shame that Miss Boyd has passed, Lord bless her.' Mrs Cottingley bowed her head for a moment.

'Indeed. A terrible shame,' I echoed. 'She was... a wonderful mistress, and a great talent.' I took a gamble in saying it, but from what Mrs Cottingley had said, it sounded as if Miss Boyd could realistically be considered talented.

'Indeed. And I can tell that you have education, Miss Penrose.' Mrs Cottingley poured some tea into my cup. I was relieved to see that tea seemed relatively the same as in the twenty-first century, though the sausages tasted odd and the bread was tough and grainy. 'That will aid you greatly in accompanying Lady Edith. She has a lively mind, as I say. She will expect intelligent conversation from you.'

'I'll try to entertain her, then,' I said. It was strange to think that, in the 1700s, it was so unusual for a woman to be educated in any way. I was at university, and that was pretty normal for a lot of people. Even if I hadn't gone, I'd still had a typical school education.

I looked around the table, and wondered what education these people had had. Then I thought about what I knew of the world in the 1700s; the political developments in England and the other nations in Britain, and what was happening in other countries. Without any source of news apart from the papers, and with many people not even able to read, it would be a very different existence here than what I was used to. I wondered what was even in the newspaper that Mrs Cottingley had been holding the day before. How much truth, and given through what political lens.

'Hm. I'm sure that you will be exemplary.' Mrs Cottingley drained her cup of tea and stood up. 'Shall we?'

TEN

I finished my eggs, hurriedly drank my tea, and stood up.

I'd hoped that our tour would take us outside so that I could size up the rose garden and figure out how I might magically disappear back to the present day, but Mrs Cottingley walked me around the interior of Trevarron House, pointing out everything from architectural details to paintings.

Despite it all, I couldn't help but be fascinated by what I saw. In my world, Trevarron House was a ruin. Now I was glimpsing it as a functioning stately home. A manor house packed with antique furniture and art; only, in the 1700s, it wasn't antique but relatively newly built. The history buff in me loved seeing it all in its original condition: the furniture gleamed, the paintings looked fresher, the colour of the paint more vibrant.

From my historical studies, I knew that the year we were in – 1755 – meant that we were in the period of the Enlightenment, where philosophical thinkers and scientists prioritised reason over religion, and new ideas began to emerge about people having the right to freedom.

In forty years or so, the French Revolution would overturn the rule of royalty in France and create a democratic republic with spectacular and savage force. I also knew that the American Revolution would begin in the 1770s as Britain imposed high taxes on the colonists that had moved there as early as the 1600s. I wondered how involved the Trevarrons were with the outside world, what they thought about the colonies, and how they'd see the war, being a part of the ruling class.

Next, Mrs Cottingley led me through a library packed full of whole sets of leather-bound books, most of which I'd never heard of: tomes of philosophy, religion and geography that I longed to take down and look at. I wondered what the maps would look like. Leaving aside the pure confusion of the situation, it was amazing to be within a vivid, eighteenth-century manor house, with everything working perfectly. It was like walking through a life-size dolls' house. The little girl inside the adult me wanted to touch everything, see how perfectly it fit together.

As I looked at the spines of the books on the shelves, I saw works that I knew would be considered controversial at that point in time: books about freedom from dictatorship and the rights to democracy. I recognised some of the authors: Voltaire, Rousseau, Jeremy Bentham, John Locke. What did that say about the Trevarrons? Was one of them – or all of them – a rebel, a socialist, a reformer?

I wanted to stay and look at everything, but Mrs Cottingley hurried me through to the next room which was a small parlour with a couple of delicate tables and chaises, and then a larger room, hung with luxurious fabrics on the walls and featuring a round table at its centre. It looked as though it had recently been set for a fancy dinner, because there were handwritten place names left on the table, and a neat collection of crystal goblets. As we entered, two maids who I hadn't seen before were polishing silverware and putting it back in a couple of velvet-lined wooden chests.

'This is the dining room.' The housekeeper swept regally around the wooden table. 'This is walnut,' she added, tracing her fingertips over the light wood which bwas buffed to a high shine, varnished expertly to showcase the soft grain of the wood underneath. 'The furniture in the house mostly belonged to previous generations, but Lord William invested in some new pieces a few years ago. This was made in London, as were the chairs,' she added, as if this would impress me greatly.

'Do the lords and lady have many dinner parties?' I asked, admiring the room.

'Lady Trevarron and Lord Charles enjoy parties,' Mrs Cottingley said. 'However, it's been some years since they were involved in the social scene.'

'Not William?' I asked, innocently. The William Trevarron situation was pretty strange, I had to admit. I knew that I'd be going home as soon as I could, but the fact that I had some serious chemistry with the lord of the manor hadn't stopped playing on my mind. As we'd been walking around, I'd thought about him whisking me onto the saddle of his horse and holding me there tightly, pressing me into his body. I swallowed and cleared my throat.

'You may refer to him as Lord Trevarron, or milord.' Mrs Cottingley raised an eyebrow. 'His younger brother, we call Lord Charles, and Lady Edith, or Lady Trevarron.' She regarded me coolly. 'Perhaps in your previous house you were on more casual terms with Miss Boyd. However, I would remind you that we take the formal approach here. As a mark of respect.'

'Of course. Sorry.' I'd have to try and make sure I said the right thing, here – at least, as long as I was here.

'Hm.' Mrs Cottingley's lips thinned for a moment. 'No. Lord Trevarron is not one for parties. He is a good master, and maintaining the estate keeps him busy. He tends to keep himself to himself.'

'Is he single?' I asked, then realised from Mrs Cottingley's expression that she thought that was an inappropriate question. 'I mean to say... there's no Lady Trevarron, apart from his sister? Is he engaged to be married, or something like that?'

'You are quite outspoken for a lady's maid, Miss Penrose. I imagine it comes of spending so much time with a bohemian woman such as Miss Boyd,' Mrs Cottingley observed; her emphasis of the word *bohemian* suggested that she disapproved of the idea of an independent woman. 'Still, I anticipate that Lady Trevarron will enjoy that aspect of your outlook. No, Miss Penrose. Lord Trevarron was once wed, but she died in the first year of their marriage. He remains a widower, and is pursued by many society ladies. However, he seems to prefer to remain a bachelor.' Mrs Cottingley's tone implied that she disapproved.

'That's tragic. I'm so sorry to hear that.' I frowned. 'He must have been quite young. How did she die?'

'He was of marriageable age. He was still in the Navy at that time, and planned to continue his career there, but I believe that Lady Elspeth's death shook him so deeply that he was unable to.' Mrs Cottingley looked at me curiously. 'She had a terrible accident. I wonder that you do not know this already, Miss Penrose. It was quite the society news when it happened, some years ago. Miss Boyd would have told you, perhaps? Or someone else?'

'I... I was not aware. Miss Boyd was not concerned with society gossip,' I invented, wondering what to say. 'And before that I wasn't a lady's maid to anyone at the right... level.'

'Indeed.' Mrs Cottingley nodded. 'Well, it was the talk of the town, and beyond.'

'He must have been crushed. Were they very much in love?' I felt terrible for William.

'He idolised her. She was the darling of every room she entered.' Mrs Cottingley shook her head sadly. 'Never was there a more vivacious, prettier girl. She was accomplished, too. French, piano, embroidery. Such a shame.' She paused, a shadow passing over her sharp features. 'If those rumour-mongers had seen how devastated he was, they never would have made up all those falsehoods about him.'

'What falsehoods?' I asked, curious, but Mrs Cottingley tutted as she looked up at the face of a large grandfather clock in the corner of the room.

'Oh, dear. I need to get you up to Lady Trevarron's quarters post haste. I didn't realise the time, and she will be wanting to go out for a ride shortly. Come along, now.'

She nodded curtly to the maids who were tidying away the crystal. I glanced at the open cabinets at the edge of the room, which held stacks of fine porcelain dishes and plates, glass and silverware. All of this would be worth so much to a modern-day antiques dealer; the opulence of Trevarron House amazed me.

I wondered what had happened to all of these possessions and treasures: had they all been lost to time and the fire? What had happened to the Trevarrons, and why was the house derelict and uncared for in the time that I had found it? And what did Mrs Cottingley mean about gossip surrounding Lady Elspeth's unfortunate death?

I followed Mrs Cottingley out of the room and up the main staircase leading to the upper level. As we ascended, we passed a number of large portraits; Mrs Cottingley had pointed some of them out to me earlier as Trevarron ancestors. But one stood out to me, and after what she had just told me, I could see instantly who it depicted.

William Trevarron stood in the centre of the picture, dressed handsomely in what I assumed was his Navy uniform. One hand rested on his dog's head, and, next to him, stood a beautiful young woman, also looking up at him adoringly. The scene was of woodland, and, in the distance, the artist had conveyed the jagged black rocks of the north Cornwall coast, and the tumultuous sea below.

I peered at the bottom of the frame, where a small golden plaque held the title of the painting. LORD WILLIAM DE VERE TREVARRON AND LADY ELSPETH MARY TREVARRON, 1750, it read. And, under that, the words, UNDYING LOVE.

ELEVEN

'Good morning, Lady Trevarron. May I introduce Miss Tegan Penrose, your new lady's maid.'

Mrs Cottingley led me into a large and ornate sitting room. The walls were covered in what looked like hand-painted wallpaper featuring pea-green water lilies and vivid blue kingfishers against a golden-brown background. Large, lead-lined windows were hung with thick velvet curtains in a deep gold hue and held back with thick, cabled ties of the same fabric. The wide wooden floorboards were mostly covered by two vast matching rugs, which matched the pea green of the water lilies of the wallpaper and were edged with a soft gold border in a filigree pattern.

It was beautiful. I was still awed by seeing everything downstairs, and Lady Trevarron's quarters were even grander. It gave me butterflies, looking at everything.

Edith Trevarron sat on one of three rococo-style sofas in the room which featured gold-painted wood and blue satin upholstery. Next to her were a stack of leather-bound books piled up haphazardly; she was flicking through the pages of one of them and held another open with her spare hand. She was dressed in a long white shirt, rolled up at the elbows, a pair of breeches and her chestnut brown hair fell over her shoulder in a messy plait. She was barefoot.

I realised that she was the same woman I had glimpsed briefly as she'd passed me in her carriage, by the gates to the estate. However, that woman had been dressed formally with her hair in ringlets and, in the moment I had seen her, had seemed startled.

Now, Edith Trevarron jumped up and strode confidently over to us, holding her hand out in greeting.

'Miss Penrose!' she exclaimed with gusto. 'Jolly nice to meet you. I trust Cottingley has been showing you the ropes?' She shook my hand vigorously and grinned at me; I couldn't help but grin back at her. I'd been expecting a formal lady in an elaborate dress, but Edith Trevarron seemed brisk and friendly, and her energy was both impish and surprisingly down-to-earth.

'Er... yes, thank you, Lady Trevarron.' I curtseyed, but Edith tutted.

'No curtseying for me, my dear girl. Can't abide it. Tegan, is it? Funny, I don't remember that name, but it's been a while since I contacted Miss Boyd's family about you.' She cocked her head slightly to one side, like an inquisitive bird. I liked her immediately, though I felt wary, again, about lying about who I was.

'Yes. Tegan.' I wondered whether I should be trying to speak in a more old-fashioned way, but I didn't want to come off as weird, so I tried to keep it as simple as possible. It was fortunate that Edith didn't remember the name of the original lady's maid. Suddenly, I worried again about the real maid turning up, and needing to explain who I was.

'Of course. Well, Tegan, sit down and tell me about yourself. And, please, call me Edith. Lady Trevarron makes me sound so old.' She rolled her eyes.

'I was just instructing Miss Penrose in the more formal ways of address, Lady Trevarron,' Mrs Cottingley interjected.

'Oh, Cottingley. Please. What you choose to do is up to you, but I require Tegan to call me Edith, because that is my name,' she said, smiling coyly at the housekeeper, but her tone was cool. 'Please don't be such a bore. You may leave us now.'

'Yes, Lady Trevarron.' Mrs Cottingley began to drop into a curtsey, until she caught Edith's eye and recovered herself. 'I will take my leave.'

I sat down carefully next to Edith – mostly because I wasn't used to wearing a corset and underskirts, and it was pretty difficult to move about in them at all, never mind perch on what was quite a delicate piece of furniture. Clearly, women weren't expected to sit down much in the eighteenth century. I thought for a moment about how car seat belts in the twenty-first century were not tested on women's bodies, and reflected that not much had changed in the world when it came to considering women in the engineering and design of most everyday items.

'Now, Tegan,' she said earnestly, and took both of my hands in hers. 'I need to ask you a very important question. And it will determine whether you and I will be fast friends from now on, or whether we will be mere polite acquaintances. I, for one, would prefer the former.'

'As would I, Lady Trevarron,' I replied, seriously, then caught the look in her eye. 'Edith,' I corrected myself.

'Good. The question is this: do you enjoy poetry?' She gazed at me seriously.

'Um. Yes, I like poetry...' I tried to think of the poets we had studied at school, and which ones Edith might have known – it wasn't any use mentioning the World War I poets, for instance. I'd taken English literature at up until age eighteen along with history and art, and I'd always quite enjoyed analysing poetry.

'You do! Ah, what a boon, my dear Tegan. I had, of course, hoped, given your time with Miss Boyd, that you would. She was someone I much admired. I have all the copies of her periodical, you know.' She went to a side table that stood between two of the sofas and brought back a small, black-and-white printed pamphlet and gave it to me:

The Snail: Or The Lady's Lucubrations

Being entertaining letters between a lady at St James's, and her friend at Dover, on new and curious subjects

'Right. Yes.' I nodded, and handed it back to her. 'She was... a very interesting woman.'

'Ah, she must have been,' Edith sat back down and looked wistful. 'I wish that I could publish a periodical. You know that Miss Boyd was part of a group of three women, the Shakespeare Ladies' Club? And that, because of them, Shakespeare has become popular again. Why, the London theatres are chock-full of his plays now. I do wish I could see one, but we get precious little theatre down here in the middle of nowhere.'

I wondered how much I would have to make up about Miss Boyd. Had I been back in the twenty-first century, I'd have just looked her up on the internet, but that wasn't possible here.

'Might I borrow one of the periodicals, to remember Miss Boyd by?' I thought at least I could do that, and maybe learn something about Miss Boyd in the meantime that might help me lie convincingly about being her lady's maid.

'Oh, of course!' Edith handed me the stack eagerly. 'Take them all. I've read them cover to cover, multiple times. You know, Tegan' – she looked thoughtfully at me – 'I can tell that we will be great friends. I like for my maids to also be friends, but it hasn't always worked out that way. But there's something about you: I can sense a soul connection between us. Do you believe in the soul, Tegan?'

'Yes, I do.' I blinked, unprepared for Edith's sudden gear change. I got the feeling that being around Edith for any amount of time would mean that I'd experience mercurial shifts like this. It wasn't a bad thing at all. I liked her.

'Oh, so do I. So do I.' Edith pressed my hands in hers. 'The philosophers nowadays, they say that we should rely on science. And science is indeed a wonderful thing. But they are men, and –

like my brothers – they can have cold hearts, sometimes.' She sighed. 'Have you found that, about men?' she asked me.

'I suppose so. I don't have brothers, and my dad – my – father,' I corrected myself, thinking that *dad* probably wasn't a colloquialism in the eighteenth century, 'well, I've never known him. I can see how you would think that about men.' I imagined that gender expectations for behaviour were pretty different in Edith's world than the modern one. Yet, it was still true that men weren't expected to show emotion as much as women. I thought about what an old and outdated idea that was.

'Hm. Our parents passed when we were young; my mother in childbirth with me, and my father... some years later.' An unreadable expression passed over Edith's face. 'Anyway, I fear that men do not sense the mystery and the wonder in the world as we do. Charles laughs when I talk of the soul, and William... When we were children, he was such a sweet boy. But when he went into the Navy, it changed him. And when Elspeth passed...'

She glanced at me as if to check that I knew what she was talking about, and I nodded. 'Well, then, I think he gave up on the soul altogether. Gave up on life, really.' She sighed. 'We hardly talk anymore. It makes me sad.'

'I'm sorry to hear that, Lady Trevarron,' I said, and I meant it. I could tell that Edith was terribly sad about her brother: it was a tragic thing to happen to anyone.

'Edith. Please.' She squeezed my fingers and then let them go. 'Ah, he is a mysterious one, my brother William.' She shook her head. 'I do love him so dearly, and he manages the estate flawlessly. Goodness knows that it is a difficult task... but I worry for him. There is a darkness in his soul, Tegan. And I wonder whether it will ever be lightened.'

'I heard that there were... rumours about Lady Elspeth's death,' I said, bluntly. I had been wondering what Mrs Cottingley meant, and now it just came out.

'Oh. Yes. That.' Edith frowned. 'Tegan, you mustn't think badly of us because of those awful rumours. Please, say that you don't.' She took my hands in hers again, and gazed at me with wide eyes.

'I don't think badly of you. I haven't heard them. I was... curious to know.' I decided that being honest was the best plan.

'Oh. Yes, dear Tegan. I understand. You wish to be assured you are safe at your new employer.' Edith nodded. 'Well, it is not a secret, and if you asked Cook or one of the maidservants, then I'm sure that they would likely furnish you with a half-truth. So, I will tell you.'

She took in a deep breath, and let it out.

'When Elspeth died, she was found in the woods, here on the estate,' Edith began. 'She had gone out for a walk, as she liked to do. She would often pick flowers for the dinner table, or enjoy the sunset on an evening walk. Of course, we thought she was safe, walking on her own. No one would dare to assault the lady of Trevarron on her own estate,' Edith said this as if anticipating that I would say Elspeth's death was somehow her own fault for being out walking alone.

'Of course,' I agreed. As far as I was concerned, a woman should be able to walk around at any time of day, wherever she wanted, and be completely safe, but that was admittedly more of a modern view. Edith looked slightly mollified.

'That day, she had gone out in the evening as she often did, but she was not back by late and so William went out to look for her. He found her with her foot trapped under a tree root. She had fallen and hit her head on a rock. There was blood all over him when he returned to the house, carrying her in his arms.'

Edith's voice hitched, and I could see that she was holding back tears.

'Oh, no,' I breathed. 'And... the rumours?'

Edith stood up and went to the window. She remained there for a moment, looking out. Her hands were behind her back and she wrung them, anxiously.

'People said that William killed her.'

'What?' I did a double take. I don't know what I'd been expecting, but it wasn't murder.

'I know. It's perfectly horrible. I hate repeating it.' Edith shivered. 'But if you're going to live and work here, you have a right to know.' She turned around to face me. 'I wonder that Miss Boyd did not discuss it.'

'She was not one for society gossip,' I said again; I had no idea whether Miss Boyd, my pretend previous employer, enjoyed gossip or not. However, Edith seemed to accept my lie.

'Indeed. Miss Boyd was far too much of an intellectual to entertain such tittle-tattle. I wish that we lived in London; perhaps there, people would be less engaged in deleterious gossip.' She sighed. 'The rumours were that Elspeth was running from him, and she tripped and fell. That he was violent and animalistic as a husband, and that their brief marriage had been filled with torture for poor Elspeth.' Edith's face flushed. It was clear that talking about the accident was desperately difficult for her.

'So... not murder as such. He chased her in a threatening way, she was afraid of him, but she slipped and fell?' I clarified. 'I mean, that's still awful.'

'Yes. But even so... none of it is true. William would never be violent. He was always kind to Elspeth. He loved her.' Edith wiped a tear from her eye. 'The rumours were awful. We stopped receiving invitations to balls and parties. Our friends excluded us. The story was written up in the papers in a most sensational way. William was painted as a dark puppeteer, a villain, even though there was absolutely no evidence to suggest that. It was an *accident. She slipped and fell.*' Edith wrung her hands miserably. 'The rumours did nothing except make Elspeth's loss all the more acute.'

'I'm so sorry that you had to endure that, Edith,' I said. It was true; I felt desperately sorry for anyone who had had to go through a death in the family that was then gossiped about by all and sundry. It must have been horrible.

'Thank you.' Edith pursed her lips. 'People say that the house is cursed, because of Elspeth's death. Even the staff are skittish about going into her old room. I have assured them all that there is no curse, and the house isn't haunted. But servants can be so superstitious. If you'll forgive me saying so.'

'Why do they think the house is haunted? Have they seen anything?' I asked, curiously. In my time, Trevarron House was a ruin, so it wasn't difficult to imagine ghosts. I didn't believe in curses, but I could believe that bad energy could stay in a house after something terrible had happened.

'No, dear. Not as far as I know,' Edith assured me.

I thought of the painting I had just seen on the stairs.

'When did Lady Elspeth pass away?' I asked. The painting had been dated 1750.

'1749. A terrible loss,' Edith repeated. I assumed that the painting must have been made as a memorial. *Undying love*, it had said.

Was there any truth to the rumours about William hurting his wife? I knew that Edith was being a loyal sister in denying them, but I also trusted her judgement. She seemed sensible and intelligent, but then again, you never knew what people were capable of.

Suddenly, I had a terrible thought. I wondered if *William* was the lord that Aunt Bill had told me about: the criminal that had disappeared into thin air when the local police had come to arrest him.

Edith didn't know what I knew.

Edith hadn't seen her house in ruins, or heard the legends about Trevarron. She hadn't seen its dereliction. And, she hadn't heard Aunt Bill talking about a lord of Trevarron, a criminal, who had done something terrible and then disappeared.

It could have been another Lord Trevarron. It might well have been; there was no way for me to know. But the thought nagged at me. If that story was about William, then was the criminal offence he had murdered his wife, or at the very least scared her so badly it led to her death? Aunt Bill had never said.

I knew I was on dangerous ground here, but I told myself sternly that the most important thing was surviving until I got home. Edith's protection was key to that plan, so I resolved to think or say no more about it until I could work out what on earth was going on.

That evening, after dinner, I went up to my room, exhausted. I peeled off my bodice and underskirts so that I was just in the shift I wore underneath and hung up the garments in the wardrobe, then unpinned my hair.

I went over to the dressing table to put the hair pins in the little jar they belonged in, and accidentally hit the table with my hip. Swearing, I saw that the impact had pulled the dressing table away from the wall a little.

I shoved it back in, but it resisted, and I realised that the table didn't actually sit flush to the wall. There was something behind it.

I knelt down and peered up and under the table. Perhaps the wall was uneven; perhaps the back of the dressing table had a drawer sticking out the wrong way?

But instead, I saw that there was a small door in the wall behind the dressing table.

I was immediately curious. Who would put a door in the wall

and then put a piece of furniture in front of it? It wasn't anything big enough to be a normal door to walk through. I pulled out the dressing table a little to see it better.

It was a door of varnished wood, approximately one and a half feet square, set into the white-painted wall. There was a small catch opening to it. I reached up, but there wasn't enough space to open it fully; it came open just an inch so that I could get my fingertips inside, but no further.

Damn it.

I had to know what was inside, so I pushed the dressing table away further – but in my tiny room I could only move it so much. The mirror, which stood on top, wobbled and almost fell off, but I caught it in time.

Finally, there was room for me to reach inside.

I opened the door and peered in.

Inside, there was nothing except for a piece of paper, folded up.

I removed it curiously, and took it back to my bed. I sat down and opened it, holding the page up to the oil lamp by my bed.

Dear Tegan, I read, and the sight of my own name made my heart hammer with panic in my chest.

If you are reading this, then you have travelled from your own time back to Trevarron, the letter began.

What?

My eyes flickered to the top of the first page.

The letter was dated 8 February 1689.

8 February 1689

Dear Tegan,

If you're reading this, then you've travelled from your own time back to Trevarron.

You know, in your heart of hearts, that you have always had a connection to history.

It isn't just an academic interest. There's something about our family that's tied to Trevarron House and its past like a ribbon on a kite tail.

I still don't fully understand it, not yet. I believe that you will find out, one day, what it is that draws us back to Trevarron. I hope that, one day, you'll be able to explain it to me.

I'm banking on you finding this letter when you do travel to the past. I don't know for sure if this will work. Perhaps the letter will disappear into the ether, but I'm going to try anyway. If you do find it, then I hope it acts as a reassurance for you.

I never told you because I believed that you had to come to it in your own time, at your own pace, when the portal was ready to open for you. And I think if I'd said anything, you would have thought I was crazy. Crazier than you already think I am. Ha ha!

My mother never knew how she got from our daily reality to the past. It happened by accident for her, just twice. The first time, she came back. The second, she didn't. I still wonder whether she'll return, one day. I'd like to see her again.

I've stopped going now. I no longer visit Trevarron House, so it can no longer take me. My experiences were, on the whole, good, but the risks became too large.

You'll come to realise what they are, in time.

I've never been able to pinpoint what it is that enables the time slip, and I know that it only works for a select few. If there are other people that have done it, I don't know who they are. I found that I knew when it would happen to me, somehow. I sensed it, and when I went to the house, it happened. The first time was an accident. The times after that, I relied on my instincts.

You may find another way of going back and forth, or you may never go. I have faith that this letter will find you if it's meant to, and when you get home from your adventure, I'll be waiting.

Your loving

Aunt Bill

I turned the letter over, but that was all there was. I stared at it, not believing what I was seeing.

Aunt Bill had travelled back in time too? How was it that I had never known?

I never told you because I believed that you had to come to it in your own time, at your own pace, when the portal was ready to open for you. I read it again. She hadn't told me on purpose. I wished that she had, though. Perhaps she could have told me more about how to get home, because I had absolutely no idea. The fact that Aunt Bill had relied on her *instincts* to get back to our own time was no help. Annoyed, I wondered why she had bothered to write me the letter at all if she wasn't going to be helpful.

Still, what my aunt's letter did tell me was that she had travelled to the past, and she had returned. That gave me hope.

The fact that Aunt Bill's own mother hadn't returned, though, was troubling. The letter mentioned risks. Surely that meant the risk of being stranded in the past forever...?

I folded up the letter and tucked it into the drawer of the dressing table, pushing the table back so it was flush against the wall again.

Aunt Bill had been here, at Trevarron House, but in a different year, 1689. And yet she'd been in this room. I wondered if she'd slept here; how long she'd been here. I wondered, suddenly, if she too was currently at Trevarron House, somewhere else on the spectrum of time. It was possible, though not likely, as she'd been in the cottage when I left. Still, I didn't know how the time travel thing worked. The thought that Aunt Bill could be in the same room as me at the same moment in a different time – if that was possible – made me shiver.

I felt horribly homesick. As beautiful as it was here, I wanted more than anything to see my aunt again, and the letter made me feel at once closer and further away.

I lay down on the bed and closed my eyes. There was something about she and I that drew us here, and made time travel possible, or so Aunt Bill thought. What was it?

FOURTEEN

It was more difficult than I imagined to find a reason to get to the rose garden.

After I found Aunt Bill's letter, I considered using her technique of relying on my instincts and 'feeling' the right time. However, I didn't feel all that confident in my intuition. I had no idea how to feel when the right time was, and, more to the point, it could take years for me to feel anything. I preferred logic.

Logically, it stood to reason that, since the last instance I had found myself in my own time was when climbing up the outside of the rose garden, the way back would be there, if anywhere. I had no other plan so far than to retrace my steps and hope for the best. I wasn't exactly a time travel genius, and anyway, that wasn't a thing. Time travel didn't exist.

Apart from the inconvenient fact that it *did*. I'd travelled here, to 1755, somehow, and my aunt and my grandmother had also both travelled in time. I didn't know how it had happened, and apparently neither did they. I didn't know how to get back, but I reasoned that there must be a mechanism to it somehow. It was just a case of discovering it.

I'd thought that it would simply be a case of slipping out unnoticed to the rose garden in the evening, after I'd finished whatever

Edith wanted me to do for the day. But it turned out that being a lady's maid – or, being Edith Beresford Trevarron's lady's maid, as I hadn't exactly had any experience of doing it for anyone else – wasn't a nine-to-five position.

I woke up early the next morning with Betty opening the curtains and setting out my clothes for the day. Groaning at the fact that it was only just dawn, I used the bathroom down the hall and got dressed with Betty's help, then went down to breakfast with Mrs Cottingley, Mr Cooper and the rest of the abovestairs staff. Betty had her breakfast in the kitchen.

After that, I was to go down to the kitchen and get Edith's breakfast on a tray, and take it up to her. She had specifically asked me to do it, rather than let one of the general maids bring it. Once I finished, I planned to slip away, find the rose garden and hopefully walk back through its gate to the twenty-first century.

After breakfast, I made my way back to the kitchen and poked my head in at the door, looking for Cook, but Betty waved at me from where she sat around the table with the other maids. Cook was nowhere to be seen.

'Come in, miss,' she called out.

Compared to the formal breakfast I'd had upstairs, in the kitchen, the girls were chattering and laughing loudly, and I wished that I'd had my breakfast here instead. I still felt really strange being here at all, and the sense of being lost and rootless meant that I had to stop every now and again and take some deep breaths.

'Thank you, Betty.' I smiled politely at the kitchen maids as I walked in; they quieted immediately. 'I'm sorry to interrupt your breakfast. I've just come for Lady Trevarron's tray. Please, go on,' I said to the group of girls at the table, who immediately began chattering again. I got the impression that I would be gossiped about as soon as I left the kitchen.

'Not at all, miss. Lady Trevarron likes it all just so.' Betty left her plate on the long, scrubbed pine kitchen table and walked to one of the side cabinets where a silver tray sat covered with a linen cloth. It bore a silver teapot monogrammed with the same *T* design as the plates I had seen the day before. She set a cup and saucer on the tray and added a plate from the cupboard, placing a generous slice of what looked like a sponge cake on it and added a silver milk jug.

'I've heard that there are rumours about a curse on Trevarron House,' I said to the table of maids. I was curious to see what they'd say; I wondered if any of them had witnessed anything as sensational as Lady Elspeth's ghost.

The chatter stopped again instantly, and they all stared dumbly at me.

'Is it cursed, do you think?' I asked again, conversationally. I expected them to laugh, and probably give me some silly answers. But nobody said anything.

'Don't speak of it, miss.' Betty frowned at the table, at the upturned faces of the other maids, all filled suddenly with fear and trepidation. 'People say there are no such thing as curses, but some of us 'ave 'eard funny things in Lady Elspeth's quarters. Odd noises at night. We don't like to go in there.' She handed me the tray. 'Best not to mention it,' she said, firmly.

I nodded, surprised.

'Thank you, Betty.' I took the tray and made my way carefully up the stairs, hoping I didn't drop it.

It was clear that the maids believed that there was some kind of curse on Trevarron House. I suspected that it was a case of panic and fear more than anything, but I didn't know that for sure. I didn't know anything about the existence of ghosts or life after death. Who did? It was the eternal mystery.

There *was* a strange kind of vibe to the house, I had to admit, but thus far I'd dismissed it as part of my general unmoored feeling about finding myself in the past, in a reconstituted manor house that I had only known as a dank, burnt-out ruin in real life. That in itself was a lot to process. The idea that Trevarron House might also be cursed or haunted was almost too much to take in.

Well, whether the house was cursed or not, I still had my

duties to perform. I walked slowly up to where I remembered Edith's quarters were, balancing the tray. I still didn't exactly know what was expected of me as a lady's maid, but I had to pretend that I knew what I was doing, or Mrs Cottingley would get suspicious.

So, I let myself into Edith's rooms, found her bedroom and pulled the curtains on her four-poster bed. I was awed by the beauty of Edith's bedroom. If it had existed in the twenty-first century, no doubt they'd have been used for photo shoots and backdrops for lavish advertising campaigns. I loved the colours: particularly the gold and blue of the adjoining sitting room, the hand-painted wallpaper.

'Good morning, Edith,' I said, quietly, setting the tray down on a table next to her bed, but she only stirred. I wondered what kind of waking-up was appropriate. Cautiously, I put my hand on her shoulder and shook her a little. 'Edith?' I said her name a few times. 'It's morning.'

She opened her eyes and stared up at me blearily.

'Oh. Tegan. It's you.' She sat up as I went around the room, opening the curtains. There were three large sash windows just in Edith's bedroom, all hung with heavy velvet curtains. Unlike her sitting room, her bedroom was decorated in a dark pink, with a satiny bedspread embroidered with a floral pattern and white sheets underneath. Her bedside tables were made of wood painted dark gold, and each table held a matching glass-bottomed oil lamp. There was another untidy pile of books on one of the tables, and a half-drunk glass of beer and a plate with a piece of bread on it.

'Did you sleep well?' I asked, coming back to her bed and setting her tray on her knees.

'Like a log.' Edith yawned. 'Oh, thank you, dear. Will you pour?'

I nodded and poured the tea for her. She watched me for a moment and then directed her gaze at the window.

'Gosh. It is a most handsome day. I think I shall go for a ride this morning. You'll come with me.'

The way that she delivered the sentence as a matter of fact and not a question reminded me of William. I swore under my breath: I'd wanted to get away as soon as I could, but it seemed that Edith had other plans for me.

'I don't know how to ride a horse,' I demurred. It wasn't something I could lie about. If Edith expected me to jump onto a horse and go for a ride with her, she was soon going to see that I couldn't when I tried to and fell off. I thought briefly about being on the horse with William, two days before, and then pushed the thought from my mind.

'You don't know how to ride?' She stared at me with frank amazement.

'I'm afraid not.' I held my hands behind my back. *And hopefully I'll never have to learn*, I thought.

'Well. I'm surprised at that,' Edith put down her teacup. 'Didn't Miss Boyd ride?'

'No,' I took a gamble. 'Her... health wasn't up to it.' I had no idea if that was the case, but seeing as Miss Boyd had just died, I took the chance that her health might have been an issue.

'Hm. I suppose not.' Edith raised an eyebrow. 'Well, we cannot have everything. You will learn, as it's a skill I would expect a lady's maid to have. And, more to the point, I like to ride, and therefore so will you. We will begin today, after I dress.'

'Thank you, Edith.' I could tell from her tone that there was no point arguing.

'Not at all, dear Tegan. Riding is a godsend. A balm for the wild soul.' She smiled up at me. 'Would you read to me while I eat?' She handed me a book of poetry. 'I believe in exercising my brain in the mornings.'

'Of course.' I sighed internally, opened the book and began reading.

I had assumed that I was going to read and Edith was going to listen quietly, but that clearly wasn't how Edith liked to listen to someone read. Almost as soon as I had begun reading – it was a book of poems by Daniel Defoe, and I began at random reading a poem called 'Ye True-born Englishmen Proceed' – Edith nodded vigorously and recited some of it along with me.

'Mr Defoe is such an interesting soul, don't you think?' she asked. 'Oh, don't stop reading, dear Tegan. But he is quite the reformer. And do you think he is right? Do you think Britain is as corrupt as he says?'

I could see how hungry she was for stimulation and company. Suddenly, I got a glimpse of what her life had been like, stuck up here on her own for weeks at a time with only her brothers for company, or the maids. No one really talked to her, and she needed it. She was bright, and in the modern day, she would definitely have gone to university. My heart filled with pity for this clever, lonely woman, stuck alone in this grand house with seemingly, only her horse for company.

'Well, it's a very nuanced situation,' I replied, thoughtfully. 'I suppose he seems to be criticising the government... but some of that's always necessary, isn't it? For a healthy society. There need to be voices of dissent, when things aren't right.'

I reread what I had just read aloud.

> YE True-Born Englishmen proceed,
> Our trifling Crimes detect,
> Let the Poor starve, Religion bleed,
> The Dutch be damn'd, the French succeed,
> And all by your Neglect.

'Oh, indeed. How perceptive of you!' Edith clapped her hands in delight. 'My dear Tegan, you are so right. So many ills trouble our society today. In Cornwall, it's smuggling and the problem of the highwaymen on our roads. And the poor are such a problem. It seems that all of our attention goes to the wars abroad, and yet, life is difficult for everyone.' She sighed.

I'd grown up in Cornwall, so I knew its smuggling history well. In the seventeenth to nineteenth centuries, smuggling had boomed in Cornwall because of the high taxes for items such as alcohol, tea and sugar. There was also the fact that, particularly in the south-west, local government had tolerated the 'gentleman smugglers' of Cornwall who were renowned for non-violence, compared to the more pirate-like smugglers that operated elsewhere. Cornwall's landscape also lent itself wonderfully well to smugglers bringing in goods by boat because of the many caves along the Cornish coast-line where they were able to hide their treasure.

I hoped that when she said that the poor were a problem, Edith meant that being poor in the eighteenth century meant having a difficult life, rather than the poor themselves being a problem. I wanted to give her the benefit of the doubt, though she also seemed to be suggesting that she, too, found life difficult.

Edith was wealthy and privileged. I knew that her life was much easier than the scullery maids', who would never be able to dream of being brought their breakfast in bed and having poetry read to them. Edith was a product of her environment, and the idea that she could feel sorry for herself at all might have seemed, on the surface of it, offensive.

But it was also obvious that Edith was deeply lonely. I could see that by how eagerly she welcomed me; the way that she clearly wanted me by her side. She had so much to say that, in the brief time I'd known her, it felt like there was an avalanche of words in her, just waiting to spill out. It was clear that it had been so long since there was anyone who would listen to her; anyone that would interact with her at all.

And, for that reason, I did feel sorry for her. Because, though she was rich and privileged, Edith was still a woman in a world where women were kept like caged birds.

'I'm so glad you're here, Tegan.' She looked up at me with her wide blue eyes, and my heart broke a little. I liked Edith, and I pitied her. But I also knew that I couldn't stay.

For the first time in the brief couple of days that I'd found myself in this life at Trevarron House, I felt bad for wanting to leave. But what choice did I have? I didn't belong here. I had to find a way to get back home.

FIFTEEN

It was my third attempt to stay on Blossom, the gentlest horse in the stables.

I'd almost fallen off twice and had to be pushed back into the saddle by Tom, the groom. We hadn't even left the stableyard, but I wasn't used to the strange motion of a horse and I'd never been taught to ride. I wasn't even that much of a fitness fan; a classic bookworm, I'd always preferred to stay inside to read.

However, today, there was a hunt, and Edith was going, so that meant I had to go too.

I very much disapproved of hunting. There seemed absolutely no good reason to chase one lone fox through the countryside on horseback with a pack of baying dogs. It was cruel and unnecessary, and the argument about it keeping fox numbers down was laughable. Surely there were more efficient ways of doing that?

However, in the eighteenth century, animal rights were very much not a thing, and even Edith, who, in the modern day would probably have agreed, was dressed in her riding gear and ready to go.

'Now, this time, grip with your thighs an' hold on,' Tom muttered as he took Blossom's rein and led us slowly away from the stables. There was a spacious, well-kept lawn at the back of the house where in my own time I remembered long grass and wild-flowers, the same as the meadow in front of the house where I used to sit and read.

Tom led Blossom and I toward the lawn; I did as I was told and held on tight.

'Try an' relax, miss. The 'orse knows if yer tense. If ye can relax, the 'orse'll relax. Blossom's a good girl an' won't throw ye, but others might,' Tom chided me.

'OK.' I nodded. He frowned at me; people didn't say *OK* in the eighteenth century. 'All right, Tom,' I added, quickly.

'Right ye are, miss.' Tom began walking us around the lawn. I tried to relax while holding on and keeping my thighs taut and sitting upright like he'd told me.

The only point of agreeing to go on the hunt was so that I might be able to disappear to the rose garden while nobody was looking. I was hoping that I could lag at the end of the group and then surreptitiously ride back to the house and find my way home, though I wasn't entirely sure how it was going to work.

I'd now been here for three days and I was starting to feel desperate. Each day I'd woken again in the same dark room, hoping that I'd somehow, magically, be in my bed at Aunt Bill's and that everything would be back to normal. But I was still here.

We had tried riding on my first day with Edith, but the groom hadn't been around to help me, so Edith had given up and taken her horse out on her own for a while. I'd thought that this would have given me the opportunity to get away then, but Mrs Cottingley had swooped by like an owl and led me away to show me the laundry, giving me several hours' tutoring on how to wash, iron and care for Edith's best things. By the end of it, I'd been exhausted, and then Edith had called for me and we'd had lunch and then a walk, with more discussion of poetry.

It wasn't that Edith was bad company, or that laundry, lunch and walking was tough work. It was more that I was battling the overwhelm of knowing that I was in the wrong place, of being terrified that I was either going insane or would be trapped here forever. I didn't know which was worse.

I had had my recurring dream every night I had been here. It was always the same, and I couldn't help but feel that it was trying to tell me something. It wasn't a coincidence that I knew that place – the rocky outcropping over the sea – was at the edge of the Trevarron property. Was the fact that I was so near to it making me dream about it more, or was there another reason?

So far, I hadn't found the opportunity to get to the rose garden or the cliffside. I was curious about both, but the rose garden took precedence.

I wondered if I could just use my more superior rank to tell Tom and the other grooms that were milling around that I wanted a break, and was going for a walk. I knew that the stables weren't that far from the rose garden. I had been just about to, but Mrs Cottingley had come down to watch my progress. Despite her surface friendliness, I got the distinct impression that she was watching me; maybe she suspected that something was up.

As I was going hunting, Betty had found what she considered a decent riding costume for me. Unfortunately, this still involved a long skirt and a petticoat, but at least there was no boned under-skirt. There was a white blouse with a frill at the neck and a dark red velvet riding jacket. I wasn't required to wear a corset, which was a relief. I liked the jacket, but the skirt was a problem.

'Ladies usually ride sidesaddle,' Tom had explained when he'd first helped me onto Blossom's back. 'But Lady Trevarron likes to ride like a man. I would suggest that you learn that way too, miss.'

So, I was doing my best to cope in the saddle with a long skirt rucked up between my knees. It was long enough so that it wasn't indecent, but I was showing some leg. I wasn't particularly both-ered about it – it was only a calf – but when he'd helped me into the saddle, Tom had seemed embarrassed.

I looked back towards the house. It was a beautiful day and the sun lit up the clean white plaster on the façade; there was a wide patio around the back, edged with large, elegant stone planters which contained peony bushes. They were in bloom, and the gentle pink of the blowsy flowers was breathtakingly beautiful.

At the edge of the patio, stone steps had been cut into the sloping lawn. You could walk from the back of the house to the main lawn where I was currently clinging onto Blossom's back for dear life. On the right side, there was a croquet lawn, set up with hoops. Beyond that was a wooded area, and at the far edge of that there was what looked like a long grass walkway with two more stone pillars at the end, also topped with griffins.

Again, I felt a sense of awe and amazement at being here. There were moments when I could put my worries about being stuck in the eighteenth century to the back of my mind and enjoy the sheer majesty of my environment. This was one of those moments. The sun was shining, and, when I wasn't afraid of falling off Blossom's wide back, it was actually very lovely to sit on a horse with the amazing view in front of me.

It was a strange balance of emotions. I could appreciate the beauty and specialness of being here. Aunt Bill had obviously felt the same, since she had travelled to the past more than once. And yet, I missed Aunt Bill, I missed Yew Tree Cottage, and my actual life.

I wondered whether my aunt was worried about me. How long had I been away, in her time? If it was the same time as I had been here, and not some kind of mythical collapse of time, like in fairy stories where people might go to fairy lands for years and be gone just a few minutes in human time – it had been days. Had she told the police? Were they looking for me?

Behind us, the lawn widened on a slight descent towards a long hedge that marked the boundary of the garden, with the cliffs of the north Cornwall coast beyond. I knew from my previous explorations of the hideously overgrown garden, in the present day, that there was a point where the hedge was cut away and you could walk straight onto the perilous top of the cliffs. That was where the dais from my dream was. I knew that if I walked there, I would find it.

However, you could still see the sea from the patio. I'd never visited the garden in the winter, but for a moment I imagined what it would be like to watch a storm come in over the sea. For a moment, there was some odd slippage in my perception that I'd had before, like a blurred negative, and I could see myself standing on the stone dais, with a storm on the horizon rather than a sunset as was usually the case in my dream.

I started, and the vision disappeared. I shook my head, trying to concentrate on what I was doing. But the vision was disturbing; I didn't know why I kept having these dreams about Trevarron, and I didn't know what had drawn me back here. But the longer I was here, the more I felt that I had some kind of deep connection to the place, as if it was part of me and I was part of it.

Mrs Cottingley stood on the steps that led from the patio, watching me with her arms crossed over her chest. I wondered if she too was suspicious that I didn't ride. It was probably something that a lady's maid was supposed to do. I couldn't read her expression from so far away, but I wished she'd disappear.

The other riders were gathering for the hunt. There were a couple of local farmers helping out, plus Edith and me, and I guessed that William was coming. Tom had told me that we were expecting some other lords and ladies to join, and he was complaining because he had to get horses ready for them too.

Tom helped me off Blossom. 'All right?' he asked, and I nodded. I didn't feel at all confident on her, but I knew that I didn't have much choice about it.

'Charles – you old buffoon!'

I jumped and turned around. From beside the stables, I watched as a tall, handsome man dressed in a smart red riding jacket and black breeches, with long black boots, came around the side of the house. He wore his sandy hair back in a smart ponytail like all the men did, and had a short, neatly trimmed beard. The man would have turned heads even in the modern day; he had that kind of effortless masculinity and swagger, confident and with a twinkle in his eye. Compared to William, who was sullen and often silent, he seemed ebullient and expansive.

He was accompanied by a delicate-looking woman of about Edith's age who was dressed in a variation of the riding jacket and full-skirt riding outfit.

The man strode purposefully over to a portly fair-haired man who was probably in his thirties, though he had the unhealthy look of someone who drank too much. His nose was already a little bulbous and red at the end, and his riding jacket looked tight.

I assumed that this was Charles Trevarron, Edith's other brother. I hadn't yet been introduced to him, and I gathered he was often out.

'Simon. It's been too long, old fellow.' Charles clapped the other man on the back.

'Ah, Lady Trevarron. What a vision you look today.' The man named Simon bowed deeply as Edith approached, leading her own horse by its reins.

'Good day, Lord Favisham. You are too kind.' Edith inclined her head politely. 'Clara! I'm so glad you came.' She embraced the young woman next to Simon Favisham with genuine warmth. She gestured to me, and I walked over to join them. 'Tegan, this is my soul friend Clara Favisham. Clara, my dear, this is Tegan Penrose, my new lady's maid.'

I curtseyed to Clara.

'Good day, Lady Favisham,' I greeted her. She was such a slight little thing that she made Edith look athletic, and Edith was tiny.

'Good day.' Clara nodded to me politely.

'Tegan's previous employer was the poet Miss Boyd,' Edith continued, her eyes glowing at the mention of someone she clearly admired. I was still feeling bad for misleading her about it, but there wasn't much I could do. 'And we have had the most diverting conversations about literature so far.'

'How marvellous, dear Edith.' Clara smiled wanly at her friend. 'I am glad for you. It must be lovely to have a good lady's maid that one can consider a friend. As you know, I do not currently have a companion in my employ.' She looked sad, and I got the sense that Clara Favisham was quite a melancholy character.

'Come now, Clara,' Simon Favisham boomed. He had been conversing with Charles and now turned a bright smile on us. 'We keep you busy at Penlivet, do we not? And you have your needle-work, and your charities. My sister is very active with the paupers, Miss Penrose, is it? She has the heart of a saint.' He held out his hand to me, and I took it. 'What a pleasure to meet you. Will you be joining us on the hunt today?'

'It is a pleasure to meet you too, Lord Favisham.' I curtseyed demurely again. 'Yes, I am accompanying Edith, though I am not an accomplished rider.'

'Ah, indeed, indeed. A bookish type, I'll wager?' He raised a kindly eyebrow and I nodded gratefully. 'Not to worry, dear girl. Charles isn't a particularly strong rider either. He will look after you, I'm sure.'

Charles looked underwhelmed at the prospect of lagging back with me at the rear of the hunt, but he was too polite to say so, and merely nodded.

'Miss Penrose, Edith has not stopped talking about you. It is a pleasure to make your acquaintance,' he said instead, a little stiffly.

'Thank you, Lord Trevarron,' I replied. 'I am honoured to be at Trevarron House.'

'Indeed. It is a fine old place. Now, then.' Simon took my arm. I was slightly surprised at the sudden contact, but he seemed polite enough about it. I had to remember that the social norms were different here, and, in Lord Favisham's eyes, I was a servant, albeit one who was allowed to walk among the lords and ladies. 'Shall we get you onto a horse, Miss Penrose? I believe Tom has one waiting for me too, don't you, Tom?'

He guided me back into the stables without waiting for me to agree.

However, at that moment, William appeared. He looked very smart in a riding jacket that fitted him perfectly, emphasising his broad shoulders and muscular figure; his strong, wide thighs seemed to stretch the material of his breeches. He watched me as Tom helped me on to Blossom's back, his expression unreadable. However, as I moved closer to where William stood, I saw that a smile had begun to play around his lips.

I didn't smile back. I was concentrating on not falling off the horse.

Behind me, I could hear Simon Favisham's voice barking orders, and, as the others milled around, he rode out past me suddenly, startling Blossom.

She bolted forward, and I wasn't enough of an experienced rider to know how to quiet her or hang on. Blossom started to canter away, following Lord Favisham as he rode off in a showy circle around the collected attendees.

I cried out, but it was too late. I slipped off the horse.

SIXTEEN

'She's coming around. Give her some air,' a deep voice said, very near to me. I opened my eyes and tried to sit up, but as soon as I did, pain cut through my head and I slumped backwards. An arm prevented my head from hitting the ground again. I groaned.

'Are you dizzy, dear?' I looked up to see Mrs Cottingley's face above me, her expression concerned. 'That was quite a tumble.'

'Yes. I'll be all right. I...' I started, and tried to sit up again.

'Whoa, girl. Just lie back for a moment.' William's voice was low and comforting, although I picked up on the fact that he said *whoa* as if I was the horse. 'Just wait. Get your breath.'

I realised that he was holding me, and had gently moved my head onto his lap. I didn't feel strong enough to object. There was a certain comfort in the solidity of his body and the sudden intimacy we found ourselves in.

'I'm so sorry, miss.' Tom stood next to where I lay. He sounded anxious; I opened my eyes and tried to smile. 'Lord Favisham... I wasn't expecting him to go past you like that,' he added.

'It's all right, Tom. I'm just a terrible rider.' I felt sorry for him. I didn't want him to get into trouble. He twisted his hat in his hands and I could see he was very concerned.

I tried to sit up again, but a stab of pain cut through my neck and my head once more.

'I think we should get her up to bed with a cold compress, and some willow bark to chew.' Mrs Cottingley knelt next to me and put her hand on my forehead. 'Poor dear.'

'Tegan!' Edith had come running over. 'Tegan, you poor thing! What beastly luck!'

'I'm all right,' I said, weakly. Actually, I wasn't. I felt very dizzy and the pain was quite bad.

'Oh, no, you aren't at all!' She frowned. 'Simon shouldn't have ridden past you so close and so quickly. Poor Blossom startled. He knew you weren't a confident rider,' Edith tutted.

'I'll take her upstairs, Cottingley. Bring the bark and the compress,' William instructed.

'As you wish, sir,' Mrs Cottingley replied.

'She will be all right, Edith. She needs rest.' William added.

Edith nodded. 'I'll come and see you after the hunt, Tegan.' She pressed my hands briefly in hers.

Before I could protest, William scooped me up in his arms. It was as though I weighed nothing. He cradled my neck carefully with one arm and positioned the other under my thighs. I could sense his strength; I could feel the muscles in his arms, and, finding myself so close to him again, I remembered the width of his shoulders. There was no softness in his chest, just hard, corded muscle.

I closed my eyes, feeling dizzy. My head throbbed.

'It's all right, maid. I've got you,' William murmured to me as he began walking back towards the house. *Maid* was a Cornish endearment; something you used to describe a young girl. I was too much in pain to protest, but I realised that I wouldn't have, even if I could.

I liked William calling me *maid*. I liked the way that his voice had softened, talking to me. I had never been picked up and carried before, like a little girl. There was something so comforting about it that I almost cried, but it was also strangely delicious. Even though my head hurt and I just wanted to lie down, being pressed against his body, being carried, being so vulnerable with him, was arousing, and I had no idea why.

He carried me up the lawn, onto the patio and into the house, striding along effortlessly.

I felt us going up stairs; the rhythm of William's steps changing. He was slightly out of breath, now, but still carried me confidently. I had wrapped my arms around his neck when he had first picked me up, and now I clung on tighter.

'It's all right, maid,' he said, again, his voice still that deep murmur that sent tingles through me. 'I won't drop you.'

Finally, we reached my room and I opened my eyes as William laid me carefully on my bed.

We were alone; I guessed that Mrs Cottingley was following orders and had gone to get me a cold compress. I felt feverish, and as he laid me on the bed, I thought suddenly of Elspeth, his young wife. The rumours had said that she had tripped and fallen in the woods because William was chasing her, because he had been a violent brute to her.

The way that he laid me on the bed so carefully belied that idea, but people could be changeable. I wondered if there was any truth in the rumour about William being violent. I shivered at the thought, suddenly worried about being totally alone with a potentially unpredictable, angry man.

'What is it, maid?' he asked softly, seeing my distress.

'This jacket is too tight,' I said. I didn't want to explain my thoughts, and it was true anyway – I was hot and the fabric was constraining my ribcage. My breath was coming in short gasps; it might have been the shock of the fall. William nodded, and, without comment, began unbuttoning it.

I was aware that I wasn't wearing a bra, and the soft white blouse I wore under the tight jacket was fairly translucent. As he unbuttoned my jacket slowly, I felt the surprising softness of William's touch. His fingertips grazed my breasts through the gauzy material.

As the jacket opened, he took in a long, slow breath. My head was beginning to clear, and I opened my eyes to meet his intense gaze and I was suddenly alive to the thrill of his touch.

Was it ridiculous to imagine that William Trevarron would have murdered his wife? Did a killer lurk behind that handsome face? I had no way of knowing. Yes, he was usually gruff and rude, but he was also now showing me a gentler, more sensual side of himself.

Without saying anything, he continued to undo the buttons. I knew that he could see my nipples through the blouse; see the curve of my breasts as I lay there, helpless and unable to do anything.

His gaze flickered to my breasts. He undid the final button, and his hand rested on my stomach. His touch was warm; both comforting and deeply sensual at the same time.

'Better?' His voice was husky.

'Y... yes. Thank you,' I breathed. I knew that my eyes were wide, my heart beating madly; I was also, I was mortified to realise, wet between my thighs.

'Good little maid.' His voice was magical, somehow; I felt a deep resonance of pleasure when I heard it, as if it had struck a drum in my belly that vibrated pleasantly through my whole body. He smoothed the hair from my forehead gently; his touch was soft. 'I...' he began to say something, and his eyes met mine with a burning passion.

My lips parted involuntarily. He leaned in towards me, his face inches from mine.

'I...' he began, his voice low.

I wanted so much for him to kiss me. My whole being yearned for him. It was so unexpected, so powerful, that I couldn't understand it. Yet, I felt as though I was captured in a whirlwind, powerless to resist being taken by it.

At that moment, Mrs Cottingley bustled in. William removed his hand from me, and stood up.

The energy between us broke, as if the whirlwind had

suddenly blown out, and I was dropped back to the earth without warning.

'Thank you for carrying the poor girl up, milord.' The house-keeper's tone was polite, but I could hear a hint of steel in it. 'I'll take it from here.'

I wondered if Mrs Cottingley thought anything inappropriate was happening; her tone suggested that she did. I supposed that she might consider herself the guardian of my honour, and that made me wonder whether it was not the first time that William had had an intimate relationship with a staff member – in those days, I guessed that would have been viewed as a very bad thing.

Or perhaps Mrs Cottingley doubted that William was a good man – perhaps she thought that he had killed his wife – directly or indirectly – and if so, was she protecting me?

Regardless of propriety or what Mrs Cottingley thought, there had definitely been a moment, between us, just now. I knew what I felt; I knew how William's voice had softened. I knew how he had touched me, and that his gaze had clouded with lust when he had unbuttoned my jacket.

The attraction between us was unmistakeable.

William nodded.

'Of course, Mrs Cottingley.' His voice was back to its proper lord-of-the-manor tone. The soft huskiness of a moment ago was gone. 'I will leave you to it. I hope the girl feels better soon.'

He left without addressing me directly. Despite my headache, I felt that was rude. But I also had got swept away in the moment with William just then; the wetness between my thighs didn't lie. He had touched me so softly, and yet so full of sensuousness. His gaze on mine was obvious.

We had wanted each other, in that moment. We were just man and a woman, obeying their instincts, unable to deny the bond that drew us together like magnets.

I didn't know what to think about the rumours that surrounded William, but as I lay there, collecting my thoughts, I decided that I would keep my distance and make up my own mind, based on any evidence that came my way. Ultimately, I hoped to find a way back to my own time, and that had to be my focus.

'Now then, Miss Penrose.' Mrs Cottingley sighed and sat down on the end of my bed. 'Let us hope that this is the last of your unfortunate accidents.'

SEVENTEEN

I'd waited too long, and I couldn't wait any longer.

Despite what had just happened between William and me, I knew that living in the eighteenth century was completely untenable. Realistically, I had no idea how long I had here before I caught something there wasn't yet medicine to cure, or consumed some eighteenth-century bacteria in the food that I was eating. Never mind the fact that I *couldn't* live here: I hadn't been born yet. There was something basically wrong with physics and time and space by me being here at all. I was a twenty-first-century woman, and the world that I was used to was a million miles away from all of this.

After Mrs Cottingley had left me, and Betty had brought up my dinner on a tray – I'd picked at it, I wasn't hungry – I waited for the house to quieten down. I knew that the main doors would get locked at around nine p.m. I knew that I needed to slip out before then. It would still be light, unfortunately, but I hoped that it being after dinner would mean that the grounds of the house would be deserted.

Still dressed in my riding outfit – I had re-buttoned my jacket in the event I did meet anyone on my travels, though it was uncomfortably tight – I crept down the narrow stairs and down again to the main corridor that ran through the house. No one was around. Good.

For a moment, I looked along the long corridor. I now knew that, at the other end, it led to the East Wing, where Lady Elspeth's rooms were. Betty had pointed them out to me the day before, but she'd refused to go in. I'd wanted to, but she had shied away.

'No, miss. I'm tellin' you where they are so's you don't make a mistake an' go in there,' she'd whispered to me. 'Milord says the rooms're out of bounds, an' we don't want to go in there anyway. Noises at night. Creakin'. Wailin'.' She'd shaken her head, looking scared. 'Promise me you won't go in there.'

I'd promised, but I was intrigued. I wanted to look inside Lady Elspeth's rooms.

However, right now, time was of the essence, and I needed to get out of the house as soon as possible. I resolved to peek into Lady Elspeth's quarters another time. If there was one.

I made my way downstairs, creeping silently, very like a ghost myself, and opened the heavy wooden front door. I grimaced as it creaked. Still, no one appeared.

I slipped out of the door, ran down the front steps and onto the gravel drive and then around to the back of the house. A couple of the kitchen maids were pottering around in the vegetable garden to my right, but they didn't see me as I flitted past. When I was out of their sightline, I ran.

I knew where the rose garden was. I remembered being dragged from there to the house by Cook; I wasn't likely to forget that in a hurry. I ran a jagged line with the kitchen garden behind me, keeping to the shadow of the hedges where I could, until it loomed ahead of me.

I stopped, and caught my breath. No one was inside, as far as I could see. Unhesitating, I moved towards it. I didn't have any time to lose, and I wasn't going to risk being found again.

I pushed the wrought-iron gate open and walked inside. How

would this work? Was it the act of climbing over the railings that made the time portal open, or was it just being in the rose garden itself? But, if that was the case, why didn't everyone who ever visited the rose garden get transported through time? Aunt Bill said it was a select few that were in some way special. How was I special? What was it about some people that made this all possible?

I looked around me warily. The roses were as soft and blowsy as before; their sweet, heavy perfume hung in the evening air like a fug. I detected the same unpleasant scent of rot as before, under the sweetness. The rose smell on its own was almost too much, without the manure or whatever it was as well.

How would I do this? Was there something I'd touched, originally, that had made the transfer happen? I walked up the pathway to the middle of the garden and touched the water fountain at its centre. I dabbed some of the water on my face. Nothing happened.

I walked back to the gateway and touched the large, elaborate letter T in the centre of the ironworks. It really was beautiful. I felt a terrible sense of loss and shame about the fact that I knew, in the future, what a ruin it would become.

I thought again of Aunt Bill and felt homesickness and worry tug at my heart.

I ran my hand over the bars of the gate and the wall of the enclosure. Nothing happened.

Damn.

I looked up at the railings, then out at the lawn beyond. I'd found my way in by climbing up those railings, to escape the barking dog. Was that the key to it? It was worth a try.

There was no one around. I walked to the outside of the rose garden and, without thinking about it too much, started to climb.

It was even more difficult to climb the railings wearing full eighteenth-century ladies' horse-riding gear, but I was determined. If this was what I had to do to get back to my own life in my own time, then I would do it.

I got to the top of the railings and looked down fearfully. I could break my neck jumping down if this skirt got caught on anything; I could be hanging here for hours until anyone found me. Carefully, I tied as much of the skirt and its petticoat as I could into a kind of knot at my side, made sure that no one was watching me, and jumped.

I landed safely this time, on both feet, without injuring myself. But the garden remained unchanged. It was still as beautiful as it had been five minutes ago; the roses were still in bloom, and nothing was overgrown.

I swore under my breath. This was where I had somehow crossed time. Was there no way to go back? How had I done it?

A shadow passed the edge of the railings. I pressed myself against a thick rose bush to conceal my presence, and hoped that whoever it was wasn't intending to come in. The shadow stopped for a moment. There was a cough and the smell of tobacco, and then the sound of someone treading past quietly.

My heart was beating hard. I didn't want to be discovered here. I didn't want to be here at all, but it seemed as though I had to be. I couldn't find a way out. The hope that I'd held – that simply entering the rose garden would be enough – dissolved like sugar.

I waited for the sound of footsteps to disappear, and poked my head out of the gate. Still no one was around.

Devastated, I began to walk along the edge of the gardens, keeping the hedge at my side so that I would stay reasonably hidden. I didn't know what to do. Getting to the rose garden had been my one plan: I didn't have anything else up my sleeve. How was I going to get home now?

I came to the end of the long walkway that bordered the woodland. At its entrance, the two stone pillars towered above me. The griffins stared down, as if judging me, assessing whatever it was in me that had drawn me here.

'Help me. Please,' I whispered, gazing up at their impassive faces. I wondered if they were the spiritual guardians of this place, somehow; totems that represented a kind of magic. *Was* Trevarron

House magic? The missing stone griffins at the gate were a local legend, but legends were one thing, and magic was another. Magic wasn't even real. Everyone knew that.

Then again, everyone also knew that time travel was impossible. And here I was.

Did this old manor house possess some kind of mystical quality that had enabled me to travel here? Was it a sort of quantum physical nexus, a bridge between many realities? Wasn't there that theory that an infinite number of alternate realities existed at once, and we could possibly even be shifting from one timeline to another whenever we made a decision?

If that was true, then why had I shifted timeline to 1755? What decision had brought me here, other than a desire to find a quiet place to read?

I didn't know. But I needed help. I was desperate. Aunt Bill's letter was no help at all.

I walked along the grass-covered parade, the waist-high hedge to my left, and the view of the sea and the cliffs beyond. I knew that if I followed it, I would come to the place that had dominated my dreams for so long, and it felt like the only place I could go, now. I was drawn there and I couldn't stop myself; a force greater than I could control powered my feet until I was almost running.

The sun was setting, and the sky was striped with orange and cerise. It was a beautiful sight, exactly like my dream. And when I came to the black rock, elevated from the rest of the cliffside, and the break in the hedge, it was all exactly where I knew it would be.

Cautiously, I stepped up onto the rock and looked out to the sunset.

In that moment, it was as if all the dreams I had had about this place — all the moments that I had stood here with the mystery man in silhouette next to me, holding my hand — all of those moments coalesced into one, as if they were pages in a book being closed, or the photographic negatives I had before now experienced slipping and rubbing against each other, now forming one clear picture. The same image, over and over, clarifying into one image, one moment, finally drawn into focus.

As soon as I stood on the black rock, I experienced such a rush of emotion – grief, love, yearning, loss – that it almost knocked me over. I was finally here, where my dreams had been leading me. Finally, I was back where I belonged.

EIGHTEEN

'Good evening, Miss Penrose.'

I nearly jumped out of my skin. The moment had been so intense that I hadn't heard anyone approaching. Standing on the black stone was an almost spiritual experience; I felt outside of time, as if I was floating.

'Goddamn it! You frightened me to death!' I cried out. I'd still been deep in a wave of emotion in that moment, with that powerful mixture of grief and love and longing that felt like a clenched fist inside my heart. I felt nauseous, full of a sickening loss that I couldn't name, as well as an intense poignancy like a sepia photograph. A feeling of coming home.

It was like being inside a kind of living hallucination. I was totally transported into a surreal but also super-real state of being. As if my dream world and my real world had come together in perfect synchronicity, and it was a shock to be jolted out of it so suddenly.

'I can't believe you didn't hear me approach,' William replied, crossly. 'There is no need for such foul language. I must say that it does not befit a lady of your position.'

'What? I... I didn't hear you. I was just...' I trailed off. *Goddamn it* was clearly vile language in the eighteenth century. I tried to make myself sound less fraught and distracted than I was, but I heard a wobble in my own voice.

I tried to think of a reason why I would be standing where I was, and failed. As far as William was concerned, I should have been tucked up in bed, which was where he had left me after my fall. I knew as well as he did that a lady's maid wasn't expected to be roaming the estate at night.

The lord of the manor, however, apparently had carte blanche for whatever wandering he chose to do. He owned it all, after all. Including me, as he had once said. A flash of irritation at the unfairness of it all rose in my stomach.

'You have a very odd way of comporting yourself, Miss Penrose,' he retorted, gruffly. 'But you are Edith's maid and not mine. I do not take any interest in what you do and do not do.' He jammed his hands in his pockets. 'It is a becoming sunset, however.'

'It is,' I agreed. I wanted to be alone. Whatever had just happened on the stone was strange, but that didn't change my overall plan to get back to my own time.

But as I looked up at William, I felt irresistibly drawn to him once again. The orange and pink sunset bathed him in a warm glow, darkening his black hair and dark eyes and making him even more strikingly handsome. He turned away from me and looked out at the view, and in that moment I saw him in silhouette in the dim evening light.

I took in a sudden breath.

It was him. Without a doubt, William's profile was the same profile I had been seeing in silhouette in my dreams ever since I was a teenager. I was sure of it.

'How is Edith? Are you helping her prepare for the duke's ball? I believe it is just weeks away,' he addressed me, politely. I supposed that he was adopting the manner of speech that was appropriate between a lady's maid and the lord of the manor.

I couldn't reply. The realisation that I'd been dreaming of William De Vere Trevarron — a person from history — almost toppled me. I wanted to sit down.

If William was the man in my dream – and it felt like he was – what was so important about him specifically? Had I had now somehow been transported back in time so we could meet? I knew the emotions that came with the dream, and they troubled me. How could I have such deep emotions for this place and this man, and not know him at all? I didn't even like him very much, though I couldn't deny the strong physical attraction between us.

Plus, there was the question of whether he was, in fact, a murderer. I hadn't learned anything new about Elspeth's death. My instincts led me to believe that Edith was right, and that William hadn't done it – it probably had been an unfortunate accident. That was the most likely explanation.

But... I didn't know for sure. I might never know. I could be standing there with a murderer. A chill went through me.

He was looking at me with a concerned expression.

'What?' I asked, blearily. I couldn't remember what he'd asked me.

'I was asking you about the duke's ball, which I would think would be the focus of yours and Edith's daily conversations, being the fair sex and concerned with these things,' he repeated, slowly. 'Are you quite well, Miss Penrose? Surely, you shouldn't be up and about after your fall.'

'I'm fine. Just a headache. I wanted to clear my head.' It wasn't a lie exactly. 'If you want to talk to your sister, you should go and see her. She's usually just up in her quarters, reading,' I added, pointedly. I wanted to change the subject, but I was also annoyed at the way Edith's brothers treated her. William's attitude to me was similarly dismissive; the fact that he clearly thought we were both simple-headed little girls, only interested in balls and dresses was irritating.

I'd only been at Trevarron a few days, but I had already seen how little social contact Edith had. I hadn't seen William visit with her at all, and he was often absent at dinner, when at least Edith would get to talk to Charles, now that he was home again.

'My duties often take me away from the house,' he replied,

crisply. 'Does she expect me to be at her beck and call all day, when there is an estate to manage? How lucky she is that all she has to engage her time with are books and piano playing. I would greatly relish such a life.' He raised an eyebrow. Clearly, William De Vere Trevarron wasn't used to anyone talking back to him. But I wasn't about to tiptoe around him, just because he was the lord.

'That's extremely unfair to Edith,' I retorted, crossly. 'You have the freedom to leave the house whenever you like. She doesn't. If she wants to go anywhere, she has to be escorted by you or Charles, because society thinks it would be indecent for her to travel without the men who own her. Books and piano playing are pleasant, but loneliness and a lack of freedom kill the soul. She needs to get out more. Why don't you let her help you in running the estate? She'd be good at it, I'm sure.'

He regarded me wordlessly for a minute, a surprised expression on his face.

'I don't believe I asked for your opinion on my sister, or the estate,' he replied, slowly. 'Though, you are correct about one thing: it is tiresome, having to accompany Edith to social occasions. I suppose that she expects Charles and me to accompany her to the duke's ball?'

'Actually, yes, she does,' I admitted. Edith had, in truth, talked about nothing else all day. It was apparently a costume ball at Lyle Manor, the seat of the Duke of Cornwall. I hadn't really listened very carefully because I had been so intent on escaping back to my own time, but now, as that might never happen, I thought with sudden horror that I might have to attend this ball and help Edith prepare her dress for it.

Not only was Edith excited about her costume and the whole grandeur of the occasion – apparently, the duke's parties were legendarily lavish – she was also excited because it was the first time in years that she and her brothers had been invited to any kind of major society event.

She'd mentioned before that the Trevarrons had been shunned from polite society over the rumours surrounding Elspeth's death, and she'd brought up the subject again that morning as I'd been helping her dress.

'The thing is, dear Tegan, that I am looking forward to the ball. But I am also nervy as a squirrel.' She had sighed as I plaited her hair and pinned it in a bun at the base of her neck.

'Why?' I'd asked. 'It can't be your first ball, surely.'

'No, of course not. But I fear that no one will speak to us, despite us receiving an invitation.' She looked up at me as I walked around to stand in front of her, making sure her hair looked neat and tidy as she liked it when she went riding.

'I'm sure they will. It's been several years. There must be some other topic for the gossips now,' I'd reassured her. But she had been pensive as she'd gone off for her ride.

I was divided about the ball. Part of me honestly wanted to go. I had spent so long studying history and fantasising about ball dresses, the masks and jewellery and elaborate headdresses and wigs. I had wondered what the food would be like, had imagined the romance of dancing to a waltz or a polka dressed in some kind of low-cut, full-skirted silk gown. I had to admit that I was intrigued.

Still, I wanted to go back to my own time. Most of all I wanted to see Aunt Bill. She was my home and my heart, and I was worried about what she would be thinking. She might think that the worst had happened; that I had been kidnapped or murdered.

But I realised suddenly, Aunt Bill might also suspect where I'd gone. Because she too had come here.

William swore under his breath, pulling me out of my musings.

'Ugh. I despise balls and parties,' he muttered.

'Some people enjoy them. People who enjoy the company of others, and fun things like dancing and music,' I answered, sarcastically. I sensed that William liked to seem misanthropic, but I wondered if he really was, underneath it all.

'I do not,' he answered, shortly.

'Charming.' I looked out at the sea and the sunset, calmed by its beauty. Neither of us said anything for a moment. I wondered again if Aunt Bill knew I was here. It was a somewhat reassuring thought that Aunt Bill might not assume I was dead and be deep in grief.

'Trevarron has always had a specialness about it. A feeling of power. Perhaps for being so close to the sea,' William said, after a pause.

'I can see that.' I nodded. The view was spectacular; as the sun set on the horizon, it grew bigger and redder, looking to all intents and purposes as if it was an immense cherry, dipped in the sugar syrup of million-degree heat. The slick, shiny black granite cliffs that cleaved down to the blue-green sea below contrasted savagely with the cerise and red sky; it was like being on another planet. The sheer intensity of colour took my breath away.

It was exactly how it had been in every dream.

We were close enough to the cliffs for the sharp tang of salty sea air to fill our lungs; I breathed it in gratefully. At least the taste of the air here was the same. Nature hadn't changed: it was just everything else that had.

Gently, I felt his hand find mine in the gap between us.

'I'm glad that you can see its beauty. I have always been so grateful that this is my home. Despite everything.' His tone softened, suddenly, and I looked up in surprise. I knew that he must mean his wife dying, but I didn't want to mention it. I didn't know if I was supposed to know.

'Trevarron is a beautiful house,' I replied, carefully. I was all too aware of his fingers entwined in mine. The same feeling overtook me as earlier, when he had carried me up to my room.

My head still ached a little from the fall, but I knew that I was basically all right. No, now, my pounding heart and the butterflies in my stomach were being caused by me touching William, and him touching me.

'It is,' he said, staring out at the horizon. I wondered whether he felt what I did: whether his heart was beating wildly in his chest; whether he felt as if he was caught in a whirlwind of passion and emotion. It wasn't just sex, though I felt the same arousal at being with him as before. It was more than that, but I couldn't explain why.

'The grounds are stunning,' I added, truthfully. 'The rose garden, in particular...'

Despite the fact I was distracted by the strange feelings that held me in their grip, I was focused enough to mention the rose garden in case William might tell me something important about it. Perhaps it was haunted? Perhaps there was some kind of mechanism or invention in it that I'd missed? But William just chuckled.

'You are drawn to that place. I can only assume that you are an amateur gardener, or suchlike.' He stood a little closer to me. I could feel a prickling sense of electricity in the space between us, flowing like a current.

'No... I just like roses,' I lied. I did like them, it was true, but I couldn't tell him the reason for my interest in the rose garden.

'Hmm.' He turned to me, and I started as I felt his hand on the small of my back. 'A rose for a rose.' He stared down intently into my eyes, and slowly drew me closer to him.

I could have protested. I could have pulled away from him and run, but in that moment, I didn't want to. Ever since I had met William De Vere Trevarron, I had wanted him, and I was chagrined to realise it about myself, bearing in mind that people said he had murdered his wife. That was, in anyone's book, a red flag. Did I believe it? I didn't think that I did, but I didn't know for sure.

Yet, I wanted him, nonetheless. I stared up at him, feeling my pupils dilate and a wave of desire wash over me. He made a wordless growl at the back of his throat, and lowered his head towards me.

His lips met mine, and I closed my eyes and let out an involuntary sigh as a deep sweetness enveloped me.

First, the kiss was soft. I thrilled at the sensation of his full lips against mine. He caressed my mouth with his, and I felt my lips part. His breathing grew heavier, and the kiss grew deeper. He held me to him firmly with his arm still in the small of my back, and his other hand cupped my chin, raising my mouth to his.

A searing, electric line of pleasure lit me up inside from my mouth to my heart to the pleasurable soft tightness in my stomach and to the wetness at the top of my thighs that William seemed to unleash whenever he was nearby. I had never, ever felt this before; had never been taken and kissed with such raw abandon. I heard him moan in the back of his throat and grip me harder, pushing his mouth onto mine, caressing my lips with his tongue.

The pull between us was so intense that it managed to overrule all of my feelings of overwhelm, fear and worry about being trapped here, or the fear that I was going mad and I was stuck in a padded cell somewhere, having the mother of all hallucinations. Whatever it was between us was such a strong magnetic pull that it overrode all of those feelings.

I knew that I was protected in his strong arms, but there was another feeling there too: one of submission to his touch. He held me firmly, as if I *belonged* to him, and I found the thought of being his, and wanted by him, strangely erotic. I hadn't ever really been *into* the idea of men like that before; I had never had fantasies about a lord and master who would devour me in the bedroom and make me obey him without question. But now, I got it.

I felt completely under William's spell. I wanted to press my face against his chest and breathe him in. I wanted... I didn't even know what I wanted. I had entered a strange, deeply erotic fugue and all I was doing was responding, not thinking.

I wanted to touch him, to strip off his clothes and worship his body. To taste him, consume him, spend all evening kissing him.

But as soon as I returned his fervour, he broke away from the kiss and shook his head.

'I'm sorry. I... shouldn't have done that,' he muttered, running his hand through his unruly black curls. 'I do not wish to dishonour you, Miss Penrose.'

'You haven't.' I caught my breath, confused at his abrupt change of manner.

'I... I must go,' he said, and turned to leave. 'It would be... improper... for you to mention any of this to my sister. Or to anyone else,' he added. Irritation caught my throat.

'Why?' I asked, crossly. 'You seemed to be enjoying kissing me perfectly well just now.'

'You speak out of turn, miss.' He had returned to the role of the stern lord of the manor now, and the glimpse I'd had of the man underneath had gone. He let go of my hand, and the connection between us broke. The change in energy between us was abrupt and cold after the electricity that had flowed through us just before.

'I don't see how you can think that. I'm perfectly within my rights to say what I think,' I replied. The sudden coldness between us was upsetting; I didn't know what to make of it. I felt off-balance, blindsided, disconnected from the electricity, warmth and joy I had felt just before.

'Ladies should be careful about what they say,' he retorted. Gruffness had returned to his tone. I wondered at the change in his demeanour, and considered again what I'd heard about him: the rumours about Elspeth, his violence, his anger. Maybe I had been wrong to dismiss it all. 'However, I suppose I should remember that you are just a maid,' he added, cruelly. I shivered at the sudden change in his manner, and his use of words. He had called me *maid* when he had laid me on my bed, but then, it had been a Cornish endearment. Now, it was a cold statement of fact.

'Really? Then I won't trouble you any longer with my company,' I replied curtly, and turned away.

'You know that it is unseemly, for the lord to have... relations... with the staff. If you were a lady, I would court you.' He reached out and caught my hand. The bond re-established itself immediately. I felt the warmth in his touch and the flow of electricity resumed between us.

I wanted him to draw me into his arms again. I wanted to be connected to him, but I was also furious. I pulled my hand away.

'But I'm not a lady?' I finished the thought for him. 'Thank you. What a gentleman you are.'

'You are a lady's maid. I would dishonour you by taking things any further. I do this to be gentlemanly,' he muttered. 'I am protecting you.'

'You're using me,' I snapped, angrily. I felt rejected and embarrassed. I had responded to William so enthusiastically – more than I ever had with anyone before, because of whatever crazy chemistry we had between us – and he'd cut me dead. It hurt.

Before he could respond, I walked away. I heard him call out my name, but I ignored him.

I'd had about all I could take of William, the eighteenth century and everything in it for one day. I just wanted to go to bed, and wake up to find that it had all been a dream. But it wasn't. It was much stranger than that.

NINETEEN

'Whoa. Steady.'

It was a couple of days later and I was kneeling on a woven mat, helping Edith while she shoed her horse, Balthazar. She had told me to hold his hoof while she changed his shoe. I was fairly sure that there were stable hands that were supposed to be doing this kind of thing, but Edith had insisted.

Of course, I had absolutely no experience with horses and Balthazar obviously knew that, because a few moments after I gingerly took his hoof onto my lap, he whinnied and tossed his head.

As I held the hoof, I was mulling over a conversation I'd overheard between Mr Cooper and one of the parlour maids, Letty. I had passed them on the back stairs on my way out to the stables to meet Edith, and noticed their heads inclined together. I'd walked by, giving them a brief nod, but as I'd done so, I'd picked up the mention of something that had made me stop around the corner and listen to their hushed conversation.

'... it's not right, 'im bein' a lord of the manor an' all,' Letty said. 'Cook says 'ee's out at all hours, an' 'ee comes back late wi' the carriage filthy.'

'Taverns, it is,' Mr Cooper replied in a whisper.

'I know that. Everyone knows that,' Letty scoffed; evidently, then, it was well known that William presumably liked a drink. 'But there's other funny things. I walked in an' seen 'im countin' money into a chest. 'Ee says, "Letty, be a good girl and go and get the fire started," but I sees 'im hide it away. Now why does a lord 'ave to hide money? An' 'ee was streaked black wi' dirt an' wet through.' She shook her head. 'Mark my words, milord is up to no good.'

''Ee's always up to no good,' Mr Cooper replied, and then their voices faded. I'd peeked around the corner and seen them walking away.

Now, as I held Balthazar's hoof, I wondered what they meant and what William was up to. My reverie was broken by Edith shouting my name.

I looked up to see the horse kicking out at me.

'Tegan!' Edith cried out again. I ducked out of the way, dropping Balthazar's hoof and letting out a sharp exclamation. He hadn't got me, but I knew it had been pretty close, and my heart pounded in panic.

'Careful, there. Are you all right?'

I looked around to see William kneeling down next to me, wearing a concerned expression. 'You almost got kicked in the face. You should be more careful. Never sit in front of the hooves, never stand in front of the horse.'

'I'm fine. Thank you,' I said, primly, getting to my feet and dusting myself down. I bristled immediately on seeing William, after he'd been so rude to me the other night. 'I didn't ask for your advice.'

'It wasn't really advice, as much as a warning.' He raised an eyebrow, coolly, probably sensing my tone. 'Edith. Why are you and your lady's maid in the stables? We have staff for this kind of thing.'

'William. Please don't be such a bore.' Edith rolled her eyes at her brother. 'I am allowed to come down to the stables if I wish, and Tegan is accompanying me. That's her role. She accompanies me. We pay her to be my friend.' Her tone with her brother was caustic.

'That is hardly an appropriate comment to make,' he retorted. 'Really, Edith. There is a way to be seemly in front of staff.'

It rankled with me that he was referring to me as staff. I *was* staff, but that hadn't made a difference when he'd kissed me. For William, it seemed, I was a variety of things, depending on his mood.

'William. If I wanted to be lectured, I would ask.' Edith sighed theatrically, and I stifled a chuckle. I'd never seen her be like this with her brother, and rather than being gruff and rude in return, William looked confused and a little mortified. I was reminded of a picture I'd once seen of a small girl gesturing angrily with a stick at a bewildered-looking bear.

Edith shot me a compassionate glance. 'Are you all right, dear Tegan?' she asked me, her tone softening.

'I'm fine, Edith.' I smiled. 'Just a little surprised.'

'Good. See? She's fine,' Edith retorted to her brother, who nodded.

He shrugged, a little dramatically. 'Well, I can see I'm not needed here.'

'Oh, look who has decided to be a big grump.' Edith's tone lightened; a smile crept over her features. 'He's upset because we made fun of him, Tegan, my dear. I think he wanted to play the hero.'

'Edith. You are ridiculous. I was just responding to a lady in distress,' William protested, but I saw a faint blush appear on his cheeks.

'We are not ladies in distress. I am an accomplished horse-woman, as well you know,' his sister continued.

'Miss Penrose's skills leave something to be desired,' he replied, also now smiling a little. Now, it was my turn to blush. It had been mortifying when I'd come off the horse before, and that whole episode just reminded me of the erotic, fleeting moment I'd had with William, alone in my room.

'Hm. She's learning,' Edith said, loyally, though actually I hadn't gone back for any more riding lessons yet. I was still thinking that there was no point doing that if I was going to find a way back through the portal at any time. 'But I think I need a groom to help me today. Tegan, I won't be long. Come on, Balthazar.' She clicked her tongue and led the horse out of the stable and into one of the other enclosures.

There was a silence and William cleared his throat.

'I hoped to find you today,' he said. All of a sudden, with Edith gone, William looked tremendously awkward.

'Really? Why?' I asked. It *was* pretty awkward between us; the last time we'd seen each other, we'd kissed, looking over the cliffs and at the sunset, then he'd insulted me and I'd left. He'd said nothing to me since.

'I realise that I was a little rude to you the other night. It was ungentlemanly. I wished to say that I am sorry.' He shot me a surprisingly shy smile.

'Thank you. That's very kind,' I said. There was a silence. I tried to think of something to say.

'Well, perhaps I can ask you to meet me again. It has been a long time since I had such an interesting conversation.' He paused for a moment. 'I appreciate the fact that you love the land and the sea as much as I do. As a sailor, and lord of Trevarron, I confess I am, perhaps, a little superstitious, as all sailors are. I like to believe that this place has a special power. It was... pleasant to converse with you about that and not feel ridiculous.'

'I hadn't considered that sailors would be superstitious, but I suppose they might be, being at the mercy of the sea.' I looked up into his dark brown eyes and was surprised to see a softness there. 'It's such a perilous mistress.'

'Indeed.' His eyes crinkled up at the edges as he smiled. 'A perilous mistress. Hm...' He stared at my face for a long moment, as if trying to understand me; as if trying to see into my head, my heart. I stared back up at him, feeling a spark of something new blossom between us. It was a different sort of energy; a kindness, a warmth that I hadn't expected from him. He was so changeable; I didn't know what to think of William. The other night when we'd kissed and then argued, I'd reconsidered the fact that he could have murdered his wife. Now, the idea seemed the furthest possible thing from the truth.

'The wise women of Cornwall are known to sell wind charms to sailors and fishermen, and many's the time I purchased such a thing from a local pellar when I was in the Navy.' William shrugged. 'I sometimes heard my colleagues scoff at these old traditions, but if they did, they weren't from Cornwall. It is part of the culture here. Part of the way we do things to respect the old ways, and the magic of the land. I accept that there are things we cannot explain. Sailors have seen odd things on the oceans for hundreds of years. I myself have experienced strange things.' He gave me an unreadable look. 'I have always felt the power of this land. Can't you?'

It was a long speech for William, who was usually gruff and relatively monosyllabic. I was surprised at his sudden urge to open up to me.

'Yes. I've always felt that too,' I said, without thinking. 'I mean... since I've been here. Trevarron is a powerful place.' I meant *always* as in, since childhood, when I'd visited Trevarron with Aunt Bill, and, then, afterwards, alone, I'd felt that power. I'd felt it in the ground under my feet and in the wide skies and the cliffside views as well as the grandeur of the house itself – even when it was a ruin, it was grand in its way.

But I couldn't tell William that.

I also thought about the rumours that Trevarron was cursed or haunted. I wondered if it had always had a strange feeling about it, even before Elspeth's death; perhaps the oddness that the maids felt in the house was more to do with a power that zinged through it, rather than a curse? After all, I'd grown up with the myths about the missing griffins on top of the gate at the entrance to Trevarron House, and now I knew that my aunt and my grandmother had travelled here. There was a deep oddness to Trevarron House, despite my liking for logic and facts – and, as much as I might not care to admit it, there were things that I couldn't explain.

'You are a surprising woman,' he said. The eye contact between us was unbroken, and it felt as though we were connecting on a different level. As humans, not lord and lady's maid. I felt that he was trying to tell me something about himself; he was trying, perhaps, in his own way, to apologise for his behaviour before now.

I looked up as Edith cantered past, now sitting on Balthazar's back. 'I should go,' I added.

'Of course. I don't wish to delay your ride,' William nodded. '*Are* you riding, today?'

'Apparently so,' I sighed, and William chuckled at my obvious distaste for the idea.

'Then I wish you the best of luck. Though perhaps I should stay close by, in case you need carrying back to your room again,' he suggested, drily. I shot him a shy smile.

'I don't wish to delay your day's work either,' I said, but he shook his head.

'Believe me, Miss Penrose. There is nothing in my day that would be half as diverting as watching you on horseback again.' A smile tugged at the edge of his lips. 'Nothing at all.'

TWENTY

I woke up suddenly from a nightmare and sat up in bed, my heart beating wildly.

I didn't remember exactly what the dream was, apart from the fact that I was running. I was being chased, and I was afraid.

I gathered the blankets of my bed around me and blinked into the darkness. At the edge of the window, where the heavy curtains were open a crack, I could see the milky sheen of moonlight outside.

I stood up and went to the window, pulling the curtain back and gazing out into the blackness.

The view from my window overlooked the sea at the edge of the house grounds, and tonight the moon was bright, shining down on the black water. The stars sprinkled the velvety blackness like a blanket of diamonds. I blinked away sleep as I stood there for a moment, watching them sparkle.

I took some deep breaths and tried to calm down a little.

As I watched, I realised that there were a couple of lights much further down than the heavens, blinking on the water. And then, as I watched, I saw one lone light on the shore.

I frowned. The light on the shore flashed a couple of times and then stayed steady. I wondered if someone was out there; a fisherman, perhaps?

It was cold, in the room, but I was used to Aunt Bill's cottage which had no central heating either. In the winter when I stayed over the holidays, we would manage with hot water bottles and blankets, and huddle together for cosy breakfasts in the morning. Downstairs, Aunt Bill would start the log burner and make a big pot of tea, and we'd talk about our funny dreams. Aunt Bill was, like me, a vivid dreamer.

It runs in the family, I remembered her saying one day as she poured me a large mug of strong amber tea from her beloved blue teapot. *All the Penrose women dream big dreams. In other times we would've been pythonesses, livin' in caves, impartin' wisdom.*

I didn't know about pythonesses, but right now I missed Aunt Bill terribly. Her comments about pythonesses – which I thought were some type of Greek priestesses, oracles of some kind – made a bit more sense now that I knew Aunt Bill and my grandmother had both travelled through time like I had. I wished I could talk to my aunt; I had so many questions for her. What had she seen? What had happened in her trips into the past, and how many had she done? What were the negative side effects she had written about in her letter?

I'd read her letter so many times, tracing my fingertips over her handwriting, my heart aching for home. I'd wished that there was some kind of magic that would transport me to her, just from having that link to Aunt Bill in my hand, but of course, it hadn't happened.

Suddenly, I heard a creak outside my door. I jumped, turning around to face the direction of the noise.

Trevarron House was old, even in 1755, and I'd got used to its creaks and noises to some degree. But this was different.

Someone was walking, or tiptoeing, in the hallway outside.

I got up, heart hammering, and walked as quietly as I could to my door.

The creak stopped for a moment, then continued, as if someone was walking away hurriedly.

All I could think about was what Betty had said about Lady Elspeth's ghost, haunting Trevarron House. We were nowhere near the East Wing, which was where the maids had said they'd heard sounds of pacing in the middle of the night.

Yet, for a moment I wondered if I would open the door and find the ghostly visage of Elspeth Trevarron staring back at me.

I opened the door and looked out, but there was nobody there.

In the distance, a door slammed.

I slumped against the doorframe, trying to calm myself down.

It was just the wind, or the floorboards creaking, I thought, trying to reassure myself. But as I closed my bedroom door and got back into bed, I couldn't help thinking about Elspeth Trevarron, and what she might want with me.

TWENTY-ONE

I'd left the house in the evening, in the company of Eric, the footman, to run an errand for Edith.

Three weeks had passed since I had watched the sunset with William. Three weeks had passed since we'd kissed.

I'd hardly seen him since that afternoon at the stables. Edith had kept me busy up in her quarters, preparing for the upcoming ball at Lyle Manor, and when I had asked why she hadn't seen William much at dinner, Edith had shrugged and said that she imagined the work of the estate was taking her brother into town and beyond.

I did see Charles around, here and there, but he mostly seemed to go out and come back drunk, or spend the day painting in his studio. I knew that he visited Simon Favisham often; Edith said that they were close friends. She always glowed a little when she mentioned Lord Favisham, which surprised me. On the whole, she seemed underwhelmed by men, but he was different – she seemed to have a little crush on him.

I didn't like Charles's paintings and neither did Edith, but Edith was kind about them when he was around. However, I didn't think they were very good at all. His draughtsmanship was terrible and he seemed to have no sense of proportion. All the paintings were also somehow flat and lifeless, and the faces of the people in them looked deathly. I didn't think it was a style as much as they just weren't very good, which was in itself impressive, considering all the time Charles had spent in Italy, apparently learning from the masters of his day. I could only assume that he'd spent more time in taverns than at the canvas.

On the few occasions that I crossed paths with William, sometimes around the stables when I was there for my riding lessons, or around the house when I was carrying Edith's dresses down to the laundry to be pressed or washed, he had acted as if he hadn't seen me at all. He didn't stop me to say hello. I'd thought that we'd perhaps become friends, but he seemed to have reverted to his previous cold manner with me.

That hurt. *I suppose that it doesn't matter what century you're in; a man will still ghost you given half a chance*, I thought.

'Go carefully, my dear Tegan.' Edith had pressed both of my hands in hers concernedly as I left the house. 'There are vagabonds on the roads, as well you know. God speed,' she said, seriously. I hadn't specifically said that I hadn't been attacked by a highwayman on my way to the house, which was the convenient story that Mrs Cottingley had dreamed up for why I'd arrived in what they thought was my ripped underwear. They seemed to believe that it was likely, and I wasn't about to argue.

'I'm fine, Edith,' I reassured her. 'I'm just going to town and back again.' I thought of all the times I'd walked home alone through towns and cities and up the country lanes around St Nantes, but said nothing. Life was so different here; even Edith, the lady of the manor, had to worry about her safety leaving the house. She had such limited independence, and now, I had less than I was used to.

It was the day before the masked ball and the reason that I was being sent out in the evening at all was that the Greek goddess circlet headpiece that Edith had ordered to be made specially by the jewellers in town was finally ready. She'd given up on it, and we had made one out of leaves that afternoon that I thought was pretty enough to be worn for a few hours, but when she'd got a message delivered in the late afternoon, she had shown me it excitedly.

'It's ready! Just in time!' she had exclaimed, dancing around her lounge. 'Will you go and pick it up for me, dear Tegan? Mr James says in his note that you can knock at his dwelling, which is above the shop.'

Of course, I said yes. Even though Edith was a sweet girl, and she treated me like a friend, I still knew that she was my boss. There wasn't really a choice to be made.

It was an hour and a half's carriage ride into Tintagel, where Edith's jeweller was. I watched the countryside bloom around me as we trundled along, thinking that, if you were just looking at the ancient hedges and the trees and lush, swaying green and yellow fields of corn and rape and wheat and barley, you'd never know that you were in a different era.

I was glad to have an opportunity to leave the house. Now that I'd been there a while, I did understand what the maids said about it feeling cursed or haunted. There was something about it that you couldn't quite put your finger on, a feeling, a shadow that lingered in its corners. I hadn't experienced another strange episode like the creaking outside my door, but something felt like it lingered at Trevarron House. Something dark.

What's more, when I'd walked out to the carriage, something else odd had happened.

Betty had run out of the house after me and stopped me as I was climbing into the carriage. She pressed something into my hands.

'Mother says to give you this,' she said in a low voice as I looked at her, bewildered.

'Your... mother? What is it?' I turned the package over. It was wrapped in brown paper and tied with a rough leather thong.

'She says you'll want it.' Betty shrugged. 'Sometimes Mother just knows things, an' she gives me things to pass on. It's a book,' she added.

'What type of book?' I frowned, holding the package in one hand with my hand on the carriage door.

'Look inside.' Betty gave me a sudden grin. 'I seen it before.'

Then, she'd turned tail and run back into the house.

As soon as I was settled in the carriage and we'd set off, I opened the brown paper.

It was indeed a book, but not one that fit the usual description of a printed book. It was more like a personal journal or diary, written by hand and annotated with notes, diagrams and drawings. It was bound in brown leather and the pages were thick.

On the first page, someone had painstakingly printed the title: *Lines of Time – a Guide for the Unwary* by Evelyn Willcock.

I knew that Willcock was Betty's last name. So, it was presumably something made by a family member of hers. It was odd, because I'd never even met Betty's mother, though I knew she was the local wise woman, or pellar.

I began to flick through it carefully.

The first pages were maps. I realised that, though they were out of proportion and much less accurate than an actual map, they showed Britain, crisscrossed by what must have been ley lines. I trailed my fingertip over the lines that were painted in different colours, feeling the texture of the paint. The land was painted in green, with the coastal areas ringed with yellow, for sand, and then blue, for the sea. The paint was still bright, even though the book looked old.

This was handmade; it had to be the only one like it. It was beautiful, and I turned the pages with awe. There were small notes written in slanting copperplate handwriting; sketches, poems, songs.

There was a small map showing the whole of the British Isles, and then close-up maps of Wales, Scotland, Ireland and England on following pages. Finally, there were maps of certain areas within those locales: the Isle of Skye and Orkney in Scotland, Cornwall in England, Anglesey in Wales, the Boyne Valley in

Ireland. There was even a map of what I realised was Brittany in France, even though it took me a while to work that one out.

I studied the Cornwall map for some time. I could see Trevarron House featured on it, painted in brown paint alongside other places of interest: St Michael's Mount was there, as was Glastonbury Tor up in Somerset, and a stone circle I hadn't been to called the Hurlers. I'd thought about some of those places when I'd been talking with William. How on earth had Betty's mother known about that? Was that why she had given me this book, or was it just a vast coincidence?

I didn't believe in anything mystical. I really didn't. But... life had been testing me recently and there were so many things that I couldn't explain that it was hard to know where to start.

I read on.

Past the maps, the author of the book began writing. The handwriting was small, and written in an elaborate, old-fashioned text that was difficult to make out in parts, but I began to follow it after a while.

Being the secrets of the lines of power that crisscross the land and my discoveries therein, the writer began.

Let this book recorde the thoughts of Evelyn Willcock, pellar, scholar of the secret artes and maker of charmes.

I write this in the year 1662. Unlike many women I am able to read and write, given my schooling by my father, Abraham Willcock, the priest of Tintagel.

This will be a secret booke based upon my observations of nature and the subtle energies that God has woven through it. I have recorded the lines of energy in these maps and believe that the places of power the ancient ones built along these lines were not accidental. A great wisdom lies in the past, and as I witness the majesty of the trees and the power in the sea, I know that our ancestors knew something we do not: that there is a power in these lines that can be harnessed and honoured.

The reader may find the idea of a mystical link between places of power ungodly and heretical, but outside of the confines of our British wisdom, there lie many ancient worlds rich in legend. Take for instance the Orient, where unusual theories abound as to the origin of the earth and its composition. My father was a wise man and he knew that there is a glowing path to God in all countries and cultures.

In ancient Chinese mythology, the belief exists that dragons of a kind of ground energy lie under the peaks of powerful mountains and link one mountain range to another. The lines of these dragons' bodies are believed to be conduits of great power under the earth. Mountains are considered great places of spiritual power.

I have wondered whether lines of power might connect places of spiritual importance in our great lands, which are also steeped in legend and myth. Why, might not great sites of pilgrimage such as abbeys and churches, natural sites such as ancient menhirs and tors and even great castles and burial mounds be linked in lines of power across our great country, as part of those lines that extend around the world?

I have taken many measurements and looked at many maps, and, as this booke will show, there are lines of power running through Britain as surely as there are dragons laying under the Chinese mountains.

I looked up from the book for a moment. The jolting of the carriage was making me feel queasy. The rough roads that Eric drove the horses along were also throwing my back out of joint, to say nothing of the fact that I was wearing a corset, underskirt and so many layers of clothing that the back of the dress stuck to me. It was no quick outing, no comfortable car ride. At least I was alone in the carriage; Eric sat on top, guiding the horses.

I wondered if a ley line really did cross through Trevarron House. It was possible; if you believed that there were lines of mystical power crisscrossing the globe, then it was conceivable that the house could sit on one of those lines.

That would have explained why I felt a strange sort of power in the grounds of the house, and why William apparently felt it too. But perhaps it might explain more than that.

I stared out of the window and watched the trees going past, thinking.

If Trevarron House did sit on a ley line, maybe that could explain the strange time slippage. In St Nantes, the legend of the missing griffins on top of the gates of Trevarron House was well known. Maybe something in the energy of the whole estate caused that effect to happen, and, maybe, it had also created some kind of time portal between the present day and 1755.

If it had, how did that knowledge help me?

I couldn't think of a way that knowing this *could* help me find the portal or activate it. I still didn't know how I'd ended up in 1755... but it was something. Perhaps if I read on, I might find a clue that might help.

I might find a way home.

TWENTY-TWO

If I'd been reflecting that the Cornish countryside looked broadly similar whatever era you were in, when we got to Tintagel, there was no getting away from the fact that we weren't in the twenty-first century anymore.

Eric stopped the carriage outside the jeweller's, and I stepped out gingerly onto a cobblestone street, placing Evelyn's book on the seat. I was intrigued by it, and I wanted to return to reading it as soon as I could.

Because I'd visited the area so much over the years, I knew that even though Tintagel was in the modern day a bustling little village, full of tourists in the summer, in the eighteenth century it had been far less populated than it would later become. At that time, tin mining – the main source of income for the area – was decreasing and would soon stop, meaning that fewer and fewer people would be able to live in the village. Tintagel Castle, a series of ancient ruins on a clifftop, wouldn't really become a tourist destination until Alfred, Lord Tennyson would write his epic poems about King Arthur in the nineteenth century, inspiring romantic Victorians to visit it on holiday.

In the twenty-first century, Tintagel was full of cafés, pubs and tourist shops selling ice creams, Cornish pasties, mythical dragon statues and plastic swords and shields for children playing at being knights. Now, as I stepped onto the cobblestones, I was presented with a very different scene.

Most of the buildings were narrow, crabbed little terraced houses, with the occasional sign hanging from the door outside. A butcher's shop was open, but I recoiled at the display of meat hanging from hooks on the ceiling; the smell was high and ripe. Further along, a sign advertised a tannery at the end of the street, which I knew was where leather was treated with urine.

There was no sense of the busy tourist high street I was used to; instead, drably dressed men and women went about their business, carrying baskets of food or fabric, or attending to horses and carts that had pulled up along the street.

The smell was unexpected. Being at Trevarron House, a manor house, I hadn't yet really been exposed to the daily realities of the eighteenth century. The muck in the street was considerable, and an unpleasant wave of what I hoped was manure assaulted my nose.

It was still fascinating, though. The historian in me marvelled at the fact I was here, watching everyday people go about their everyday tasks, this far into the past. It struck me that although what people wore was different, and public hygiene and cleanliness was very far from the twenty-first century, people were not so different to how they were now. I watched families with small children; the children playing with hand-stitched dolls or running around with sticks. Women carried baskets of food and fabrics. People gossiped on the corners, laughed, exchanged news.

I coughed and put my hand over my face before knocking at the jeweller's door. Hopefully, I could get back in the carriage quickly and get away from the smell. I was a little concerned that I'd get the bottom of my dress filthy if I stayed in the street. Looking around, the dresses of the women I could see were there were caked in filth at the hems.

I held up my skirts protectively and knocked again.

There was no answer. I knocked a third time.

From down the street, there was a roar of noise. There was a pub at the end, and crowds of men were gathered outside it, looking like they were jostling to get in, or peering through the windows at whatever was going on inside. There was a lot of cheering, and an occasional roar that reminded me of watching wrestling on TV as a child with Aunt Bill.

Curious, I walked down the street and peered in at one of the grimy windows.

Inside, I could see a crowd of men standing around a raised dais, and on that, two men were fighting.

I turned to a man standing next to me.

'What's going on?' I shouted, above the hubbub.

'No place for a lady, miss. Best you go,' he said, frowning. Several men were staring at me; clearly, I wasn't welcome.

'What is it?' I asked again, looking back through the window.

'Tis a fight. Bare-knuckle boxing,' the man said, pushing me aside so that he could get a better view. 'Get on wi' ye, now, girl. No place for a lady,' he repeated.

I shook my head, transfixed by what little I could see through the glass. From this distance, all I could detect were the vague shadows of two men trading blows in a dark pub full of smoke and dirt. I could hear the roar of the crowd, as savage and unforgiving as how I imagined the Romans at the Coliseum, watching the gladiators fight to the death.

I didn't want to watch, but there was something compelling about it. I had never seen a real fight before – those TV wrestling matches were choreographed, everyone knew that. Aunt Bill had her favourites, and she used to grip the edges of her easy chair tightly when they'd do a special move and bellyflop their opponent. She loved their outfits, their personas, the drama of it all.

I supposed that I'd been pretty sheltered in my life until then because I hadn't ever seen anyone fight in real life. I'd been ready to square up to Cook on that day when I'd travelled back in time, but Mrs Cottingley had saved me.

I felt compelled to see more. I don't exactly know why, but I edged my way through the crowd. Inside the pub it was hot and sweaty and smelt strongly of body odour, sawdust, vomit and all manner of other unpleasant odours. The smell was so powerful that it felt like it hit me in the face with its sheer intensity, but after a moment of shock, I continued to push forward.

Eventually, I got to the third row back from the makeshift ring that had been erected at the back of the pub.

Two men, both stripped to the waist, were joined together in a rough embrace. Blood and sweat ran down the muscular back of the man closest to me. They pushed each other away, and began hitting each other again. The man opposite where I stood grimaced in pain as a blow from his opponent landed on his ribs; as he grimaced, I saw that he was missing many teeth, and blood smeared his face from what looked like a broken nose.

I realised that they weren't wearing boxing gloves, and this was nothing like as organised as a boxing ring. The dark-haired man, who had his back to me, aimed a savage punch at the other man's cheek, and I watched as his fist drove into the other man's jaw, causing some of his remaining teeth to fly loose and spatter blood onto the upturned face of the crowd. I turned away in horror.

There was nothing noble or romantic about this fight. It was just two men, slugging it out to win, in a room full of baying, drunken idiots. It made me feel sick.

I felt a hand on my arm, and looked around to see Eric standing next to me, eyeing the crowd.

'Time to go, miss. I have the package, but we have to go and pay for it,' he said, firmly. I could see that there were some men in the crowd looking me up and down, and I felt suddenly very visible in my corset and dress, which was much nicer than what most of the people standing around were wearing. 'You aren't safe here,' Eric said in a low voice, in my ear, and I realised what he meant; I still carried the money for the headpiece in my purse. I could see the expressions of many of the people standing around, who were looking me up and down in my fine dress, as if valuing what it could be sold for if it was stripped from me.

I nodded and turned to go. I'd seen enough.

Eric took my elbow and started to steer me through the crowd. There was a group of men that wouldn't let us through for a moment; they leered drunkenly at me, and shouted abuse. One reached for my shawl and pulled it off; a laugh went up as my neck and collarbone were exposed.

There was a sudden loud roar from the crowd. Eric took the opportunity of the distraction to push me through the crowd and away from the men.

'Leave the shawl,' he muttered, his hand firmly in the small of my back. I could tell that he was annoyed at having had to come and get me.

I craned my head around to see what the noise was all about. By now I was about ten rows back from the boxing ring, but just for a moment, a gap opened in the crowd and I saw a bare-chested William De Vere Trevarron, Lord of Trevarron House, standing victorious over the prostrate body of his opponent. Grimly, he clutched a wooden cup, with blood dripping from his knuckles.

And, in that brief moment, his eyes met mine.

TWENTY-THREE

It was all I could think about, the next day.

I'd hardly slept. When Eric had got me back to the house, I'd taken the headpiece to Edith and then made an excuse that I had a headache and needed to go to bed. She had been kind as she usually was, and let me go, but reminded me that it was the duke's costume ball the next day and that we had to be ready.

When Betty came to open my curtains and set a cup of tea by the side of the bed, I was awake. I had lain awake for at least two hours already, thinking about what I'd say – if I was going to say anything – to William.

Eric hadn't seen him; I was fairly sure of that. It had just been a moment, and then William had turned away from us. Eric had been facing the other way, but I'd seen. And William knew that I had.

I wondered if anyone else knew. Had anyone else seen William fight? Was it well known that he did this? Was it common knowledge? I wondered whether it had been a one-off fight, or if there had been others. And if there had, why was he doing it?

I took the tea gratefully from Betty, making small talk with her, but my thoughts were consumed by William.

I couldn't help but think about the rumours Edith had told me about how, when Elspeth died, people said that William had murdered her. That he had a violent temper.

I'd dismissed the idea, just like Edith had. Not because I knew William deeply, but because people always gossiped about things, because it seemed like an unnaturally sensational story, and because Edith didn't believe it. And I trusted Edith's judgement.

But now, I'd seen William beat another man to a bloody mess, and that would have changed anyone's mind. If William was capable of that, what else was he capable of? And if he was violent, if he had had something to do with his young wife's death, why did I feel so attracted to him? What did that say about me?

I knew that William was supposed to be accompanying Edith to Lyle Manor today, which meant that we were all going to be there together – in the carriage, and definitely at the ball itself. As a lady's maid, I was expected to go, and be there to attend Edith: help her with her costume and manage her dance card, and otherwise be of help if she needed it.

I didn't want to see him, but I knew that I would have to.

I got out of bed with a heavy heart, washed and dressed and arranged my hair, and picked up Edith's breakfast tray as usual. I had brought the book that Betty had given me up to my room when I'd got back and had flicked through some more of the pages, but what I'd seen at the tavern occupied my thoughts, and I couldn't concentrate on it.

When I got up to Edith's quarters, she was already awake and sitting up in bed. She'd opened the curtains herself.

'My dear Tegan,' Edith welcomed me as I walked in, surprised at the light room. Usually, Edith was a heavy sleeper, no doubt due to the fact that she didn't have much else to do, and because I knew that she tended to stay up late, reading. 'Did you sleep well? It's the day of the ball! Are you excited? Is your headache gone?'

She was like an excitable parrot, and, despite my worries about William, I smiled.

'I'm much better, thank you, Edith,' I put her breakfast tray over her knees and stood at the end of the bed. She poured herself a cup of tea and sipped it.

The Trevarrons favoured tea or hot chocolate in the morning, but I understood from listening to the maids in the kitchen that the staff felt both were a modern affectation. Ale was more common at this time; I knew that no one drank water, as it would be full of bacteria. Even though no one knew what bacteria was in the 1700s, they still knew enough that drinking water could often make you ill.

My body, used to drinking a litre of water every day, had suffered since I had been here. I'd had several upset stomachs just from eating and drinking what there was on offer, and I didn't like the way that I smelt, just having a shallow bath once a week – even that was considered quite high and mighty and only for the likes of lords and ladies by Betty, who had sniffed in irritation every time I'd asked her to fill up the copper bath in the bathroom for me with hot water. The fact that Trevarron House actually possessed indoor bathrooms with rudimentary plumbing was something Betty was proud of, but she also resented having to run a bath for me, even though it didn't involve her carrying buckets of water up the stairs.

'You will talk to me, if no one else does, won't you? I'm afraid that I will be left at the edge of the dancefloor at the ball, like the spinster that I am,' Edith fretted. I was starting to understand her mood changes, but they could still take me by surprise. 'I am afraid that no one will talk to us. That they will shun us.'

'Of course I'll talk to you, Edith. But I'm sure that you will be very popular, and lots of people will want to talk to you and dance with you,' I reassured her. 'And... you're not a spinster. How old are you?' I realised I had no idea.

'Oh, Tegan. You are so *bold*. I am twenty-five. Rather ancient and swiftly marching past marriageable age, I fear.' She sighed.

'Twenty-five is hardly old.' I frowned. 'We're the same age. I'm nowhere near wanting to get married.'

'Most ladies are betrothed at a young age, to bind families

together,' Edith said. 'I don't doubt that you know this. Yet, they say that a marriage is where a man and a woman may experience the love of God most profoundly.' She sounded doubtful. 'I think that I have always preferred horses to men, though. And I have always believed that a fast friend – a friend of the heart, another woman to be a true companion – would be preferable to marrying a man. I do not know men very well, but my brothers, though they are gentlemen, are smelly and vulgar.' She made a face, and I couldn't help but laugh.

'I wouldn't argue with you there, Edith. Well, not about Charles and William being smelly, particularly. But men in general. Yes.'

What I didn't add, though I thought it, was how sad it was that Edith would never be able to explore her sexuality in this life. In the modern day, she might have been gay; she did seem to have a slight crush on Lord Favisham, so perhaps she might have been bisexual or even asexual or anything at all, and no one would have batted an eyelid. I could imagine Edith working in a bookshop or a library, or perhaps being a scientific researcher, an intelligent, quirky woman, full of life and fun. But here, she was pressed down, kept from living, kept from being herself.

'Oh, Tegan. You are so wicked.' Edith giggled. 'And to have the *freedom* to want to be married, or not. This is the benefit of not being a lady.' She sighed, and then caught my expression. 'Oh. I'm sorry. I just meant...' She trailed off.

'That's all right, Edith. I know what you meant.' I sat down on the end of her bed. 'When do we need to leave for the ball?'

TWENTY-FOUR

The ball was much bigger and more opulent than I'd expected, and when I walked in behind Edith, I looked around me in awe.

Lyle Manor was a much larger house than Trevarron. Edith had told me on the way over that it had been built in Tudor times, which was still a good two hundred years earlier or more even in the early eighteenth century. As the carriage finally jolted along to the end of a long, twisting drive surrounded by lawn and thick with beech trees, a wide grey stone mansion with what seemed like hundreds of lead-lined of windows stretched out in front of us.

High Gothic arches alternated with areas where the stone was covered in green shrubs. I could see that the building had various different wings, and the place we had come into ended in a circular drive where carriages were stopping while their passengers disembarked. There was a hubbub of costumed partygoers lining up to get inside the house. Two butlers were welcoming people inside.

I wondered if Aunt Bill had experienced anything like this on her trips to the past. What grandeur had she seen? What squalor? I wondered if I would ever see my aunt again, and grief clutched at me. I helped Edith out of our carriage and arranged her costume for her. She was dressed as the Greek moon and hunter goddess, Artemis, and the headdress I'd had to collect from the jeweller featured a circlet of pearls set in silver with a silver crescent moon at the front. The dress, which she'd had made by her favourite dressmaker in town, was a shimmering silver-blue satin with a white bodice, embroidered with crescent moons and stars. She carried a bow and arrow to reference Artemis the huntress. She looked lovely. We had taken a long time plaiting her hair artfully around her headdress, and I was quite pleased with my efforts.

I wore one of Edith's dresses. It was a costume ball, so we had had to think of something I could dress up as. I'd politely refused some of Edith's more culturally insensitive ideas – she didn't know that they were, so I didn't blame her, but I didn't want to dress up as an African tribeswoman. In the end, we'd agreed that simple was best. I was a lady's maid and therefore my rank meant I couldn't dress as anything like an Egyptian queen or a Greek goddess, so Edith offered me an outfit she had once worn – a flower girl.

Edith had had the dress adjusted to fit me; a dressmaker had visited the house one day and taken my measurements, then returned a week later with the remade dress that now fitted perfectly. I was curvier than Edith; she was naturally petite, but she also ate almost nothing, which I knew couldn't be good for her. However, bearing in mind the eighteenth-century diet, I wasn't convinced that the food would actually be good for anyone. My stomach was still upset almost all of the time.

My costume was a pink-and-blue dress with a wide, corseted Madame de Pompadour skirt, covered with garlands of small roses. The pink tunic was ruched with pink satin with a bodice to match. There was a white muslin apron with pockets, and I carried a large flat basket filled with flowers I'd picked in the gardens at Trevarron that afternoon. I'd curled my hair in ringlets the best I could by tying it in rags overnight and wore a white muslin cap on top of it.

I felt ridiculous, but when Betty had finished dressing me, in Edith's room, I'd come out from behind the screen and Edith had clapped her hands delightedly.

'Oh, Tegan. You look wonderful!' she had breathed, and I

didn't have the heart to say that I thought I looked like a birthday cake.

William hadn't said anything to me on the journey. He'd sat on top of the carriage with Eric, the footman, making the excuse that Edith's and my dresses took up all the room inside the carriage and there was barely room in there for Charles, Edith and me. He'd refused to meet my eye as we'd waited on the stone steps for the carriage to be brought around, making small talk with his brother.

William was dressed in what Edith told me was a French guard's uniform. He wore a rich blue coat trimmed with silver braid, which was turned back with scarlet revers on the coat tails. The coat had silver epaulettes on the shoulders and a scarlet collar that was also trimmed with the same silver braid. Under the coat he wore a scarlet vest fastened with a belt, matching blue knee breeches and white cloth gaiters covered his knees. Last, he wore a three-cornered hat that was also trimmed with silver braid.

When he walked out of the house, I'd done a double take. I didn't particularly know what he was dressed as until Edith told me, but the first thought I had on seeing William in his ball finery was that he looked like an incredibly handsome highwayman. I had deliberately looked away, because I knew I was staring and I didn't want to make a fool of myself.

However, I'd snuck another look at him while Edith was talking to Charles, and the sight of William De Vere Trevarron, black-eyed and black-haired, with the military style uniform showing off his strong, muscular physique, made my heart beat faster. I was suddenly aware that I was biting my bottom lip.

No. Don't feel attracted to a violent man, I cautioned myself. It hadn't ever been something I'd experienced before; I wasn't a girl who loved bad boys. Some women swooned over men with tempers, who shouted, who swaggered around like they owned the world and could break it between their bulging biceps if they chose to. That had never attracted me at all. In fact, I hated it. I hated bullyboy theatrics. It repulsed me.

My gaze slid to William's hands, and I saw that they were bruised and covered in cuts.

The sight was a good wake-up call. He might have been handsome, but there was no way that I was interested in interacting any more than I had to with a man who willingly would be so brutal. I had no way of knowing what had happened between him and Elspeth, but I knew what I'd seen in the boxing ring, and that gave me pause. I had told myself that I would hold back judgement and observe evidence of his criminal nature, or lack of it, as it happened.

But the fight was evidence that William held a darkness in him. And if he was able to beat a man bloody, it did make me think twice about whether he might have been able to do the same – or worse – to a woman.

William looked up and met my eyes. His mouth had twitched, and a brief flash of irritation had crossed his face before he had jumped athletically on top of the carriage.

Had William actually had seen me, the night before, at the fight? There was a possibility that I was wrong, but I knew that he had. I didn't know what to say to him. Should I mention it? Or was this just going to be a secret that I kept for as long as I was here?

I was sure that neither Edith nor Charles would know about William's appearance in the fighting ring; surely, he wouldn't be able to tell them. But, as I looked at his hands, I wondered how he would explain those injuries away.

It was the first time that I'd been at close quarters with Charles Trevarron. He had spoken to me a little before I'd fallen off my horse at the hunt meeting, and I'd seen him around the house; he was often there in the dining room when we had dinner. Although I took my breakfast with Mrs Cottingley, the butlers, footmen and the senior maids, I had dinner with Edith, Charles and William, when he was there, and Edith and I usually had a casual lunch in her rooms.

At dinner, Charles was generally full of himself and badly informed. He held forth vociferously on all manner of topics from poverty ('they should all work harder, to achieve what we have') to disease (he was a keen promoter of keeping windows closed and not washing over much, to avoid letting bad humours enter in) and, of course, painting.

There were so many times that I'd had to bite my lip and not retort when I heard him opining about the issues of the day. As a historian, I was fairly well informed about events in the eighteenth century and found that Edith was, in general, much more perceptive, well-read and intelligent than her brother. Edith read the newspapers, scientific, poetic and art periodicals and ordered new books all the time, keeping up with new ideas and thinking about things deeply. She was an abolitionist, being against slavery, while Charles – cementing my bad opinion of him – argued passionately for it.

Charles seemed to form his opinions from the headlines in the gutter press. I found it particularly difficult to listen to him comment so loudly and confidently about the 'benefit' of slavery to humankind, and the fact that he believed it was a practice God approved of and had in some way inspired in the hearts and minds of good Christian men. On those occasions, I'd excused myself from the dinner table.

In the carriage on the way to the ball, Charles – dressed as Julius Caesar, complete with the laurel-wreath headpiece and the white robes – regaled his sister with tales of his exploits with other artists and socialites in Italy, which she was customarily kind about, but which I thought made him sound immature. Everything Charles said centred around a key theme of him being cleverer than everyone else. Perhaps Charles believed that he was Caesar; the fact that he had dressed as a Roman emperor didn't escape me.

Maybe it was normal for men of the time to assume their own birthright of superiority; but even though he was often gruff to the point of rudeness, I'd never really felt the same with William.

There were also several points in the conversation where Edith tried to tell Charles about the poems she had been working on, but

Charles made fun of them, and instantly changed the conversation back to himself.

I'd read the poems and was impressed. At one point, after Edith had mentioned her poetry twice and been made fun of, I'd interjected that I thought the poems were very good, and that Charles should read them.

Charles had stared at me without saying anything for a long moment, and then resumed telling Edith his story about making fun of an Italian chef in Naples. Clearly, my opinion was not of interest to him.

As we walked inside the house entrance, we were met by serving girls carrying trays of drinks as well as jugglers dressed as medieval court jesters. There was a large cloakroom, staffed by a number of men in smart uniforms – I assumed it was the staff uniform for the footmen and butlers at Lyle Manor – where ladies and gentlemen were leaving cloaks and wraps, revealing elaborate costumes underneath.

Edith grasped my hand with excitement. Her eyes were glowing as she looked around; I could see that she was already entranced.

We followed the line of attendees ahead of us into the ballroom.

There were already what seemed like hundreds of people there. This was no small, cosy gathering. I'd expected a crowd, but nothing quite like this.

The room was huge; bigger than a sports hall or a decent-sized nightclub. It was probably two hundred feet square, and everything in it was opulent and grand.

Golden chandeliers holding hundreds of glowing lights – I assumed they were oil lamps – hung from the ceiling. The walls were hung with rich tapestries and ornate, gold-edged mirrors, and a string band and a pianist in the corner were playing something fast and upbeat. In the centre of the ballroom, there were already couples dancing, and the rest of the attendees stood at the edges, drinking wine and talking noisily.

I looked around me in amazement. It was a beautiful scene, and just for a moment, I let the majesty of the moment envelop me in all its twinkly magic. How amazing that I was here; I still could hardly believe it. It was perilous, but also remarkable.

Now that we were at Lyle Manor, William had to at least give the illusion of being a functional part of the Trevarron family. He had strode ahead of Edith, Charles and me, and was greeting the duke warmly as we arrived at the entrance to the ballroom.

The duke, a man possibly in his sixties with long grey hair tied back with the customary black ribbon, slapped William on the back and seemed pleased to see him.

The Trevarrons were ushered to a queue of lords and ladies waiting to be announced to the already assembled crowd. They took their turn presenting a portly, middle-aged man in a smart uniform – I guessed that it might be Lyle Manor's head butler – with cards, which he read aloud in a booming voice to announce them.

When it was Edith's turn, I watched as her name was read aloud with her brothers. She blushed happily as her name was announced. William's expression was blank; I got the impression that he would rather be anywhere but at the ball, and was merely being polite. Charles, by complete contrast, bowed deeply as his name was said. I had to consciously concentrate on not rolling my eyes.

When the Trevarrons were announced, they drew attention from the crowd. But unlike the lords and ladies who had been announced ahead of them and been greeted with cheering, whistles of appreciation and smiles and waves, many of the ball attendees turned to each other and started chattering in low voices when William and Edith descended the steps. There was some laughter, but it wasn't joyful as before. I saw some of the women side-eyeing Edith and then looking away disdainfully, and, as William walked onto the ballroom floor, several of the men and women stepped out of his way altogether.

I could tell that Edith had noticed their reception, and that it had dampened her spirits. I felt for her; she'd been so nervous in the carriage ride over. However, she smiled brightly at me.

'It's so busy!' she breathed. 'Look. There's the Duke and the Duchess of Marlborough. And Viscount and Lady Falmouth.' Edith pointed out various richly dressed figures to me. I could see why she'd been so excited about the ball – for a vivacious young woman who spent so much time alone, it must have been wonderful to finally be among so many of her peers.

For me, though, it felt strange. For one thing, I didn't know any of these people, and for another, I was staff, and not a real guest. Lady's maids and valets were allowed to attend balls if their lords and ladies wanted them there, but Edith had told me before we got in the carriage that I shouldn't necessarily expect to be asked to dance.

'Tegan, dear,' she had said, those amber eyes wide with concern. 'You know that if I was able, I would change the rules. But, as a lady's maid, you may not get very many dances.'

I could see that she was awkward, and I wanted to put her at ease.

'Please, Edith. Don't fret.' I'd taken her hands in mine, and seen the dawn of relief in her eyes. 'I'm not much of a dancer anyway. And I'm just here to support you.'

'Thank you, dear Tegan.' Edith pressed my hand in hers. 'Oh! Lady Claire and Lady Fenella are here.' She waved at a couple of young women our age who were standing nearby. 'Let us go and say hello. They are old friends.'

I followed Edith towards the young women who were dressed in lavishly jewelled gowns. Some of the costumes at the ball were definitely costumes: I recognised pierrot-type outfits with hand-held masks, shepherdesses in white and blue ballgowns carrying crooks and men in French-style outfits with bog hats and long swords, like I remembered the four musketeers from the movies I'd watched as a child.

Lady Claire and Lady Fenella didn't seem to be wearing specific costumes. Lady Claire wore a gold damask satin gown with a fleur-de-lys print in white and Lady Fenella wore a deep pink gown with ruffles at the sleeves. Both followed the fashion of the day being dresses that were low-cut, square necks at the front with a bodice that highlighted small waists, and wide skirts supported by the punishing corsetry and constructed underskirts I knew were underneath.

'Dear Claire. Fenella.' Edith stretched out a hand to her friends, but they both stared coldly at her and did not respond.

'Isn't the ball lovely? I declare that I have never seen any decorations as handsome,' Edith continued, nervousness edging into her voice. Claire looked away, as if she was embarrassed.

'Lovely.' Lady Fenella nodded. 'Lady Trevarron. We were most surprised to see you and your brothers here.' She stared directly at Edith, unsmiling. Her tone implied that Edith wasn't welcome.

'The duke invited us,' Edith replied, querulously.

'It has certainly been a while since we saw you,' Lady Fenella continued, her eyebrow raised. 'I hardly thought you would dare attend a ball again, given your brother's... misfortunes.'

I stared at both of them, distaste in my mouth. I wanted so much to be able to tell them that they were both being horrible to Edith and they should stop being so bitchy, but I knew that I couldn't. A lady's maid being so outspoken was unheard of, and it wouldn't help Edith's case for me to tell them off. As much as I wanted to say something, I remained silent.

'It has been very sad for us all after Lady Elspeth's unfortunate accident,' Edith said, slowly. I got the impression that she had rehearsed that statement from the way that she said it so formally. Like a politician reading out a prepared statement. 'Yet, it is four years hence, and we are allowed to live our lives, though we miss her gaiety and grace every day.'

'Your brother spends most of his time in alehouses, I hear.' Lady Claire looked over to where William stood, alone, watching the dancing with a glowering expression on his face. 'Is that where he is living his life? Where he is commemorating Lady Elspeth's grace and gaiety, perhaps?'

'That is unfair and untrue. William works hard to maintain the estate,' Edith protested.

'Indeed. I wonder that you can bear to live there after what happened,' Lady Claire continued. 'I could not. But you are so... loyal... to William.'

The inference was clear: Claire and Fenella were suggesting that not only was William a murderer, but that Edith was in cahoots with him. That she lied to protect him, perhaps.

'Of course I can bear it. It is my home,' Edith replied. I could see from her face that she was upset, but she was also too polite to turn around and flounce out of there like she should have done.

'Indeed. And at least Lord Trevarron is at home, Claire.' Fenella tapped her friend lightly on the wrist. 'Lord Charles has just come back from Italy, I hear. Presumably with an array of canvases for us to admire.' She smirked. 'Will he be undertaking an exhibition, Lady Trevarron? In London, perhaps. At one of the galleries there.'

Edith blushed. So, it was common knowledge that Charles's art was an expensive hobby – and that he wasn't very good.

'Hm. I fear that I may be too weak of stomach for the... *subject* of Lord Charles's paintings.' Lady Claire smiled, but I could see from her eyes that there was no warmth in that smile at all. It was the smile of a crocodile about to devour its prey.

'The subject?' Edith echoed.

'Oh, yes. I believe there is a fashion in Italy, as there is in many foreign lands.' Lady Claire fanned herself as she spoke. 'Painters become so friendly with their assistants, and, I have heard, often paint them as muse. Of course, the artistic temperament is a mystery to me.' She feigned an innocent tone. 'I am content with my embroidery and leave great art to the *men*.'

The way that she emphasised *men* didn't leave any of us in doubt of what she meant. She was suggesting that Charles was gay, and that – presumably – Claire and Fenella were suggesting that he had come back to England with a chest full of paintings of his Italian lovers.

'Excuse me... I have to attend to something.' Edith's blush had deepened, and now her face was splotched with outrage. She picked up her skirts and dashed to the other side of the ballroom, completely humiliated.

I followed her, shooting Lady Claire and Lady Fenella a look of disdain. I hoped they knew what I thought of them, even if I couldn't say it.

'Edith... wait,' I panted, trying to slip past the dancers in the middle of the ballroom and navigate the crowds in my wide dress.

Yet, when I caught up to her, she was sequestered in a corner by Simon Favisham.

'Lady Trevarron. It has been many weeks since I laid eyes upon your deific beauty. What a boon it is to see you this evening,' Simon purred smoothly, bowing deeply and doffing his hat, a red three-cornered affair with a long red feather. He had a dandyish type of costume – all white and red, and I didn't know exactly what he was dressed as. Edith gave him a beaming smile. 'Good evening, Lord Favisham' – Edith curtseyed politely –'you remember my lady's maid, Tegan Penrose?'

'Miss Penrose.' Lord Favisham bowed in my direction. 'How beautiful you look this evening. A maid dressed as a milkmaid. Charming.'

He was as polite and solicitous as he had been before, when I'd met him at the hunt.

'Is Clara with you this evening?' Edith looked around hopefully, but Lord Favisham shook his head.

'My sister has been danced away, I fear,' he replied. 'My weeks have been bleak without the blessing of your countenance.' I looked surreptitiously at Edith, wondering if she was taking all of this flowery language seriously, but her expression was rapt. I knew that she'd been looking forward to seeing Simon at the ball, and that quite a few letters had been going back and forth between them over the past few weeks. After our experience with Lady

Fenella and Lady Claire just before, I was glad that there was at least one friendly face for Edith there. 'May I ask for this dance?'

'Certainly.' Edith took his outstretched hand.

Lord Favisham whirled Edith onto the centre of the dance-floor, where a group of dancers were just beginning a routine. I didn't know what it was – Edith had asked me if I knew all the modern dances when we had been talking about the ball, and I'd lied and said that I did. I'd thought that I shouldn't say I had no idea about what dances were popular in the eighteenth century, because that seemed like the sort of thing that a lady's maid should know. I didn't want Edith to get suspicious, and I needed to fit in as well as I could, until I found my way home.

I watched the dance for a while. It seemed quite intricate and involved couples standing opposite each other: a line of men and a line of women, who would take turns to promenade down the middle the aisle in various different patterns, and then change partners, twirl and go again. I tapped my foot along with the music and accepted a glass of wine from a serving girl.

I watched as the dance finished, and a new tune began. As it did, many of the dancers swapped partners, and there was a small melee of excited to-ing and fro-ing as gentlemen asked ladies for the next dance. However, Edith remained alone in their midst, and I watched with a sad heart as her face fell, realising that no one else would ask her.

I watched as Lord Favisham put a proprietary hand on her arm and said something in her ear. The dance began again, and I noticed that Lord Favisham held her very tightly, and his eyes never left Edith's as they danced.

'Miss Penrose. You look very pretty this evening.' I looked up, startled, to find William standing next to me. His hand was on my elbow. 'I think we need to have a little conversation. Don't you?'

TWENTY-FIVE

'Enjoying the ball?' William steered me out of the ballroom, his hand on my elbow still. There was a large open door at the back of the room that led onto a square courtyard dimly lit with lamps. It had got dark, and I saw that some couples had taken refuge out here. My gaze flickered to a couple of dark corners, where I could see couples embracing.

Regardless of the era, people would always find an opportunity to slip out of a dance to kiss in the corners, I thought.

'Yes, thank you. Are you?' I pulled my arm away from his grip and frowned up at him. I wasn't sure of William. I couldn't predict what he would do, and even though there was a lot of chemistry between us, I was still wary of him. Especially now that I'd seen him bare-knuckle fighting just the night before. It had been savage and raw, although there was a part of me that had also reacted in a primal way to seeing William, stripped to the waist, his hard-muscled back and torso smeared with sweat and blood, raining blows on his opponent.

But I'd already decided that I wasn't going to think about William in that way anymore.

'No. It is exactly as I expected it would be. A poisonous gossip mill, dressed up in taffeta,' he muttered. I wondered if William had endured some of the same cruelty as Edith had; though he was rude and insufferable, I did feel some sympathy for both of them at being subjected to the sort of bitchiness I had already heard this evening.

'You saw me last night.' He changed tack; there was no preamble. William crossed his arms over his chest and frowned down at me. All of his previously friendly manner was gone; it was as if the conversation we'd had about the sea being a perilous mistress, about sailors buying wind charms from wise women, and the magic of the land – as if all of that had never happened.

'Yes. I did.' I lifted my chin defiantly. There was no point in lying about it. He had seen me.

'Have you told anyone?' he asked, his eyes narrowing.

'No,' I replied, truthfully.

'Not the other servants? Or my sister? You two seem to be very intimate,' he continued, gravely.

'No. I think you'd know if I'd told Edith. She would have come straight to you.'

He nodded.

'That is true. My sister has no guile.' He regarded me cautiously for a moment. 'And you, Miss Penrose? Do you have guile?'

'If you're asking me if I am devious and a liar, or if you think I'm going to extort you over something that you obviously keep secret from your family, then no. I am not, and I won't do that,' I replied. My heart was beating fast; William was the lord of the manor. He was my employer, and despite the fact that Edith was fond of me, if William decided that I was leaving Trevarron House, then I was leaving. I couldn't do that; the rose garden was the only way back that I knew of, and I had to work out how to use it to travel to the modern day. Otherwise, I would be stuck here forever.

So, I had to play ball. For now. With a dangerous and powerful man.

'I see.' He stared deep into my eyes. 'Come with me.'

He strode out of the courtyard, through a stone arch and onto a wide, well-kept lawn. It was quieter again out here, although there were ornamental gardens to our left where some ball attendees were talking and laughing.

I could have walked away; I didn't have to follow William, but where would I go? He was clearly used to being obeyed, and the rebellious part of me considered running in the other direction, or running away from the ball altogether and living a peasant's life in the village or in the woods. But I knew that I wouldn't survive long, doing that.

'Walk with me,' he commanded, and led me along a pathway that emerged into a stunningly beautiful long pergola walkway, covered in vines. I could see that it would be lovely in the daytime. As well as grape vines – with fat purple grapes hanging in rich bunches – the pergola was strewn with flowering jasmine. Now that it was evening, lamps were arranged all the way along it, lending the walkway a mystical, flickering light. 'It is more private here.'

I followed him, my heart beating wildly. I was nervous about what he might say, but I was also very aware that I was alone at night with a man that my most primal nature wanted to lose myself in. He looked incredibly handsome, and his troubled frown did nothing to turn me off. Very much the opposite: there was something about William's gruffness, frowns and deep gazes that made me tingle all over.

No, I reminded myself. *Remember who he is.* I made myself look at his bloodied and bruised knuckles. *Remember what he might have done to his wife.*

'This is far enough.' He stopped in the middle of the walkway and turned to me.

I stopped, and watched him expectantly. There was a silence. I could see from his expression that he was unsure how to begin the conversation.

'Are you going to tell me why you were fighting?' I prompted him. 'You've walked me all the way out here, away from everyone, so I assume you want to. Or you're going to ravish me.' I raised an eyebrow; I wasn't about to let William De Vere Trevarron get the better of me just because he thought he was superior in rank and by birth. I knew that was rubbish, even if he didn't. I was better educated than he was, and I'd been vaccinated against things that might well kill him. I was up on two fronts, at least, even if I didn't possess vast inherited wealth.

'You are very plain spoken for a woman.' He stared at me, still frowning. 'Still, that is refreshing,' he sighed. 'Yes. I was fighting.' He nodded. 'I never intended for anyone to find out. Well...' He corrected himself. 'No one that matters.'

'Is it something that you do often?' I guessed from what he said that it hadn't been the first time. He nodded again.

'I have been fighting since my Navy days. It began with the other sailors; we boxed. That was gloved, like gentlemen. I found that I had a... certain talent... for it.' He looked uncomfortable, talking about this, but I sensed that it was important for him to tell someone. Perhaps he'd never been able to talk about it before.

'I imagine that isn't unusual, in those types of occupations,' I said, evenly. He nodded.

'It isn't. I became an unbeaten champion. One night, when some of my colleagues and I were enjoying some shore leave in the Indies, there was a fight in a hostelry. The boxers were fighting without gloves. My companions volunteered me. I didn't want to fight, but they had bet on me to win, and I didn't want to let them down. I fought, and won,' he said with a shrug.

'And then?' I prompted him. I realised that I was interested to know the story; and I also realised that I wanted a reason to believe that William was a good man. I wanted to like him. I didn't want to believe he had murdered his wife. It was unlikely; Occam's Razor held that the most reasonable explanation for something was the most likely, and the most likely thing was that Elspeth had had an accident. I desperately wanted that to be true.

'I didn't do it again for some years. I returned home and got married. I got promoted to captain. Things were going well. I still boxed, in the proper way. Then, we lost Elspeth. She died... very suddenly.' William's tone hardened.

'I heard... Mrs Cottingley said...' I began, then paused. I had to ask him about the rumours – whatever they were – that had surrounded Lady Elspeth's death.

And yet, as soon as I began speaking, I realised how rude and inappropriate it was of me to ask him what I wanted to ask. If he had killed the woman he loved.

There was no good way to broach that subject. I could feel my face turning red.

'What did she say?' he barked.

'Oh. Nothing. Forget I said anything,' I stammered, feeling awkward.

'No, I can see that there is something you wish to ask me. Ask it,' he ordered.

I didn't want to, but I couldn't think of anything else to say.

'Mrs Cottingley said... that there were rumours about how Lady Elspeth died. It was... an accident?'

He stared at me for a long moment without saying anything.

'She fell. She was running through the woodland and caught her foot in a tree root. When I found her, she was dead,' he said, brusquely. 'She hit her head on a rock as she fell.'

'I'm so sorry,' I said. I was sorry. 'That sounds horrific. Why was she running?'

He narrowed his eyes at me.

'I see. I take it that you are fully aware of what the rumours are.' His voice was a thin, hard line of contempt. 'Kindly trouble me no longer with your salacious interest in my wife's death. Good evening, Miss Penrose.'

And he strode away, his back squared, emanating anger.

TWENTY-SIX

'William!' I ran after him. 'Wait!'

He stopped, yards from the maze. He didn't turn around, and I could tell that he was furious.

'William. Please forgive me.' I reached out a hand, gingerly, and touched his arm.

'Lord Trevarron,' he corrected me.

He spun around and squared up to me. I took a step back, instinctively wary.

'Don't' – his voice was steel, now – 'don't torment me any further.'

'I don't intend to torment you.' I tried to keep my tone steady, even though he was scaring me. 'I just asked an innocent question.'

He searched my face for a moment.

'Fine. If you do not wish to torment me, then you will not ask.' He frowned heavily. 'The loss of my wife has weighed heavy on me for many years. Only recently do I feel some degree of lightening of this burden.'

'Because of the bare-knuckle fighting?' I asked. He nodded, briefly.

'I don't do it for the money. I give anything I earn from the fights to the poor on the street.' He looked chagrined. 'After

Elspeth passed away, I was furious with the world. I still am. She was...' He trailed off, unable to complete the sentence. 'She was everything that was good in the world. Gentle. Sweet. Loving.' He flexed his right hand; the pain made him wince. 'The fights are the only way I can survive her loss. I can direct my anger at another man who has agreed to be there. I lose myself in the fight. I sacrifice my blood. I do not care if I live or die.'

'I'm sorry that you lost her,' I replied; it was hard to know what else to say. What he had said was shockingly raw and dark, but I didn't want to dishonour his honesty by remarking on that.

I still wondered why the rumours had begun about William's temper, about him being an abusive husband. Was it just the fact that someone had seen him fighting, and made an assumption that he was a violent man? If so, it was a reasonable assumption. I could understand why someone might have thought that.

'So am I.' He looked blank for a moment. 'But what you saw must remain between you and I, Miss Penrose. Edith cannot know. I realise that word may get around about my fighting. Goodness knows that enough people attend the alehouses' – his expression turned grim – 'but *Edith* cannot know. I do not care about anyone else knowing. Let them talk.' He cast a baleful glance back at the ballroom, and I realised that William must be all too aware of the gossip about him that was still swirling around the hundreds of lords and ladies and their servants in there, like a virus, a poison in the air. 'Promise me.'

'I promise. Your secret is safe with me,' I agreed. 'But surely, word will get back to Edith eventually?' I thought about the whispered conversation between Mr Cooper and Letty on the back stairs. The staff were clearly already well aware about this or at least about the fact that William was taking part in activities outside playing the part of the lord of the manor. Lady Claire and Lady Fenella had all but said, just now, that there was continued gossip about William in the town.

'Edith lives a quiet life, on the whole.' He stared into the ballroom. 'Tonight is the first society event she has been to for some years. Other than that, she has her friend Clara, and some ladies she corresponds with.'

'The servants know, William,' I said, but I was thinking about Edith and her narrow, pressed-in little life. It made me sad to think about it. 'And if your fighting has been going on in the past few years when all of you stopped going to social events, that's the only reason why Edith doesn't know. If she goes to a few more balls, someone is going to tell her.'

I knew that William was aware of what was being said about him, but I also thought that he didn't care that much. He cared when he had to come to a ball to find himself shunned, but in the rest of his life, he seemed quite content to be alone, angry and scowling at the world.

'Hm. Indeed.' He gave me a long look. 'If the staff gossip, I cannot stop them, but I do at least have the option of terminating their employment,' he said, simply. 'And considering our experience at the ball this evening, I wonder if we will be invited to many more. The duke has been kind to invite us, but the Trevarron name is still mud in Cornwall.' He glowered at the dancers in the ballroom; their shadows like marionettes, jerking in the lamplight.

I wondered what it must be like to have absolute power over your immediate environment like William had.

'It's hardly ethical to give your servants the sack if they tell Edith something you should have told her yourself,' I argued.

'The sack? Why would I put them in a sack? I am not a monster.' He looked at me, confused.

'It's a turn of phrase.' I reminded myself to try and keep my language appropriate for the eighteenth century.

'Hm. Well, ethics do not enter into dealings with servants.' William frowned at me. 'I can only assume that Edith has been influencing you with her bizarre ideas about society.'

'Edith's a progressive thinker. She reads a lot about ethics and philosophy, and she's probably more educated on new ideas than you are,' I replied crisply. 'You and your brother would do well to listen to her more.'

'Indeed. And who are you to tell me what to do?' A light of passion flared in William's eyes, and he took a step closer to me.

'I'm myself. But that doesn't mean I can't have an opinion.' I didn't care if it was unseemly as a lady's maid to be arguing with the lord of the manor. I couldn't just listen to what he was saying and take it. 'What about your peers, here at the ball? Do you think they know about your fighting?'

'I suppose it is possible.' He stared down at me with an unreadable expression. 'I care not. All I care about is that the news does not reach Edith. You must not tell her,' he repeated.

'I won't.' I refused to drop his gaze. I refused to back down to William De Vere Trevarron, just because he was a lord and I was a lady's maid. 'Why can't Edith know, though? You don't seem to care about anyone else. Why her?'

'I don't have to explain myself to you,' he replied, his voice gravelly.

'I don't think you have to explain yourself to anyone very often. And you should have to. Everyone should be accountable to someone,' I argued.

I could feel a growing passion in me and crackling between us like a thunderstorm.

'Dear God, woman. Do you ever relent?' He ran a hand through his hair. I could sense his frustration with me, but it was a tension that had been there ever since we'd met and we both knew that it had been moving toward something.

'No.' I met his eyes; my gaze held his, fearlessly. If he thought that I would cower to him, just because he was tall and muscle-bound, or because he spent his time beating men bloody in taverns, then he was very much mistaken. The fact that he was Lord William De Vere Trevarron did not impress me in any way. That was just an accident of birth.

This was the moment.

I knew it in my bones as well as I knew my own name. There was a desire between us that pulled us together like a lace draws the two sides of a bodice closed. All the time that I had been at

Trevarron, I had felt myself being drawn towards William, as if I was the lace in that bodice, being pulled tighter and tighter towards him.

I'd resisted it when I'd been appalled by William's violence, and the thought that he might have had something to do with Elspeth's death. But now that I knew something more of his story, my heart had softened towards him a little. I still didn't know the truth, but I had to rely on my instincts.

'So it would seem,' he growled, and before I knew it, he had grasped both hands around my waist and drew me to him.

'William!' I cried out, but he crushed my mouth with his so that my exclamation was dampened with his kiss. For a brief moment, I pulled away from him, shocked, but the raw need in his eyes when I looked up into them drew me back to him. I had never been looked at like that before. I had never been so wanted before.

I kissed him back. He seemed surprised for a moment, then grasped me roughly again and kissed me, hard. He made a growl at the back of his throat.

'Tegan,' he murmured. 'You are... you...' He trailed off, his kiss deepening and the passion between us growing. He smelt so good that I wanted to be even closer to him; I wanted to run my hands over his chest, nestle my head into his neck.

Behind my eyes, the vision of the sunset bloomed. It was a memory of my dream as well as the scene we had just witnessed. There was a sense of rightness about being in William's arms that was like coming home, as well as filling me with deep tingles of excitement.

The kiss was rough and passionate; I could barely breathe, but I didn't pull away. I wanted him as much as he wanted me, and I pressed my aching breasts into him, wanting to be touched, wishing that we were naked together under the wide Cornish skies.

Panting, he pulled away slightly for a moment and looked at me with a dark wickedness in his eyes.

'You kiss like a harlot,' he muttered. He kept me pressed to him tight; the tone of his utterance wasn't disapproval – more like wonder. 'No lady kisses like that. Are you secretly trained by a brothel keeper?'

It was the second time someone at Trevarron had asked me if I was a prostitute, but in that moment, I didn't mind William asking me. I knew that sexual mores were different, then, though from the other illicit, groping couples I'd seen sequestered away in the corners outside the ballroom, maybe not so very different, after all.

'No. Just a woman that knows what she wants,' I murmured, and reached up for him again, tangling my fingertips in his hair and drawing his face down to mine for a kiss. 'If that makes me a harlot, then so be it.'

William made a grunt of passion and pushed me up against the side of the pergola. I parted my legs to stand steadier, and he groaned with passion and thrust his hand between my thighs. I still had many layers of fabric between me and his hand, but I could still feel the heat of it, cupping the most sensitive part of me. I pushed against his hand, instinct taking over.

'I have wanted you as soon as I saw you. You are an enigma. You do not express yourself like any woman I have ever known. You are different...' he murmured in my ear as we stood there, embracing like teenagers. 'I should push your skirts up and have you, here and now, like the harlot you so deservedly are. And, yet, I do not wish to dishonour you.'

Despite the sudden heat that had engulfed us both, I knew that I also wanted more from William than a quick fumble in a pergola outside a ballroom. I leaned back a little from his body, putting a few inches between our faces. What I wanted, I couldn't say, but I knew there was something between us: more than this animal attraction that he so obviously felt, too.

'What, then?' I breathed.

'I do not know.' He took a step back, taking a deep breath and shaking his head. 'But not this. Not here.'

He walked away, into the darkness, leaving me alone. My heart was beating wildly, and I could feel the slick wetness between my thighs. William's touch was electric, and every time I was near him, I was completely powerless.

As a lady's maid, and a woman in the eighteenth century, I was already fairly powerless. By contrast, William was a man, and, not only that, a lord. William De Vere Trevarron held all the power, and I held none – apart from the fascination he apparently had for me.

I had rendered the lord of Trevarron House almost weak with lust, but what good would it do me if I was stuck here, in the past, forever? How could I, a lady's maid, have any sort of relationship with him – chemistry or not?

Whatever attraction there was between us, whatever had just happened, couldn't happen again. Either I found a way home, or I'd have to stay – and if I stayed, there was no possible future for me and William. *Was there?*

TWENTY-SEVEN

On the way back to Trevarron from the ball, Edith had been reserved. I'd thought she was tired, but, the next day, when I went up to her room, she protested when I opened the curtains.

'Don't, Tegan. I'm staying in bed today,' she said, weakly. I sat on the edge of the bed and looked concernedly at her.

'Are you tired? It was a late night,' I asked. We had all got back about one in the morning and Edith had gone straight to bed. I knew that Charles had stayed up drinking alone in the parlour, and William had jumped down from the top of the carriage and walked swiftly away from it as soon as it had slowed into the drive. I'd slept fitfully and woken up late.

She shook her head.

'I am, but I feel a little unwell. Leave me, dear Tegan. I do not wish for company.'

Her voice was small, vulnerable somehow; I felt worried for her.

'Are you sure, Edith? I brought your breakfast up,' I said. 'Do you need the doctor?'

'No, don't fuss. It's just women's problems.' Edith curled up into a ball under the covers. 'Leave me. Please. If you want to do something, you could take my tiara back to the jeweller. I do not wish to keep it,' she added.

'All right.' I went to her side table and picked up the tiara she'd had made specially for the ball. It had been placed carelessly in its box when Edith had got home and taken her costume off. I'd offered to help her, but she'd waved me away, insisting that she could do it herself.

'You're sure you don't want to keep it? Will the jeweller even take it back?' I asked doubtfully. There had been such a fuss to get it in the first place that I was surprised at Edith's capriciousness. She'd been so excited to wear it; I wondered why she was suddenly so uninterested.

'He will. Ask for a full refund,' she said, shortly.

'As you wish.' I picked it up, in its box and went to the door. 'I'll check on you later.' I added. She grunted from under the sheets.

I pulled the door closed and headed downstairs. I knew that I'd have to ask one of the footmen to take me into town on the carriage again, but I also realised that I had the whole day unexpectedly free, and that meant that I could spend a good amount of time trying to find the portal.

Casually, I walked out of the house and to the rose garden. I was lucky; no one was around, even though I'd waited until midmorning to take Edith's breakfast up to her room, knowing that we'd come back late and she probably wouldn't wake up that early.

The garden was blooming still; the roses were fat, blowsy and fragrant. As I walked in, I remembered my first entry to the garden, and how strange I'd felt. I still felt strange here.

I'd brought the ley line journal with me too, intending to spend some time studying it.

Beyond the wrought-iron gate, the rose garden unfolded like a sanctuary steeped in perfume and softness. The air was heavy with the scent of the roses, rich and intoxicating, like walking through a department store floor of luxury perfume counters. Roses blushed in crimson, peach, pink and ivory; their petals were thick, and I had the urge to sink my nails into them, knowing that they would leave a mark, like on flesh.

The gravel path crunched softly underfoot. I looked around me, making sure I was alone.

Sunlight filtered through the climbing roses that spilled over trellises, casting lacy shadows on my sleeves. It was quiet.

I still didn't know what I was looking for. Just the notion of a place having a particular 'power', like time travel – who knew what else, maybe some places on the ley line made you invisible, or gave you the power of flight – was ridiculous. I was embarrassed for thinking it. But the rose garden was my only link to home.

I sat on a nearby wrought-iron seat and opened the book, picking up where I'd left off:

Great powers seem to be bestowed on certain souls in the vicinity of a line of energy. This is what I have observed and I record in this booke of wisdom that must remain secret.

I have spent my lifeblood following the lines of energy to mystical sites around this country and beyond. I have found a curious phenomenon that occurs when certain moments occur or when the celestial bodies are aligned. Time appears to line up like rows of corn, and one may jump from one line to another if one is so inclined, and if one is predisposed somehow.

The predisposition may be a birthright, for I have observed that my owne mother has jumped the lines and I have also. And yet none of my friends have done so, despite trying.

I do not know why this is the case. Perhaps there is a demon in our blood that allows it, which is all the more reason why we must keep this secret, for fear that we will be put to death as witches.

I looked up from the book, thoughtfully. It would definitely have been true that is Evelyn Willcock found that she could time travel, she would have been considered a witch and probably burned. I knew that in the sixteenth and seventeenth century, thousands of innocent people were persecuted as witches, usually because they were inconvenient in some way, and not because they were in cahoots with the devil.

When certain moments occur when the celestial bodies are aligned. I wondered what that meant.

I flicked to the back of the book where I'd seen a mysterious chart of symbols. I looked at it again. There was a row of shapes that I realised represented moon phases: crescents, circles with empty centres and centres filled in black. I assumed that the black moons were the dark moon phases where the moon seemed to disappear from the sky, and the circles with empty centres were full moons. The last symbol was a circle with a line through it.

Against the symbols, Evelyn had written something in a language I didn't understand. I thought it might be Latin, and racked my brains thinking about the tiny amount of knowledge I had, but I came up short.

quando luna inter solem et terram transit, ianua aperietur

Portae multae sunt, itinera infinita

Via est tantum paucorum; caute ambula si es donatus, nam lineae potentiae ad caelum et infernum ducunt

I knew that *luna* meant moon, and *infernum* probably meant hell. Other than that, I was in the dark. Finally, there was one small note.

Cum luna eclipsatur, chaos regnat

Evelyn had written the English translation for that one: *When the moon is eclipsed, chaos reigns.*

I shivered. There seemed to be a sense of threat in what she'd written; *chaos reigns.* Plus, I didn't like the reference to hell that I suspected was in that text I couldn't understand.

There had been a solar eclipse on the day that I'd travelled in time back to 1755, not a lunar eclipse. But maybe something else happened on the day of a solar eclipse – not chaos, but, maybe, something happened to the lines of energy that meant time travel was possible? I frowned.

I stood in the centre of the garden and turned my face up to the sky. In the distance, I could hear seagulls, but then everything went quiet.

I realised that a total silence had blanketed the garden all around me. I looked around, but nothing moved. It felt as though the air had stilled; no leaf or petal in the garden stirred.

Time felt like it had slowed. I could have been standing in the rose garden at any time; it was a kind of timeless moment, completely still.

The quiet intimacy of the space was strange. The longer that the stillness continued, the more odd it felt. I walked to the middle of the garden, by the water feature, and stood there, watching the water flow.

Every petal of the garden felt alive, like it was watching me, and yet the stillness was all-pervading. As I watched the water, tinkling and flowing prettily, I frowned.

For a moment, the water had stilled completely. I was sure of it.

Had I imagined that? I watched it closely. It resumed its flow, from the main pool at the bottom through the body of the mermaid, and out of the top of her head. The water cascaded down the mermaid's body again, making a pleasing sound when it hit the surface. I realised that I could hear the sound of seagulls again.

But just as quickly as it had resumed, the water suddenly froze again. The mermaid looked up at me in mute appeal. All sound was deadened, as if the garden had had a blanket draped over it.

I looked around me. A bee that had landed on a rose nearby was caught in perfect stillness.

What was happening? I looked around me.

At the end of the walkway I could see out into the wider garden, beyond. And, for a moment, there was nothing there of the kitchen garden, the green lawns or Trevarron House standing grandly above.

For a moment, all that I could see was the long, tangled grass of the meadow as I'd known it, and the house as it had been in my time: ruined.

Oh, my goodness.

I ran towards the gateway.

I could see it. Home was so close, I could almost touch it.

All I had to do was walk through that gateway, and I would be back in the twenty-first century. I could see Aunt Bill again. I could go back to university.

A mixture of grief and joy clutched at my heart; the pain of being away from Aunt Bill and her cottage had been awful. It had been my real, spiritual home, and she was one of just a small number of people I could count as family; the thought that I might not get back to her had scared me.

Yet, as I reached the gateway, the vision dimmed. There was a moment of slippage, where it was as though the picture of the long grass and the ruined house *jumped*, like an old piece of film that had come off a projector, and the tended gardens and the house of 1755 returned.

No.

I threw myself towards the final couple of feet of the walkway, feeling myself falling.

In the last second, I opened my eyes. The long grass reappeared for a moment. I reached out a hand to touch it and felt its texture on the tips of my fingers.

Please, please.

Aunt Bill! I screamed, desperate. *Please, can you hear me? Come and find me, please!*

Then, it was gone.

I lay on the hard gravel, and started to cry.

TWENTY-EIGHT

The note had been slipped under my door at some point in the day. I only found it when I got back, finally, to my room, after going into town in the carriage to take back Edith's tiara and drop off some letters at the post office.

I had needed to get away. I was shaken up by what had happened in the rose garden and needed time to process it.

The trip into town had been uneventful, but I was grateful for the time to sit in the carriage and think about what had happened. I'd seen my own time through the gate in the rose garden. I'd seen the time slippage happen, before my eyes, and I'd witnessed a kind of time slowing whilst I was looking at the water in the fountain.

Overall, it gave me hope. For the first time since I'd travelled through time, I had seen for myself that the rose garden *was* some kind of portal. I'd stood within it as time had changed outside it. All I needed to know now was, why it had happened then, and why it had happened before, when I'd travelled back to 1755.

On the journey to and from Tintagel, I read more of Evelyn's book.

In the Orient, it is said that these 'dragon lines' of energy that link mountain ranges have strangely demonic powers. There are reports of odd happenings in areas rich in this dragon energy, which cannot be proven. I note it here as evidence of a strange effect which may be similar to that which my family has experienced.

I read on, but Evelyn seemed very reluctant to discuss exactly what these 'odd happenings' were. I wondered if time travel was one of them.

Her notes in Latin intrigued me. I wondered if I could ask Edith to translate them for me; I knew that she spoke and read Latin, but I was reluctant to share Evelyn's book with her. If she asked me what it was, what would I tell her?

Meet me at the gatehouse. I looked at the note again.

I hadn't seen his handwriting before, but I knew it must be from William. The handwriting was perfectly copperplate, written in a dark blue ink on thick cream paper monogrammed with William's initials in an elegant font: *WT*.

I held the note to my chest for a moment until I could think clearly.

I couldn't go.

I shouldn't.

Damn him.

I hadn't seen William since the ball the night before. For the rest of the evening, he'd avoided me, and when it was time to leave, he'd sat on top of the carriage once more, leaving Edith and I to put up with a very drunk Charles on the return journey.

I threw the note on the floor and ground my heel on it.

I don't think so.

If anything, he probably wanted another illicit fumble, and if that was how he thought this was going to go down, then he had another think coming. I couldn't deny my attraction to William, but I could resist becoming his occasional whore. He'd even called me that. A *harlot*. Because I kissed him back, and didn't go limp in his arms like some kind of doll.

I stared out of my window, at the wide gravel drive at the front of the house and the drive that snaked away from it, through the trees and past the well-kept lawn that was a wild meadow in my time.

I knew where the gatehouse was. Since I'd been at the house, I'd learned where all the parts of the property were: the stables, the kitchens, the washhouse and the privy that the servants used.

The gatehouse sat at the opposite end of the property to the end I knew – the gateway to the estate that boasted the stone griffins on top of their pillars. Completely at the other side of the house, the grey stone gatehouse sat at the edge of a deeply wooded half acre of land. There was another drive into the house from there – the way that the tradesmen and suppliers usually came in. The gamekeeper, Cedric, manned the gatehouse sometimes if a delivery was expected, but I knew that it lay empty a lot of the time. The reason that I knew that was because I'd overheard some of the kitchen maids complaining that it was a nice little house, going to waste: they would have liked to live there, probably, as opposed to their narrow beds in their maids' rooms.

It was already getting dark outside. The house was quieting down. I stood at the window, fighting my feelings. I wanted to see him. My body and mind and heart cried out for him.

However, both times that we'd kissed, he'd pulled away. *Not here. Not now. You're just a maid. A harlot.* He'd denied what was happening between us and denied me. And it had made me feel cheap and used and unwanted.

Now, he wanted to see me. Clearly, William De Vere Trevarron was used to getting anything and anyone he wanted, whenever he wanted them. But that wasn't going to be me.

Pinning up my hair swiftly under a cap and wrapping myself in a long, dark shawl, I let myself out of my room and crept down the back stairs. If William wanted to meet me, then I'd meet him, and tell him exactly what I thought of his behaviour.

TWENTY-NINE

'I didn't think you'd come.'

He stood at the window of the gatehouse, half in darkness. The room was lit by candlelight and an oil lamp; he hadn't lit a fire in the hearth.

Not planning to stay long, I thought. *Not setting the scene for a romantic tryst. Fine. I see where I stand.*

It was a sparse room, obviously not usually lived in. The furniture – a small dark-wood table and two high-backed chairs – was basic. A couple of rifles leaned against one wall, and a wooden shelf with a few cups and bowls piled on it sat on the other side of the room.

'I got your note. Mustn't disobey the lord of the manor,' I replied, smartly. I'd come, but I was angry about him summoning me, and angry about the cloak-and-dagger way he'd done it.

I wasn't Aunt Bill's niece for nothing. She's brought me up to be independent and distrustful of men, and to know my worth.

'You are rude and sharp-tongued.' He stared at me wolfishly. 'Take off your shawl. You look like a washerwoman.'

'What I look like is none of your business.' I walked up to him and poked him in his chest with my finger. 'I only came to tell you that you've behaved abominably. We might have had a bit of a moment at the ball, but that doesn't mean you get to treat me like your whore, to be summoned at will, every time you want a bit of a fumble. It's fine if you regret what happened. We're both adults. But we do both have to live in the same house. I—'

I wasn't finished lecturing him, but he took a hold of the hand that I had poked him with and clasped his own hand around it, drawing my fingers downwards and behind my back. He drew me to him, not as roughly as before, and with the other hand, peeled off my shawl.

'Stop it,' he said, in that gravelly tone. 'Stop talking. You know why I asked you here.'

'No, I don't.' I pulled away. 'Who do you think I am? You think I'm your prostitute for hire? You know absolutely nothing about me!' I raised my voice. I'd walked over here with anger brewing in my belly, and every step I'd taken had made me crosser at William's behaviour. I'd thought that I would either give him the benefit of the doubt and give him an opportunity to apologise, or I would tell him off. 'I'd really recommend you never tell a woman to stop talking ever again.'

Seems like I'm not about to get an apology anytime soon, I thought, which made me even more furious.

'I don't know what to expect from you. Surely you knew what I meant when I left the note. You came.' He kept my hand behind my back, but I twisted free from his grasp.

'Oh. That extensive, six-word treatise of love and devotion. Yes, that was totally clear.' I didn't care that my voice was dripping in sarcasm now, because William De Vere Trevarron was being an absolute bastard and I was not standing for it. Even if he was a lord and I was a lady's maid. I didn't have it in me to defer to him a moment longer, and there wasn't anyone to overhear and be shocked at my lack of propriety.

No, he was going to get it. I wasn't about to hold back.

'Do you think the fact that I came here is some kind of consent for sex?' I stared mercilessly into his eyes and registered shock there. I doubted that anyone had ever spoken to him this frankly, and definitely not a woman. Perhaps his young wife had, or his mother, but I doubted it. If they had, he might not have been so badly behaved. 'Do you think that six words on a piece of monogrammed paper is enough authority for me to come here and drop my panties?' I saw the confusion on his face at the word – *panties* were a modern invention, and I wasn't wearing any. The norm was to be naked under your underskirts.

'I don't...' He looked confused.

'Raise my skirts for you. Let you take me over the table, because you're the lord and master.' I stood with my hands on my hips, facing him. 'How dare you assume that I'm yours for the taking because you own this house. You don't own me. You can't own people.'

'I know that.' He ran a hand through his hair. 'If I misread the situation, I apologise. But you and I both know that there was... something... between us, at the ball, and on the cliff. And I have been unable to stop thinking about you today.'

He turned away from me and opened the door that I had closed behind me when I'd come in. 'Go, then. If you want to. If you can honestly say that you don't feel what I feel, then go. I will not stop you, and I will not interfere with your employment with Edith. I am not the monster you think I am. Perhaps... just a little unused to a woman as plain speaking as you.'

I was still angry, but his confession took the wind out of my sails. His shoulders sagged; he looked suddenly different, full of regret. I relented slightly.

'I... I am attracted to you, William. That should have been obvious. But I'm not here to be some kind of whore for you, whenever you want. You can't use me like that.' I knew that being this honest was dangerous. I didn't know William at all; I didn't know if he was an honourable man or not. But I had to be honest. It was who I was.

'You're right. I'm sorry, I just... don't know how to do this.' He turned to me and I saw a softness in his eyes that I'd never seen before. His voice was low. 'I want you, Tegan. I might have gone about this all wrong, but I do... more than I have ever wanted anyone. I've felt this...' He trailed off and shook his head. 'This odd feeling about you, ever since I saw you with your bloody knee in the rose garden. That I have known you before. You have a familiarity about you I cannot name... I have... dreamed of you.' He closed his eyes, a blush stealing to his cheeks.

'You've dreamed of me?' I repeated, not believing what I was hearing. I'd dreamed of him for so many years, not knowing it was him. My heart twisted in my chest. I swallowed hard.

'Yes. Obsessively. Since you got here. Erotic dreams. And...' He looked haunted. 'Before now. Before I ever saw you. I dreamed of you.'

'How?' I breathed. I was thinking of my dream of the silhouettes against the sunset, but I didn't dare mention it.

'I do not know. It seems impossible. And yet, when I saw you, it all rushed back to me. Years when I thought you were a fairy. A dream woman to keep me company in the long years at sea and abroad. I had a sailor's life. It was lonely. I returned and became engaged to Elspeth. And I suppose that a part of me put her face on that dream woman and imagined that she was my destiny. I loved her.' He broke off and shook his head. 'But as soon as I saw you, I knew that it was *you*. How can that be?' He stared at me like a lost child, uncomprehending. 'How can I have known you for all of my life, and only now find you standing here in the flesh? And, when I touch you, I can hardly breathe with the wanting of you.'

He walked towards me and took both of my hands in his. At his touch, my whole body felt like it had been bathed in a warmth I had never known. I took in a deep breath and met his eyes; I knew that mine were wide with surprise at the sensation. It was so sweet, so deep and true that I never wanted to let him go.

'Tegan. Please, please forgive me. Please know that I'm not a brute. Very far from it. I have... had no women since my wife died. I have done nothing but fight and concentrate my energies on the estate. I have been half a man, and I was satisfied with that. I would have stayed that way forever, but you appeared. And you turned everything upside down.'

He stared into my eyes and I felt his gaze light fires within mine.

'I... I didn't know this was how you felt. I just thought... you wanted to use me. You called me a harlot.'

'That was crude of me. You just... took me by surprise. The way you kissed me... I have never been kissed like that before. I have never felt that way before. Like an untamed beast. And yet...' He traced the line of my cheek gently with his forefinger, and a line of electricity zigzagged from my cheek to my lip and into the tip of my nipple. 'Yet, you intrigue me. Even without you being my dream woman, you would have fascinated me. You are bright, beautiful, *caustic*.' He smiled, and his smile lit connecting circuits of heat under my skin '... and brave. You are enticing. I cannot think of anything but you.'

'Oh.' After all of my lecturing him, now I couldn't think of anything to say. I hadn't expected this heartfelt confession.

'Oh,' he echoed, and kissed me.

This time, it was a world away from the first time we'd kissed, when it had been so passionate that my lips had felt bruised afterwards from the savagery of William's mouth.

This time, his kiss was gentle; his lips brushed mine with a longing I'd never felt before. I heard his breath catch.

His hand brushed my hair away from my face.

'And so very beautiful,' he murmured. 'If you didn't know that already, which you must.'

I felt something in me open at his sudden tenderness; this time, it was a rush of emotion that enflamed my heart and made me feel like I wanted to cry. I had no idea why such intense feelings had me in their grip, but when I opened my eyes and saw his deep brown eyes staring down into mine, I felt my heart open again. It ached, like a rusty door that had been closed for so many years might have protested at being opened. Tears welled up unexpectedly. William's eyes widened in concern.

'Oh, blessed child,' he whispered, holding me tight to him. 'Do not cry. I do not wish to upset you. I only wish to bring you pleasure.'

'It's all right,' I stammered, trying to control myself and failing. 'I feel... there's a strange connection between us. As though I've known you for a long time, and I didn't know I missed you until now.'

I thought suddenly of the book: the strange occurrences that happened along ley lines. Was this connection between William and me also linked to that? I had no idea, but it was definitely strange to hear William's confession that he had dreamed of me all his life.

It might have been a lie to get me into bed, or it might have been fanciful imagination on William's part, transposing my face onto a recurring dream of his. But what if it was true? How could anyone explain that? Had some kind of mystical energy line running through the earth, under Trevarron House and its grounds, affected William's dreams?

'Tegan. I feel it too,' he murmured, tilting my face up to his. 'I don't know what it is. All I know is that I cannot think about anything except you. And...' He shook his head. '...somehow your... emotion, your open heart – yes, I can feel it – connects to mine. I feel what you feel. How can that be?' Gently, he kissed away the tears that had fallen on my cheeks.

His act of tenderness only made me want him more. There was something so deeply seductive in the knowledge that my honest, unpredictable feelings had brought out a protective tenderness in this usually dismissive, gruff lord of the manor.

'I'm sorry. You must think I'm being so silly.' I was embarrassed. It wasn't like me to be like this at all; I was usually more guarded.

'No. It makes you all the more desirable,' he replied, tracing the line of my neck gently with his forefinger. 'You are a woman in command of her honest nature. That is... irresistible to a man.'

I kissed him again, softly, but I felt as though I couldn't get close enough to him. I wanted to inhale him, taste him, devour him.

He sighed deeply as my soft lips brushed his. I opened my mouth, and his tongue caressed my top lip gently. I kissed him back, my tongue finding his, and the kiss deepened.

He growled in the back of his throat. His arms circled my waist and drew me to him again, and now I could feel that he was hard.

'Tegan. I want you. Urgently,' he muttered, his lips finding my neck.

In response, I wrapped my arms around his neck, and whispered in his ear. 'I want you too. Now.'

He swore under his breath. He was like one of his stallions, how they were in the stables when they wanted to get out and run. I could sense his tensed muscles, his hardness, like a beast that was desperate to ravage something.

'You know that I cannot hold myself back much longer. If you wish to remain untouched, you must leave now. Or I cannot be responsible for my actions.'

'Take me. Now,' I breathed, meaning every word.

He exhaled, a groan of lust escaping his throat, like an animal. William picked me up. Carefully, as if he was carrying an item of great value, he carried me up the stairs.

THIRTY

'Take off your dress.'

He stood at the end of the bed and watched me, a gleam of lust in his eyes.

He had carried me up the creaking wooden stairs to the single room above and lowered me onto the edge of the bed, where I sat and gazed up at him. Obediently, I began unlacing my corset.

'Hm. That's right. Good little girl.' He bit his lip, watching as I slowly removed layer after layer. Soon, though, he grew impatient. 'Stand up and turn around,' he ordered, and I did as I was told. With a few practised moves, he wrenched my skirts down and the corset free and threw them on the floor of the room.

He stared at me with glazed eyes.

'You are beautiful. So *pure*. Your skin is so smooth and soft,' he marvelled, drawing me to him. Kneeling, he pulled me closer to him and pressed his face into my thighs. He began kissing the soft skin there. 'Gods. You smell so good,' he murmured, and pushed me back on the bed. I fell back willingly, and spread my legs. I knew what he wanted, and I wanted it too.

When his warm mouth met my opening, I made an involuntary moan. He kissed all of me, running his tongue gently all over me. Then, he parted me with one hand and sat back for a moment, inspecting me. I was already too aroused to feel self-conscious.

'Such beauty.' He met my eyes, looking up at me from between my legs. 'So perfect. So wet already. I wasn't wrong, was I? About being a harlot?' He smiled; I knew he was making a little joke with me, and I didn't care, anyway. He knelt over me and rested one warm hand on the mound of my pubis, and kissed me softly. I could taste myself on his lips.

'More... please,' I whispered.

He smiled lazily.

'So greedy. Rest, little one. I will give you all the pleasure you desire, and more,' he murmured. The weight of his hand on me was driving me wild, partly because it made the whole of my clit and my G-spot tingle, wanting him, wanting more, and partly because it felt proprietorial. William rested his hand on my body like he owned the whole thing. And unlike before when I'd been offended by the very idea of it, now I found the idea deeply erotic.

'You like that?' He smiled, watching my face.

'Y... yes. Like you own it,' I stammered. I knew that I was already dripping wet for him.

'Oh.' Surprise registered on his face for a moment, followed by a look of such primal desire that it made my heart pound. 'I see. You like that idea.'

'Yes,' I panted. In that moment, I did.

'Then you should consider me your lord and master while we are here, little one' – he smiled wolfishly – 'because I own every-thing here. The land, the house, the carriages. Your wet little opening is not exempt from that list. Say it.'

'You... own all of me,' I whispered.

'Indeed, I do. I am your lord and master. Say it.' He gently reached his index finger out and began circling my clit slowly. I gasped with pleasure.

'You are... my lord... my master,' I murmured.

'Hmm. Good.' He kissed me again, continuing to stroke me. 'Now,' he murmured. 'I am going to return to kissing you there.

And you are going to take it for as long as you can without climaxing. When you feel that you cannot wait a second longer, you will beg me to finish. And, if I am feeling very kind, I will. Do you understand?' He raised an imperious eyebrow.

I was his so completely in that moment that I wouldn't have been able to disagree even if I'd wanted to, which I very definitely didn't. I was completely in William's power, all the more because I knew that he was playing this game with me because I liked it. He was concentrating on my pleasure rather than his own, because he wanted to please me. And that generosity of spirit moved me deeply.

I nodded mutely.

'Good.'

He lowered his head and I gasped at the sensation of his mouth on me again. The softness of his tongue was perfect: just enough pressure, but not too hard. He seemed to know the perfect spot; I moaned loudly. It was so good that I never wanted him to stop.

I had had lovers before; not many, but I wasn't a virgin. Yet, most of the young men I'd been to bed with had given my clit cursory attention at best, and though some of them had gone down on me enthusiastically, there hadn't been much finesse to it, or much focus. The scattergun approach – move around! Hit all the bases! – was what I thought they might have been thinking, but that didn't work for me. I had touched myself enough to know that I had a couple of very effective areas and they needed consistent touch at a consistent pressure or it wasn't going to work.

William, by contrast, was both the most sexually desirable man I had ever been in bed with and the man that most clearly knew what he was doing. I'd never been so overwhelmed with lust before, and completely at the mercy of a man so in control, so... masterful.

The orgasm started building immediately. It was like it had been waiting inside my body for this moment, for someone to come along and touch me in exactly the way I needed to be touched. As William's velvety soft, firm tongue lapped at me, I felt as though there was a hitherto untapped well of sweet pleasure connecting my clit to my heart and the top of my head, and he had poured the first line of electric warm honey along it to activate the connection. My senses swelled with bliss. My heart grew like a rose. I could feel pleasure suffusing my whole body, and it kept getting more intense. I could feel the contractions begin: one, then two, then three small, pre-climax peaks of pleasure that meant something much deeper was on its way.

I writhed around, desperate for more. As if he knew that I was getting close, William slid two fingers gently inside me, stroking where it was sensitive.

'Oh God... I can't... William, please...' I cried out. I knew that it would only be seconds until I couldn't control myself anymore, and I wanted to come. I wanted that swollen, wet spot inside me rubbed and stretched. I wanted the hot sweetness inside me to explode and cover me with its ecstasy.

'Are you begging me to finish?' he asked, keeping his fingers inside me and stopping licking me for a moment.

'Yes,' I panted. 'Please, William!'

'What do you say?' He had pushed down his breeches and my eyes widened as I saw how hard he was. I reached for it, but he caught my hand. 'No. Be a good girl. What did I tell you?'

'My lord and master. Please. I'm begging you to let me come,' I babbled; I wasn't aware of what I was saying. I'd say anything for the pleasure that I knew was only seconds away, and I wanted him.

'Fine,' he grunted. I knew that he had been holding himself back, and that he too wanted nothing more than to lose himself in me.

Slowly, he lowered his head back to me and resumed his licking, his tongue warm and wet and insistent. Leaning up, I saw that he was touching himself.

I cried out; the ecstasy of seeing him pleasure himself at the same time as serving me was more than I could bear. I wrapped my legs around him and forced his head further into me.

He grunted again, and I knew he was trying not to lose it immediately.

'Harlot,' he muttered, looking up at me briefly. Him stopping pleasuring me was unbearable. 'So wet. So wanton.' His eyes met mine. I could see his hand moving faster, and the pleasure had glazed his eyes. I knew that his self-control was wavering. He wanted to let go, but I knew that he was staying present with me so that I could climax first.

'Yes. My lord. Yes,' I panted. He smiled and resumed his attentions. Now, I was only seconds away.

I felt the orgasm coming. The pressure of his tongue was irresistible, like a train. I could feel myself tensing up around him; he groaned, muffled by my thighs. His words were nonsense now, like mine, we were both lost inside our pleasure and passion.

I lost all of the restraint I was holding on to. I let myself go and pushed myself hard against his face.

It was as if the wave of pleasure waited behind a wall that had to be broken down, and the moment that the wall broke was greeted in my body by orgasmic contractions which were so deep and hard that I felt as if I would crush William with the sheer force of my ecstasy. My legs kicked and my arms flailed, and I *screamed* as I came. I felt as though I climaxed over and over again, and I heard him lose control, and groan deeply as he came, too.

THIRTY-ONE

We lay there, panting, side by side. Neither of us spoke for a few moments.

I didn't know what had just happened. I did, of course, know exactly *what* had happened, but I had no idea *how* we had gone from me stamping into the gatehouse, angry at William, to us making love in the way that we just had.

'That was... unexpected,' he said, his voice gravelly.

'Yes, it was,' I replied, getting my breath back. 'That was... probably a mistake.'

William turned onto his side, propped his head up on his elbow and stared at me.

'I don't think that it was,' he said, seriously. 'Why do you think that?'

I took a moment to reply.

'Because. There's a huge power imbalance here. How can this ever be anything other than a mistake? I'm your sister's maid. Nothing will ever change that.'

Not unless I leave this timeline and manage to return home, I thought. But I couldn't say that to him.

'Come to me. Come here. I want to hold you.' He held his arms out for me; I couldn't resist his touch. I took in a deep breath of him as he held me against his chest; it was a kind of nectar, the smell of him. It did things to the most instinctive part of my brain; it made me want to wrap my legs around him again. *Babies, fill me up with babies, healthy, strong babies*, that was what my mind was saying. He smelt right. It was primal and animalistic, but it was still true.

'William. Don't,' I mumbled into his chest, but I didn't mean it. I couldn't pull myself away from him.

'Tegan. You know that this is something real. I felt it. You felt it.' His voice rumbled in his chest. There was something so reassuring about it; I wanted to snuggle up in his arms and never leave. 'Let us have this. I need this. I need you. And. I think you might need me, if you let yourself.'

'What future can we have?' I pulled away slightly and looked up at him. I wanted him to understand my concerns. 'You know that you hold all the power here. I have nothing if you decide to cast me away,'

I wanted to add, *like Elspeth*, but I didn't. I believed him. I think that I now believed that what had happened to her had been a terrible accident, but there was a tiny part of me that asked, *What if it wasn't?*

'I would never cast you away,' he said, seriously, unblinking.

'You say that now, with the flush of an orgasm still in your cheeks,' I replied, a little tartly, but I didn't think he was taking this as seriously as he should. 'What happens when you think this through and decide I'm right? That it's untenable?'

'Untenable?' He frowned at the word. It was clearly an unfamiliar one in this time.

'Impractical. Doomed,' I clarified.

'Tegan, my sweet girl,' he sighed; the pet name made me tingle. 'I have been doomed for many years. Every time I step into the ring to fight, I risk my life and my health.' He examined his ruined knuckles, still covered in deep cuts. 'Before you, I did not care if I lived or died. This is the first time I have felt anything like hope in a long time.' His eyes met mine again, now fleetingly. What he was saying was difficult for him.

'You should stop the fighting. You'll die from your injuries, or a blood-borne disease,' I said. I'd been concerned for William when I'd seen him at the fight, and I still was.

'Diseases come from the air. Blood is merely blood,' he replied. I sighed. I couldn't begin to bridge the gap between our world views. Even things like a basic knowledge of germs and medicine were so different between us, and I could never tell him the truth. Partly because he wouldn't understand it, and partly that in telling him, I would have to reveal where I was really from.

'I can't believe that you do it at all. It seems so... unseemly,' I said, slightly changing tack.

'I told you. It's a compulsion' – his voice was low; he was being honest, even if the truth was hard to say – 'it's been all I have.'

'It's not all you have. You have the house, the estate, a family...' I wondered how he could think that he had nothing. Compared to most people, he had everything.

'None of that means anything. It's just things and power I never asked for. Inheritance. An accident of birth. Family... I have my brother and sister. That is all. Not my own progeny.' His face darkened. 'I never will, now.'

'You might,' I argued. 'And owning Trevarron does mean something. If you truly had nothing, you'd know the difference.'

'Perhaps you're right. You have the conscience I do not,' he said, gruffly.

'All right, but...' I was about to try and explain myself again, but William caught me in a kiss.

'Please. Just be with me,' he said, quietly, and I nodded. I still had my concerns, but I felt as though it taken a lot for William to say what he just had. 'I know that we think differently. I know that you are a good soul: compassionate, wise. I am a brute, but I occasionally believe that I can be a better man. Lying with you makes me believe it.'

He held me to him, and I felt him relax. I wondered when the last time was that he had opened himself to someone so honestly. I suspected that it had been a long time.

I wondered what he meant by calling himself a brute. Did he just mean the fighting, or his rudeness, or something else that I didn't want to consider? I was too far gone, now. I could not accept the idea that Elspeth's death wasn't an accident.

'Dear maid,' he murmured into my hair. 'A pure angel. With you I feel at peace, finally.'

I laid my head on his chest in reply. After a few more minutes, his breath deepened and I realised that he had fallen asleep.

I lay on my side, still held in his arms, my head still rested on him. I felt my own eyes closing, and half dreams flitted in front of my eyes. My body wanted rest, and my mind wanted to escape. I let myself go.

I didn't know how much later it was that night, but it was dark when I woke up in the gatehouse bed, and William was gone.

'William?' I sat up, discomfited, and called out his name, but no one answered.

I got up and padded carefully down the stairs to the room below. No one was there.

I went back up to the bedroom and got dressed, feeling spooked by the utter darkness and waking up in the unfamiliar place, which, now that William wasn't there, felt wrong. I didn't want to be there any longer than I had to.

I didn't know if I'd be able to get back into the main house. Usually, the doors were locked in the late evening, and if I couldn't get back to my bed, I didn't know what I'd do. The weather wasn't terrible, but I still didn't want to spend the rest of the dark hours outside on my own.

I started back towards the house, walking quickly and sometimes breaking into a run. The night was so still; the moon was high in the sky, and owls hooted in the trees.

The shadowy shape of Trevarron House loomed ahead of me as I made my way towards it. In the dark of the moonlit night, it seemed to sit ponderously in its gardens, crouching like an immense toad.

I had followed the long path back to the house, but as I walked along the edge of the property, along the side that led alongside the coastline, I looked out over the sea, marvelling at the silvery sheen of the moon on the water. Tonight, the tide was almost flat, and there were none of the dramatic waves breaking on the cliffs I'd seen before.

Perhaps it was because it was such a still night that I noticed a wavering light at the edge of one of the caves, down at the bottom of my eyeline. I stopped and peered over the wall where I stood. I knew there were caves all along this part of the north Cornish coast; under Tintagel castle there was the famous Merlin's Cave, which you could walk all the way through at low tide if you didn't mind a scramble through the rocks at one end.

I blinked, watching the sea. It had probably been a boat coming in; a fisherman going out early, perhaps. I turned away, but then turned back when I saw the light again. Now, I could see that it was a lamp on board a small ship, and it seemed to be flashing in a certain rhythm.

Like a message, I realised, watching it.

I had no idea what the message was, but I watched, fascinated. I knew the boat wasn't sending a message to me; they probably couldn't see me. It would be for someone else. But who? And why?

I stood against the waist-high wall at the boundary of Trevarron House and watched. In the distance, I could hear raised voices. Listening, I began to hear another noise, like something being dragged, heavy things being dropped. The voices continued, distant, but present, like a spell chanted into the wind.

Carefully, I leaned over the wall as far as I could go, and looked down.

At the bottom of the cliffs I saw a small beach. The moonlight lit up the fine sand and the black rock behind it.

A couple of boats had pulled up on the beach, and a large crew of men were hauling crates from the boat and onto the sand. A gang of men stood on the sand, taking the crates and loading them onto a carriage that stood close by. I realised that a rough dirt track led onto the small beach, which was how they had got the carriage all the way down there.

It was hard to lean out far enough to see what was going on, and if it hadn't been such a bright moon that night, I wouldn't have seen anything. But, as it was, I could see quite a lot, and because there was virtually no wind for a change, I could hear reasonably well too. The voices echoed up the rock to me, like a kind of amplifier.

There was a general hubbub of voices, though I could tell that they were trying to act quietly.

I couldn't see their faces. They were looking at each other and not up at me. Yet, something made one of them look up, and I caught my breath. In that moment, I did see his features, and I was shocked to see them again so soon.

The man on the beach was William De Vere Trevarron.

THIRTY-TWO

'I don't care what you say. This is an important offer, Edith! You have no understanding of the facts. You are my sister, therefore you will do what I say.'

As I entered Edith's quarters the next morning, having had almost no sleep at all, I walked straight into an argument between her and Charles.

'Oh. I'm sorry, please excuse me,' I deferred, curtseying. 'I will leave you.'

After making my way back from the gatehouse, I'd climbed back into the house through an open window in the kitchen and crept up to my bedroom. The clock in my room read four a.m. when I finally crawled into bed; Betty had woken me up from a fitful sleep at six thirty a.m.

As I'd tiptoed into my room last night, the thought had occurred to me that when I'd heard the creaking noise like someone walking outside my room, it might have been another maid on her way back from a secret assignation or a forbidden night out. All maids were supposed to be in bed by ten p.m., and the front door to Trevarron was locked at nine. But I knew that I couldn't be the only one that had figured out a way to sneak out.

I had rolled out of bed that morning feeling as if I was filled with sand. Betty had looked askance at my shin, which was scratched from climbing in the kitchen window, but had said nothing as she helped me dress.

I hoped that Edith would send me away; I could do with getting back into bed and having a nap – to say nothing of trying to process what had happened between me and William the night before and trying to make sense of what he'd been doing on the beach – but she shook her head.

'No, Tegan. Stay.' Edith's face was flushed and she looked furious and upset. She wore one of her favourite robes, a floor-length, dark green velvet garment with wide sleeves and a tie waist, and her dark hair was loose. I'd come in to help her dress, as we were expected at her friend Clara's house that morning for a social visit and Edith had been excited about seeing her friend all week. 'My brother is just lecturing me about my responsibilities, assuming that I know nothing.'

'You do know nothing. All you do is sit up here with your books.' Charles scowled. He, by contrast, was dressed smartly, as if he was going out. 'You need to become a wife. It is your responsibility to marry. It is what is best for the family name!' he raged at her.

'Books are important,' Edith argued, tartly, and I thought how much Aunt Bill would have liked Edith. 'How else would we know about the issues of the day? If I ever do marry, I will marry a man that understands that. Not a brute like Simon Favisham.'

I looked at Edith in surprise, and then back at Charles.

'Lord Favisham?' I asked her. 'From the ball?' She nodded.

'My brother informs me that Lord Favisham has proposed an offer of marriage,' she replied, succinctly. 'And he is cross that I have refused it.'

'This is a man's world and you cannot be expected to know anything about it. Kindly obey my wishes when you present yourself to Miss Favisham today.' Charles fixed her with a steely stare.

'I will not have you destroy a good match. I would rather that you stayed at home and consider the offer seriously rather than embarrass us all by seeing Clara today and point-blank refusing her brother,'

'Charles. If Simon has made me an offer of marriage and not even mentioned it to me directly, what does that tell you?' Edith stood with her hands on her hips. 'He does not respect me, or like me. He desires the Trevarron estate. I don't want to marry him.' Her voice wavered on the last words, and I thought back to the ball. Simon Favisham had seemed nice enough, and Edith had been excited to see him; they'd been exchanging letters, and I'd assumed that there was some kind of wooing process happening. So, what had changed since then?

Edith had been quiet in the carriage ride back, and then ill the next day, refusing to get up. That day, because I had the time free, I'd ended up experiencing the time slippage in the rose garden. I hadn't thought about much else since then.

Now, I wondered what had happened to Edith at the ball and felt guilty that I hadn't been more vigilant. She'd been her usual self since, though I realised, in retrospect, that she had been more introspective than usual. I supposed that if she was quiet, it might have been because she had felt humiliated at the ball; the Trevarrons had been ostracised. But now I wondered what Simon had done to her.

'You will marry Simon, if I have to drag you to the altar,' Charles snarled, and flounced out of the room, his coattails flapping. I stood aside to let him go; even then, he strode past me so close that he might have bumped into me if I hadn't have got out of the way. To Charles, I was invisible.

'Edith. Are you all right?' I went to her and took her elbow, guiding her to one of the chaises in the room. I pulled the curtains, letting in the morning light.

'Thank you, Tegan. I am quite well, though rather enraged by my ridiculous brother,' Edith fumed, sitting down. She ran a hand through her hair.

'Have you really had a marriage proposal?' I asked.

'Yes.' She sighed. 'Not one that I want, as it turns out, but Charles wants it.'

'That's irrelevant. Let Charles marry Simon, then.'

'Tegan. Dear.' Edith shook her head.

'Can't he marry someone, if it's so important?' I frowned. 'Is it important for one of you to get married?'

'It would be a good thing. Financially.' She sighed. 'Charles could. But he has... other preferences.' Edith looked away. Perhaps what Lady Claire and Lady Fenella had intimated at the ball wasn't wrong after all. 'He has never expressed an interest in any woman.'

'Neither have you a man, but he's putting pressure on you to marry,' I stated plainly. It hardly seemed fair.

'Charles thinks that I know nothing about anything. But I understand more about life than he does.' She got up and walked to the window, pushing up the sash and leaning out to breathe in the morning air.

'Charles has had a life of ease. He has never shouldered the responsibility of running the estate, as William has, and he never joined the Navy, like William did. He went to school and then decided that he would be a novelist, but he was rather a poor writer. Then, he decided that he would be an artist, and he has dedicated himself to the art world ever since.' She leaned out of the window. 'What a beautiful morning. You can hear the magpies chatter; listen.'

I listened to the sound of the birds in the trees for a moment. It reminded me briefly of the seagulls I heard when I was in the rose garden, and the moment when the stillness descended, and I heard nothing.

'Is he a successful artist?' I asked. Edith shot me a caustic glance.

I snorted. 'That bad?'

'He has never sold more than a couple.' Edith raised an eyebrow, and I wondered if she was also referring to our conversation at the ball. 'William has refused to fund any more trips abroad. He says that it is akin to pouring our money into the sea.'

'Goodness.' I wondered whether that was why Charles always seemed in a bad mood. I thought that Edith was probably right; the fact that Charles had essentially been allowed to do whatever he wanted probably hadn't improved his character. Edith and William had been subjected to different kinds of restrictions, and that had made them both strong and resourceful in their own ways.

'Yes. William is worried about money, I think. Though he would never say it to me.' Edith frowned. 'I wish that I could bring money into the house, but the only way that I can do that is to marry well.'

'Would marrying Lord Favisham be marrying well?' I asked.

'Technically, yes.' She shrugged. 'I was once rather keen on the idea. Until recently...' Her expression darkened.

'You must have lots of other suitors,' I said.

'Not really. I find men boorish in general, but Simon has always been a good friend. And recently, he seemed to become more interested in me. He has been writing quite romantic letters.' She blushed, and cleared her throat. 'And, as you saw at the ball, we are still ostracised. No one wants to socialise with us still, never mind marry me. Simon is the only one that has made a proposal. I realise that Lord Favisham knows of my social position, and he knows of Charles's debts.'

She drew her lips tight, and I could see what she was thinking. Simon Favisham had come to understand that he could buy Edith; that, because of the rumours around Elspeth's death, the Trevarrons had become pariahs in Cornwall, and that meant he was free to swoop in and marry Edith, thereby taking whatever stake in the Trevarron family legacy that was hers. She had little choice.

'Edith. Do you even *want* to get married?' I asked. She thought for a moment.

'I will consider it, because it would be a strategic connection for our family. The Favisham family is powerful in Cornwall, and they are wealthy. Charles says that Simon has offered a large cash gift if we marry.' She bit her lip. 'However... Simon is... untrustworthy. Rough.' Edith's eyes met mine, and I knew what she meant.

'He's abusive,' I said it for her. She blushed and looked uncomfortable.

'Clara is my great friend. I would never wish to speak of her brother in that way, it would ruin his reputation—'

'*Edith.* Simon's reputation is not your responsibility. And if he wants to treat women like animals, he deserves everything he gets. Though, I doubt he'll ever suffer any punishment.' I narrowed my eyes at her. 'Has he hurt you?'

'No... not really.' Edith frowned. 'He... has been rather too... *ardent*... in his pursuit of me, a few times. I know that I should not accept any invitation to be alone with him, or any man. That would be unseemly.' She pondered something for a moment, clearly unsure whether to say it. 'There have also been... rumours... about Simon, over the years. I had always dismissed them, because...' She trailed off.

'Because, why? He's charming?'

'Yes. I mean, he is a man. He would sometimes, when Clara and I were young, chase us, catch us, and if it was me, fondle me... I told him to stop, but it was high spirits,' Edith said.

'Edith. If he touched you without you saying it was all right, that was assault. And if he continued to do it without your consent, that was also... not all right,' I cautioned her. 'What were the rumours?'

'Clara's lady's maids. She... had a few that left, complaining about Simon.' Edith blushed. This was clearly uncomfortable for her to talk about, not least because she had now witnessed for herself who Simon Favisham really was.

I remembered that Clara had mentioned, back at the hunt, that she didn't have a lady's maid. Now, it was obvious why she didn't.

'You were happy to see him at the ball,' I prompted her. 'What happened, Edith?'

'You had gone to speak with William. We finished dancing and he tried to sequester me into a room alone. There were a few moments until anyone came in, and he... he was ungentlemanly in his actions.'

'Edith. This is important. What did he do?' I leaned forward.

THIRTY-THREE

I could see that Edith was uncomfortable talking about this, but I had to know. And it wasn't fair to Edith for her to keep whatever Simon had done to herself. He didn't deserve to walk around freely without punishment if he had hurt her.

'He... tried to kiss me. I pulled away, so he forced me back against the wall and grabbed my breast. It hurt.' She closed her eyes; I could see the fear that was on her face. 'He pulled up my skirts and put his hand...' She trailed off, unable to say it, but she didn't need to. 'His breath stank. He was drunk. But I feared that he would have gone further if someone hadn't pounded on the door. I was... frightened.'

'Oh, Edith. I'm so sorry,' I breathed.

'You have no need to be sorry, Tegan,' Edith said, quietly. 'You are the only constant I have.'

My heart broke for her.

'I'm so sorry that I wasn't there to protect you.' I felt terrible. I knew that, probably at the moment that Simon Favisham was assaulting Edith, I had been kissing William passionately outside, in the gardens. Guilt filled me with its sick dread.

'It wasn't your fault.' Edith took my hands in hers. She was so small and birdlike that her hands were like a child's.

'I should have been with you.' I shook my head. I should have been there. It was my job to be with Edith, but, instead, I'd let my passions run away with me.

If I'd been in my own time and a friend of mine had confided in me that she was afraid of a man and that he'd been aggressive towards her, we could have reported him to the police. But there was no recourse for women in the same situation in the eighteenth century. In this time, we were chattel, to be owned by men. We had no rights. And no one thought that roughness – or worse – was a big deal. It was just how men were, and we had to put up with it.

I wondered if it was really so different in the modern day. Yes, it was clear that abuse was unacceptable. And yet, I knew that most women still experienced harassment and abuse. It wasn't punished properly, and society still seemed to accept it.

'I don't think that you should consider marrying anyone that you don't feel comfortable with, just because Charles has spent all the family money,' I said, firmly. 'You're not a bargaining tool. You're a person. Your body is not to be traded. Especially not in a marriage to an abusive man. Please don't ever see him again.'

'You are so forthright, Tegan. It takes my breath away.' Edith sighed. 'But you are right. I am not currency. I will have to see him again, in society. But I don't want to marry him. I do want to visit Clara, however.' She gazed up into my eyes pleadingly. 'She is my only other friend, apart from you. I do not wish to lose her.'

'Why don't you send her a note and ask her to meet you in town, or by the coast for a walk? You don't need to go to Penlivet.' I stood up and let go of her hands. 'I'll go and get your breakfast tray, and then we can get prepared. You don't need to make a decision about the marriage until you're ready, either. Have you spoken to William about this? Surely his word is more important than Charles's?'

'Yes. I must find him and speak with him.' Edith nodded. 'Thank you, dear Tegan. I will send a note. What would I do without you?'

'I think you'd be fine, Edith, but I'm happy to help,' I said, and I meant it. Despite the restrictions she lived under, Edith was sensible. She understood more than Charles gave her credit for, and I would have trusted her over him in any situation. But she was also my friend, and a woman in need of support. I paused for a moment.

'Edith? May I ask a favour?' I asked.

I had transcribed the Latin phrases from Evelyn's book onto a piece of paper two nights ago and brought them with me to Edith's room this morning, intending to ask her to translate them. I had decided on a cover story that seemed believable, but now, it didn't feel like the right time to ask. Edith was upset.

However, I needed to know what the Latin meant. My need was pressing, and there was no other way I could think of. I didn't want to ask William, and I couldn't ask Charles.

Edith was my only hope.

'Of course, dear Tegan. Anything.' Edith rubbed at her beautiful, lambent, green-blue eyes and gazed at me kindly. She had such a good heart that the idea that anyone might hurt her made me enraged all over again.

'I... I read some lines of a poem, but they are in Latin, and I don't understand them. I wondered if you could translate?' I asked, handing her the piece of paper. She frowned, and took it from me, opening it and read:

quando luna inter solem et terram transit, ianua aperietur

Portae multae sunt, itinera infinita

Via est tantum paucorum; caute ambula si es donatus, nam lineae potentiae ad caelum et infernum ducunt.

'This is an interesting snippet, my dear. Where did you find this? I don't recognise the poem.' Edith looked at me curiously. 'Is it one of Miss Boyd's unpublished works, I wonder? She had a flair for the mystical, as do I. Although I do not recall her usually writing in Latin.'

'Oh. Yes. That's it.' I nodded, grateful for the idea. I didn't enjoy lying to Edith, but, right now, I had to. 'She gave me an unpublished poem of hers, and I couldn't understand this part.'

'Oh, how *marvellous*!' Edith breathed, turning the paper over in her hands reverently. 'Why, I feel as though Miss Boyd has reached out from beyond the grave to soothe my troubled heart with the balm of poetry.' She sighed. 'Do you think so, Tegan?'

'Perhaps, yes,' I agreed. I felt bad again for misleading Edith, but if the thought gave her some comfort, I wasn't about to take it away. 'What does it mean?' I prompted her, gently.

'*Quando luna inter solem et terram transit, ianua aperietur*,' Edith read aloud. 'That means, when the moon passes between the sun and the earth, the door will open. *Portae multae sunt, itinera infinita*. The doors are many, the paths infinite. And *via est tantum paucorum; caute ambula si es donatus, nam lineae potentiae ad caelum et infernum ducunt*... Hmmm. The way is only for the few; tread carefully if you are gifted, for the lines of power lead to heaven and hell.' She looked up at me. 'Yes. I think that's it.'

'Oh. Wow. Thank you.'

That certainly gave me a lot to think about.

When the moon passes between the sun and the earth, the door will open. That meant that the time portal or whatever it was opened during an eclipse. I thought for a moment: what that line was describing was a solar eclipse, not a lunar one. When the moon passes between the sun and the earth. I was pretty sure that was the definition.

'I would love to see the whole poem, if you would allow it, Tegan.' Edith handed the paper back to me.

'Oh. Of course.' I nodded. Hopefully, I would be able to conveniently forget the poem enough times that Edith would stop thinking about it, or I would leave and the whole matter would be moot.

'You know, seeing those lines gives me a kind of strength,' Edith mused. '*Tread carefully if you are gifted, for the lines of power lead to heaven and hell.* What beautiful words. They seem to mirror my situation, don't you think?'

'Do they?' I asked. Edith had a flair for poetry, but, though I was very fond of her, she also had the ability of the privileged to centre her own experience in more or less anything. However, I had to remember that Edith's privilege was that of a caged bird. Just because the cage was golden and covered in jewels didn't mean that she was free.

'Yes. I feel as though I am a gifted poet and observer of life, and yet I stand on the perilous boundary between heaven and hell,' Edith mused. 'Perhaps that is the burden we as women carry. I greatly admire Mr Milton's *Paradise Lost*, yet he does not consider women's lives and the hell on earth they can be.'

I didn't know what to say to that. I wanted time to consider the translation of those Latin phrases and to think about what they might mean for the time portal.

'Let me go and get your breakfast, Edith,' I excused myself. 'And we can talk more when I return.'

'Thank you, dear Tegan. My soul friend.' Edith smiled wanly, and guilt washed over me once again.

The fact that I had also spent the night before in her brother's arms, a terrible secret that I could never tell her, tore at my conscience. Edith would never understand it, and I knew that on some level I was betraying out friendship, doing whatever I was doing with William.

What was I doing? I was surrendering to a passion that I should have resisted, but couldn't.

Every step that I took towards the kitchens resonated with a combination of guilt and secret, delicious pleasure in my body.

What had happened between William and I the night before had been magical. I still wanted him. I had awoken with the taste of his skin in my mouth and the smell of him in my hair.

Yet, the intense passion between William and I shadowed the friendship between Edith and me. I was doing something I could never tell her, and my own duplicity bruised my heart. Now, as well as that, I was horrified for Edith. She was facing a terrible threat to her safety and her sanity, and I was desperately worried for her.

And then, there was the issue of what William had been doing on the beach the night before. I'd woken up alone in the gatehouse, and then seen him on the beach at the bottom of the cliffs... What was that? William was taking delivery of something, in the middle of the night?

There was only one explanation for what William had been doing, though I balked at the idea. There was only one reason why anyone would go down to the edge of the cliffs on a moonlit night, in the early hours, to meet a boat and unload a mysterious cargo.

It seemed that I had not been the only clandestine meeting in William's diary last night.

William had met some smugglers, and taken something from them. But why?

THIRTY-FOUR

'I'm worried about Edith.' I sat on the side of the bed, watching William as he washed the blood off his knuckles. 'Has she spoken to you about Simon Favisham's marriage proposal?'

'Lord Favisham? No. What proposal?' William glanced at me, frowning.

'You don't know?' I did a double take. I was sure that William must have been involved, as Edith's guardian.

'No.' He shook his head. 'I have hardly been at home.'

I swore under my breath.

'I can't believe Charles hasn't said anything to you. Lord Favisham has proposed to Edith. Charles is putting pressure on Edith to marry him, even though he's an awful man. You can't let it go ahead. Simon Favisham is a brute,' I said, my voice quick with anger. 'He takes advantage of women. Hurts them.'

'What?' William was standing at a wash cabinet in the corner of the room, and I watched as the water he poured from the ceramic jug into the large basin below it grew pinker as he washed his hands. He had a cut on his eyebrow too, and he moved carefully. I'd hardly been able to watch the fight, but I knew he'd taken a few hard blows to the ribs, among other things. 'What are you talking about, Tegan? Simon Favisham is a decent enough fellow.

They are family friends. Simon and Edith have known each other since childhood, though I confess that I never had an inkling he had a softness in his heart for her.'

'William. Listen to me.' I moved off the bed and came to stand before him, taking his wet hands in mine. 'There is no *softness* in Simon Favisham's heart. Please believe me when I tell you that he's already assaulted your sister, and other women. And he plans to somehow gain access to Trevarron House through Edith. I'm *afraid* for her, William. She thinks she has to marry Simon because of Charles's debts. She says that the estate is in financial trouble.'

'She should not be discussing the Trevarron finances.' William's expression was fierce and he was as gruff as usual, but then it softened when he saw the concern in my eyes. 'But... I know that you and Edith are close. Did he really hurt her?'

'Yes. He attacked her at the ball.'

It had been William's suggestion for me to come to the fight with him tonight. He had slipped a note under my door, like before, but this time I'd gone out to meet the carriage at the stables, and lay down inside it as we had ridden up the gravel drive. William had driven the carriage himself, sitting on top and driving the horses. When we had cleared Trevarron House and passed the gates, he'd stopped the carriage, and helped me to sit up beside him.

I couldn't say no. I felt deeply guilty being with him again, but the pull to William in my heart and in the beating pulse between my legs was undeniable. I felt bound to him by a thick, invisible thread of lust and need and want.

I knew that our secret was forbidden and unworkable. I knew that every time I kissed William or met him in private, I was in some way betraying my friendship with Edith, but I couldn't help it.

'Attacked her?' William let go of my hands; I watched as he clenched them into fists. 'She is Lady Trevarron. He would not dare. He is a gentleman.'

'William. Don't be so naïve. He's a predator. Predators don't care about rank and titles. She's a woman; that's all he cares about. And your family money isn't as important as Edith's safety.' I felt that, at least, if I could make William protect Edith, then maybe what we were doing together wouldn't be as bad as I felt it was. It was a way that I could assuage my guilt, and I took it.

'I hardly thought when I brought you here that we'd be discussing my sister.' William's brows furrowed; he began pacing around the room. I was all too aware that just half an hour earlier, he'd beaten his opponent in a bare-knuckle fight. I'd watched through my fingers as he'd grunted heavily, forcing the other man to the sawdust-covered floor and kneeling on his neck.

'It's important. Edith's safety is important. You have to protect her,' I repeated as he came to me and took me in his arms.

'I will protect her. I have always protected her.' He frowned, and kissed me on the tip of my nose. I was surprised by the tender gesture, and warmth flooded through me.

'You never told me why it was so important that Edith didn't know about your fighting.' I gazed up at him. 'You don't care about anyone else knowing. Why Edith?'

He exhaled.

'Do we have to talk about that now?' He stroked my hair. 'I had other plans for this evening.'

It was difficult to focus on anything, being in William's arms. When he held me, I was filled with desire for him. He had a way of making me feel so protected and safe as well as full of a delicious, sweet and wicked lust I had never known before. Even my concern for Edith took a back seat when I was in his arms, looking up into his deep, dark eyes.

Yet, my worry at never being able to return to my own time was growing. I was heartbroken almost every day at the thought that I would never see my aunt again. Never return to the cottage. I had to remember all of that and not get too lost in William, because if I did, I would be lost forever.

'William. Please.' I held back from his touch, just a little.

'Fine. I will tell you,' he growled, and gestured for me to sit on the edge of the bed next to him. 'I can see that your curiosity will not be satisfied otherwise. And I am learning that Miss Tegan Penrose is a challenge mentally as well as physically.' He raised one eyebrow.

'A challenge isn't a bad thing,' I retorted.

'Indeed, no.' He smiled ruefully and took my hand gently in his bruised and bloodied one. 'You know that our parents are no longer with us,' he began. 'My mother died in childbirth with Edith.'

'I knew they had passed. That's so sad.'

'Yes. She was a kind, sweet woman.' William nodded. 'That meant that my father was a widower. It drove him to drink,' he said, shortly.

'I'm sorry,' I said, knowing that it must be difficult for William to talk about this, especially considering his own loss of Elspeth.

'You have nothing to be sorry for, my dear one.' He brought my hand to his lips and kissed my fingers gently. 'However, as Edith grew, our father's drinking got worse, and I believe that he blamed Edith for our mother's death. That was, of course, a terrible belief. But he became violent. With all of us, but it was the worst for Edith.' He sighed deeply.

'What did he do?' Part of me didn't want to know, but I felt compelled to ask.

'He beat her. We tried to stop him, but we were still children,' William grimaced. 'He beat Charles too. I, at least, was able to run away. It was part of the reason I joined the Navy at sixteen.' He bowed his head. 'I still feel guilty for leaving them with him.'

'How old was Edith when you left?' I asked, dreading the thought that now came to mind.

'She was six. Charles was ten.' William closed his eyes.

'Did your father...?' I couldn't bring myself to say it. William nodded.

'I fear so. She and I have never specifically spoken of it. But... I know.' Tears sprang to the corners of his eyes. 'He died when she was fourteen, I was twenty-four. But it was long enough for her to be trapped in a house with him.'

'Oh, William. I'm so sorry.' I could feel his grief as if it was my own.

'So, you see. I have never wanted Edith to know about my fights. She wouldn't understand, and I do not wish to distress her. She is very sensitive to violence of any kind, which is not surprising.' He wiped his eye with the side of his hand. 'I sometimes worry that I am a brute like my father was. I do not wish Edith to think that I am.'

'She doesn't. She adores you.' I stroked his hand gently.

'Then I would not disappoint her,' he insisted. 'Do you understand why I do not want my sister to know of my weakness?'

'Yes. I understand,' I sighed. 'Ironically, in Edith's life, you're the only one who wants to protect her and not hurt her. You do realise that there is no way that she can marry Simon Favisham, don't you?'

'I know,' he nodded.

'You know that he's a man like your father. Cruel. Abusive. He would hurt her. He has already.'

'If he has hurt her, I will kill him,' William growled, his hands balling into fists again.

I had hated watching him fight. I told him that I'd hated it, afterwards. But there was a small part of me that had peered between the gaps of my fingers. A part of me that wanted to see William, bare-chested, slick with sweat, physically dominating another man. He was so strong, so fast and savage in his blows. When he was fighting, it was as if he was another person. There was a demon inside him, driving him to rain down blow upon blow on his opponent, hard, violent hits that would have devastated me.

As much as I hated violence, the thought of Simon Favisham and men like him filled me with rage. I wished I had William's body and boxing skills so that I could beat him into a bloody pulp, which was what he deserved. It was certainly the revenge that Edith deserved. And the lady's maids that he had assaulted, or worse.

There was a part of me that liked it. I wanted to see this primal, animalistic William. Perhaps because I'd felt something of him before, when we'd slept together. And I wanted more.

I knew that I was still in a vulnerable position. I knew that William held all the power between him and me, just like he'd held the horses' reins on the way over in the carriage. But I wanted him, and so when I'd seen the note appear under my door, I'd come.

'Promise me that you'll step in. Help Edith,' I insisted.

'I will talk to her,' he assented.

'And Charles?' I knew that Charles was creating problems and he wouldn't listen to anyone apart from William.

'And Charles.' He nodded. 'Now. Come to me.'

I went willingly. I knew that he wasn't the gruff lord of the manor, and he wasn't the aggressive fighter now, either. I knew that he was the lover who I had shared so much pleasure with before, and I knew that I couldn't keep away from him.

'Does it hurt?' I breathed as I traced my fingertips over his brow; the cut was still a little bloody, and it smeared my skin.

'Not now. Your touch is like honey.' He took my fingertips in his and kissed them softly. 'It's as though you could heal me with your skin on mine.'

'Why did you ask me to come tonight?' I breathed.

'I planned to be away. The public house has decent rooms. I wanted to see you again in private,' he answered gruffly. 'I couldn't wait any longer. All I do is think of you.'

I took in a deep breath.

'I thought about you too. About... last time.'

'What did you think about?' he asked, huskily. He was so close to me now that I could smell his scent; he had washed, but there was still his musky, manly scent that I wanted to wrap around me like a blanket.

'About you... pleasuring me with your mouth,' I murmured, shyly.

He growled in the back of his throat.

'It was a privilege to be allowed to taste your sweet nectar,' he murmured back to me, and my breath caught in my throat. 'I am your servant, Tegan. All I wish is for your pleasure.'

'You very much *aren't* my servant. I'm the servant here.' My rational self wanted to remind him of the power imbalance between us, though I was falling under his spell quickly.

'Perhaps. But, in the bedroom, when it is just us, my job is to serve you and bring you pleasure. In whatever way you want it,' he said, his voice low. 'We can do that in any way. I have always... enjoyed... pleasing a woman.'

I blushed. I wasn't used to men saying things like this to me.

'I... I... There was something else.' My cheeks burned with shame as I recalled how much I had enjoyed being made to call William *my lord and master*. I knew it had been something he'd introduced to our lovemaking; he didn't really require me to call him that, not between us. But when he had instructed me, told me what to do, taken charge, it had turned me on, deeply. I wanted that again. I wanted William to take control.

'What is it, my sweet one?' he asked, kissing me. I gasped as his lips met mine.

Outside, I could hear the crowd that had attended the fight being ushered out of the pub. The noise from below in the street was loud: bickering, braying, drunken shouts and yells. William had been the favourite to win, and I wondered how many people had made or lost money based on his performance tonight.

Yet, inside the small, humble room above the inn, it was just us.

We didn't need much. A fire crackled in the grate, and the flickering flames cast a warm, golden glow over the room, high-lighting the rugged stone walls and the heavy wooden beams over-head. The bed in the middle seemed small to me – I was used to king-size and double beds, and the beds in this time were smaller. But it was enough for the two of us, and covered with a hand-stitched patchwork coverlet. In the corner, the washstand sat next to a simple wooden chair and a wooden coat stand.

'I want...' I trailed off. I didn't know how to say it, but he chuckled, breaking off from the kiss temporarily.

'I know what you want.' He smoothed the fabric of my dress, his hands making their way to my waist.

My heart pounded in my chest, my pulse quickening. He watched me with an intensity that made my breath catch, his gaze dark with longing, his broad shoulders tense, his jaw clenched with restrained desire.

The air between us was woven with anticipation. I knew he wanted me. I felt his hands move to caress my bottom through my skirts. I looked up at him as he pulled me towards him.

'I know what you want, sweet one,' he repeated, his voice thick with desire.

The firelight cast shadows across his chiselled face. He had put a shirt on after the fight, for decency, perhaps, but now it was undone at the collar and hung loosely on his wide shoulders and muscular frame. I could see the definition of the thick, wide muscle in his arms as he reached for me, and feel them when he held me in his grasp.

'Tegan,' he said my name like a prayer, his voice low, rough with need. 'I can't wait anymore. I want it too.'

My heart fluttered at his words, and without thinking, I pressed myself closer to him, my breasts against his chest, my lips brushing his. It was a soft kiss at first, testing, tentative, but the heat grew quickly. William groaned and his lips deepened the kiss as he tugged the fabric of my gown aside to reveal my bare breasts.

'I know that you want permission to be my wet, hot little harlot,' he breathed, pulling the bodice of my dress away. 'I know that you want nothing more than to be taken. To submit to me, here and now.'

I gasped at the sudden rush of warmth that flooded through my body: I was responding to him, responding to his words and his energy and the heat of his touch. My hands moved up to his chest, feeling the steady thrum of his heartbeat beneath my fingertips. He was so strong, so solid. He winced slightly and I remembered his injury, but he held me all the tighter and kissed me, hard.

His lips trailed from my mouth to the curve of my neck, brushing the sensitive skin there. I gasped, arching into him, my breath coming faster as his kisses grew more urgent. His hands slid down to the small of my back, pulling me against him, the heat of his body setting mine aflame. I could feel his need pressing against me, and it made my knees weaken.

'I've waited for this,' William murmured between kisses, his breath warm on my skin. 'Now I'm going to enjoy it. Take off my shirt.'

'Y... yes, sir,' I breathed. He smiled darkly.

'Yes, my lord,' he corrected me. I repeated it.

'Good.'

My hands moved obediently to the hem of his shirt, pushing it over his head to reveal his broad chest. I traced the lines of his muscles, my fingers memorising the smoothness of him, the firmness of his chest. He was already starting to bruise, and I was gentle. Even so, my pulse quickened with every caress.

William lowered his head, kissing me again, this time slow and deep. His hands moved hungrily over my body. There was a raw, untamed longing in him, and I felt myself respond to it. The same longing was in me; it had begun in the gatehouse, and the fire had been raging in me ever since.

My hands moved to the buckle of his belt, my fingers sure and steady. There wasn't any trembling; I knew what I wanted. I loosened his breeches and pushed them down. He kicked them away.

He was totally naked, now, and stared at me with a fierce intensity.

'Kneel before me,' he commanded. I didn't hesitate. His voice was low, but it carried an undeniable authority. I was beginning to realise that authority made me wetter than I had ever known before. Yet, there was something comforting in his command, a reassurance that I was exactly where I was meant to be.

I gazed up at him, my breath catching at the sight of him, so perfect, so strong.

'Yes, my lord.'

William groaned at the sight of me on my knees. His hands slid into my hair; he reached under my chin and tilted my face up to him.

'Do you trust me?' he asked, his voice was steady, though the heat in his gaze betrayed a deeper hunger.

I swallowed, feeling my pulse quicken.

'Yes, my lord,' I whispered.

A small, satisfied smile tugged at the corner of William's mouth as he reached out, his hand grazing my cheek with a tenderness that contrasted with the strength of his presence. 'Good,' he murmured, before his hand slid again to the back of my neck.

I thought I knew what he was about to do, but I was wrong.

I had been kneeling, and he had been standing naked in front of me. If he had told me to take his thick, hard length in my mouth, I would have done it; I was so ready for him. But, instead, he turned me around on my knees and pushed me so that I was bent over the edge of the bed.

Before I could say anything, he parted my legs with both hands. I could hear him take in a breath and let it go as he inspected me.

'Beautiful,' he breathed. 'If only you could see yourself. Pink, gleaming and wet with desire for me,' he murmured. 'My little harlot. Wide open and waiting for me with no shame.'

He leaned over me and I felt his hard body behind me; all muscle. He could crush me if he chose to. Instead, he pushed my head into the coverlet.

'Stay there and don't move,' he commanded. I nodded, mutely. His command made the whole of my abdomen fill with sweetness; I could feel my own wetness had made me slick. It felt as though it was running down my thighs. Somehow, being commanded by William, in the bedroom, was intensely arousing for me. I didn't know why, and, in that moment, I didn't care.

'Good little maid,' he murmured, his voice thick with approval. His hands gripped my wrists gently but firmly and guided them behind my back. He held them there, and for a moment, I felt nothing but the steady pressure of his hands, the weight of his control.

His lips trailed down my neck, warm and possessive.

'You'll stay still for me, won't you?' he repeated.

'Yes,' I breathed. 'Yes, my lord.'

I felt his hand caress my back, my bottom, my thighs, as he held my wrists with his other hand. Then, I felt his fingers slip between my thighs and into my wetness. I gasped at the sensation of his fingers as they stroked me gently. I moaned, and he chuckled.

'You like that,' he said; it was an observation. I nodded, fervently.

'I see,' he mused, and continued stroking me. I moaned louder. I could feel my pleasure start to reach a plateau already; usually, when I touched myself, it would take much longer.

'Hmm.' He stopped stroking me, and, instinctively, I sat up in protest. 'No, you don't.' He pushed my wrists down into the small of my back, reminding me that I was still restrained by his hand. 'Back down you go. You promised not to move, remember? Nod if you remember.'

I nodded, my face smushed into the coverlet. I was desperate to do anything that would make him continue and lead me back to that mountain of pleasure.

'Good. Try to remember how to behave.' His voice was stern, but there was a hint of amusement at the edge of it.

His fingers resumed their gentle touch, sliding and slipping delightfully in my wetness. I moaned and wriggled against his fingers.

'Does the harlot want more?' he asked. I nodded enthusiastically. I wanted him inside me. I wanted to be pushed down by his weight. Just the posture he had me in – leaning forward over the foot of the bed so that my whole body rested on it, completely prone, with my legs spread, was deeply arousing. It was arousing to be so vulnerable, so exposed to him.

I felt him draw back for a moment and then felt a delicious pressure against my opening. I squirmed against him, wanting more, but he placed a hand on the back of my neck.

'Wait,' he muttered. 'Not until I say so.'

I whined like a hungry puppy. He chuckled again.

'Such a needy little girl. She wants it so badly.'

He pushed into me, but just a little. I moaned deeply and pushed my hips back against him.

'More,' I panted.

His breath was heavy. He leaned forward so that his weight was on me, his forehead resting against my back.

'You belong to me tonight, Tegan,' he said, his voice rough with desire. 'And you will obey me.'

'Yes, my lord,' I breathed, as I felt him enter me a little deeper.

'You do not tell me what to do or when to do it,' he continued, pushing slowly inside me. I knew that, despite his words, he was desperate to be inside me as much as I was to feel him.

'No, my lord,' I murmured.

'Apologise,' he commanded.

'I'm sorry, my lord,' I cried out. He pushed a little further inside me.

'So you should be. Beg me for more.'

'Please, sir. Please, my lord. Fill me. I need it,'

I cried out in pleasure as I felt him enter me, deeper and deeper. It felt so good, so right; a combination of comfort and delicious, sweet wickedness. He groaned, his voice gruff with pleasure.

'Is that what you wanted?' he purred, in my ear, and I nodded, enthusiastically, wanting all of him.

'Yes, my lord,' I replied, obediently. He grunted and began pulling himself out of me slowly. The sensation was as good as it had felt going in.

'Hmm. Filthy harlot,' he swore as, when he was all of the way out again, he pushed back in. I thrilled at the indescribable sweetness that his movement built inside me.

The words sent a shiver down my spine, a thrilling rush of heat flooding my body. There was no fear in me, even though he had totally dominated me with his body; even though I was spreadeagled and unable to move.

There was a deep-seated longing in me, a need to give myself completely to him. It wasn't even just sexual. It was something emotional. There was something so deep and primal between William and me; he'd said it before, like we had known each other in other lives. For long years. He seemed to know my body intimately, know what I would like, know what gave me pleasure. Like a husband.

'Yes. Oh, yes, yes,' I whispered, the word falling from my lips like a sacred vow. 'Take me, please, William.'

'As you please, my sweet one,' he muttered, and pushed into me, harder. I moaned loudly. Now, he began moving in and out of me, and my pleasure began to peak; a stream of nonsensical words escaped my mouth.

As my climax came, and the pleasure broke over my whole body like fireworks bursting inside of me, William tensed and groaned, pushing harder into me. I felt his release and revelled in his growls of deep pleasure. We were one being in that moment: my body entangled in his, his breath in my face, his weight on me.

He held me as the reverberations of pleasure continued to shake us, and, finally, we were still.

'Tegan,' he breathed my name reverently. 'Tegan.'

I had no words to give him, but something had crossed the line in me. I knew that something important had happened between us; yes, we'd enjoyed something delicious, but it was more than that. We had connected deeply.

Gently, he helped me to roll over and he gathered me in his arms. We lay together on the bed, him holding me tightly against his chest. I had never felt so loved, so safe, as in that moment. I'd given everything of myself to him, and he had held me.

He continued to hold me.

Neither of us said a word. I closed my eyes and felt all my muscles relax.

Hundreds of years away from where I was supposed to be, I finally felt like I was home.

THIRTY-SIX

In the night, I woke up to find William pacing the floor.

I sat up and rubbed my eyes.

'What is it?' I asked, blearily.

'Go back to sleep,' William said in a low voice.

'Can't you sleep?' I sat up and watched him. He was pacing in a circle, grinding his knuckles together.

'No. I am often wakeful at night. Especially after a fight,' he muttered. I could sense the tension in him. Before, when we'd made love, he had been loving and attentive, totally focused on me. Now, he seemed tense and distracted. 'Pacing helps me.'

'Do you do it often?' I blinked, trying to wake up a little. He nodded.

'Yes. Go back to sleep,' he repeated.

I closed my eyes for a moment, laying back down on the mattress and pulling the blanket over me, but the sound of the creaking floorboards made me open my eyes suddenly and sit up.

'It was you,' I said, realising the truth of my words as I spoke them. 'Outside my door that night.'

He frowned at me and stopped, standing still at the end of the bed.

'What are you talking about? What night?' he asked.

'I woke up in the middle of the night. About a week ago. Someone was walking outside my room. Like they were spying on me or something,' I said.

'No... that wasn't me, my sweet one.' William sat at the end of the bed. 'I have no need to lurk outside your room. Why would I do that?' He looked genuinely confused, then glanced away. 'However...' He sighed. 'You may not think well of me for doing this. But sometimes, when I cannot sleep, I go to the East Wing. I find it helps to be among Elspeth's things.' He paused, and reached out to stroke the curve of my foot. 'At least, I did, until recently.'

Of course. That made total sense. I wondered why I hadn't thought of that already: that it would be William who was pacing in Elspeth's room at night. Who else would it have been?

'The maids thought that it was haunted. That room,' I said, haltingly. 'I thought...'

'Haunted? By whom?' William frowned, and then the realisation dawned. 'They thought it was Elspeth?'

'You forbade them to enter the room, they said.' I nodded. 'They heard the creaking of the floorboards. I think they may have heard... crying,' I said, carefully. 'I suppose they thought it was a kind of ghostly wailing.'

'Oh,' he nodded, looking embarrassed. 'I never think about the servants. What they might hear or think. I suppose they are just... invisible to me, most of the time.' He hung his head. 'You have made me realise how wrong I have been to think in that way.'

'Indeed. They aren't pieces of furniture. They're people,' I said. He nodded, looking down at his hands.

'Tegan, I...' he began. I could see that he wanted to say something, and it was difficult for him.

'You don't have to explain.' I reached for his hand. 'It's all right, William. She was your wife. You lost someone you loved.'

'I know, but... there is something I want to tell you. About Elspeth,' he said, looking up and meeting my eyes.

'Listen, William. I understand if you're still grieving. It takes time,' I replied. 'I guess being in her room makes you feel closer to her memory. I understand.'

'It's not that. Yes, I hung onto Elspeth's memory. Yes, I would sometimes go to her quarters and be among her things,' he said, haltingly. 'But, since we have... become close, I have not... been there. I have not felt the need.'

'I see.' I nestled my head into his chest, and he put his arm around me. 'Come back to bed.'

'You don't hate me, because of it?' he asked, climbing back in bed with me and hugging me close to him.

'How could I ever hate you?' I murmured, muffled, into his chest. *I love you*, I thought, but I couldn't say it. It was too dangerous a thing to say, but I felt it.

'You might, if you knew me better.' His voice rumbled in his chest.

'Why?' I asked, looking up at him. My heart felt raw. 'Why would I ever hate you, William?'

He shook his head and lifted my chin for a kiss.

'It is no matter, my sweet one,' he murmured, gently. 'Sleep now.'

I closed my eyes again, relishing the sweetness of his kiss. As I started to drift off in the warmth of his arms, a thought struck me.

If it hadn't been William outside my door that night, who had been there? And why?

THIRTY-SEVEN

'If Cook finds out I've gone, she'll 'ave my guts for garters,' Betty muttered as she knocked on the door of her mother's house. 'Mother'll do what she can, an' then we've go to go, miss.'

'I know, Betty. I'm grateful for your help.' I gave her a reassuring grin, but my heart was pounding in my chest. I was nervous about seeing a pellar – a witch, really, or a wise woman – but I was also freaking out.

Betty had mentioned that her mother was a pellar when I'd first arrived at Trevarron, and – prompted by her mother – she had given me Evelyn Willcock's journal, which had been very helpful in piecing together what on earth was happening to me and how I'd got here. Of all people, Betty's mother might have some kind of astrological wisdom that would help me. If I could predict when the next eclipse was, then I could go home. So, here we were. I was also curious to meet the woman that was related to Evelyn Willcock. The journal was such a beautiful thing; I wanted to thank Annie Willcock in person for letting me have it.

I felt that if I knew when the next solar or lunar eclipse was going to happen, I could predict when the portal might next work. But that was easier said than done in 1755. There wasn't any handy online astrologer to tell me when it would be, and I didn't know where I could find an ephemeris that would predict what planets would be where at any given time.

I knew that people throughout history had observed eclipses. In the 1500s Christopher Columbus had consulted an almanac to discover an upcoming lunar eclipse and used it to lie to the indigenous people of Jamaica that he and his men had been living off for six months, saying that it was a sign that his god was angry with them for stopping food supplies.

The fact that almanacs presumably still existed somewhere – farmers used them, I thought – encouraged me. So, it was just a case of finding one.

It had been weird, walking into St Nantes, almost three hundred years before I had known it. It had been strange to follow the same country lane that went from the gates of Trevarron House to the little village I knew so well. There were some things that were familiar, but much that was different. Many of the houses I was used to hadn't been built yet. Here and there was a tree I remembered, though three hundred years smaller, but in the main, the woodland was laid out differently.

Cullen's farm was there. I stared at the dirt track through the gates as we walked past it. The barn was different, and the metal shelters for the cattle weren't there, but the farmhouse was more or less the same: a large stone place like I remembered, but now it had a thatched roof.

'Who does that belong to? The farm?' I asked as we strode past.

'Cullen family.' Betty nodded as we walked past. 'The sons're all bastards. I mean, not meanin' they're born on the wrong side o' the blanket, like. I mean, 'tis a bad evenin' if one of 'em decides he's set his cap for ye.' She pulled her lips into a tight line. 'The Cullen lads is partly why Ma was 'appy to see me go into service at the big house,' she added.

'I'm sorry to hear that, Betty,' I said, looking back at the farm as we passed it. I understood what she was saying: that the Cullen boys, whoever they were in that generation, were bad news. Rapists, possibly. Certainly not gentlemen.

It made me sad to think of all the thousands of years that men of all ages, classes and creeds had mistreated women, and society had just let it happen.

I also wasn't that surprised that it had belonged to the same family for so many generations; that was how things were in small Cornish villages, even now, though a lot of the old families had moved away, and a number of the properties in lots of villages had been bought up as holiday homes.

The sad truth of it was that lots of young Cornish folk couldn't afford to buy the property in the villages their families had lived in for generations anymore, and there wasn't much work, unless it was tourist related. I knew that a lot of young people ended up moving away. However, Cullens was still being run as a family business, and St Nantes had always had a thriving, tight community.

There was part of me that was wondering if we would see Aunt Bill's cottage. I knew that it was old, though I didn't know exactly when it had been built. I knew where it was, and I knew that we were walking towards it.

However, when Betty turned off the main street through the village at exactly the point I was so used to, my heart caught in my throat.

Surely, we couldn't be going to the one place I knew so well? To the place that I had considered home for all these years?

As if in a dream, I followed Betty as she led me up the same narrow lane I had walked up and down for as long as I could remember, and up the path to Aunt Bill's front door.

A woman with a kind expression opened it. As she saw her daughter on the doorstep, she let out a surprised cry.

'Elowen! What's this?' she exclaimed. ''Tis not your day off, maid?' Nevertheless, she enveloped her daughter in a warm hug and kissed Betty's cheek. I'd forgotten that Betty was a servant name, and in fact Betty's real name was Elowen.

'No. But this lady wanted to see a pellar, so I brought her to you.' Betty hugged her mother. 'Ma, this is Miss Penrose, Lady

Trevarron's lady's maid. Miss Penrose, this is my Ma, Annie Willcock. Best pellar in north Cornwall.' Betty pronounced her mother's name with pride.

'It's nice to meet you,' I replied, politely, but it was surreal, standing in front of Aunt Bill's front door, almost three hundred years before I'd known it.

The garden was similar to Aunt Bill's, but different. Instead of the roses that climbed up Aunt Bill's trellis and the fragrant lilac and butterfly-attracting buddleia bushes at the front of the house, Annie Willcock's garden was planted with a number of plants that I didn't recognise. It was neat and orderly, but I had the impression that her planting was more for use than ornament. Rows of glossy, dark-leaved plants were staked neatly in rows, but I didn't know what they were. There were other rows of recognisable vegetables: beetroot, onion, carrot tops that flourished in neat squares; in one corner, there were nettles and raspberries.

Next to the door was a large rosemary bush on one side and bay on the other. I knew from Cornish lore that both plants were considered protection for the home, especially planted by doors.

Despite the differences, it was still very definitely Aunt Bill's cosy cottage. The window frames were different; Aunt Bill's had sash windows, and these were smaller, with the kind of lead surround and handmade glass that cottages would have had at this time. The walls were in the original stone, whereas Aunt Bill's had been rendered in white. Smoke flowed merrily from the chimney.

I couldn't believe it. All this time, I had been desperate to get back to my aunt, to my life, to the cottage I'd always thought of as home, and here it was. Suddenly, as if I'd called to it and it had called to me.

I felt a deep pang of homesickness and reached out for the doorframe, feeling suddenly dizzy.

'Best come in, then, miss.' Annie stepped aside, giving me a strange look.

I walked into Yew Tree Cottage with a feeling of mounting dismay.

Inside, it wasn't the same. Aunt Bill's version had a reasonably modern kitchen and utility room. Her front room had all the usual things: a TV, sofas, cabinets, bookshelves. There were basics like electric light and an indoor bathroom that I knew this cottage wouldn't have.

This room was different, but it was cosy and welcoming in its own way. Though it was darker – the smaller windows let in less light – it was still quite charming. The wooden floorboards were bare, but the room was lit by oil lamps and candles, and a pleasantly resinous smell of pine filled the room, along with the smell of woodsmoke which I'd always liked. I guessed that Annie was burning a sweet wood like apple or birch.

A vase of wildflowers stood on a stone mantel over the fireplace, and what looked like an apothecary cabinet sat against the left-hand wall. Each of its little drawers looked to be labelled in the same careful hand: mugwort, rue, elder, hyssop. I wished I could have looked in all the drawers, but that wouldn't have been polite. An array of bowls, jars and bottles stood on the worktop of the cabinet; it was clearly in regular use.

My breath caught in my mouth again as I recognised the inglenook fireplace at the back of the room. In Annie Willcock's front room, the fireplace was the focus, and bundles of drying herbs hung near it. A fire burned behind a metal grate where Aunt Bill's wood burner stood, back in the twenty-first century.

I wanted to cry. I wanted Aunt Bill to walk in and say, *Evenin',* *maid*, and envelop me in a hug like she always did. I wanted to see her, with her curly hair and her undercut, her hippie dress and big boots from being in the garden.

But she wasn't here. I was three hundred years too early.

The room was much more sparsely furnished than Aunt Bill's version of it. There was little to no soft furnishing or ornamental knickknacks. Most things seemed there to serve a purpose: a stool next to a basket of wool halfway through being carded, a table with plates, cups and bowls stacked neatly and a basket containing vegetables next to them.

A wooden dining table and chairs sat to one side of the room, and Annie motioned for me to sit down.

'Now then, miss. 'Ow can I be of service?' Annie sat down opposite me. I'd been so focused on the cottage that I hadn't paid much attention to her, but now I stared at her in fascination. She was probably in her forties, but she looked younger. Her black hair was done up in a neat bun and her complexion was surprisingly clear and unlined, with a healthy flush to her cheeks that looked natural and not rouged. Like everyone in the eighteenth century, her teeth were yellowed and uneven; dentists didn't exist yet, and neither did fluoride toothpaste and electric toothbrushes, never mind dentures, tooth bleaching and veneers. She wore a rough-spun dark-cream linen dress like the one that Cook wore, tied with a brown sash. However, her light blue eyes were kind, and she possessed a kind of bright, impish energy that I warmed to immediately.

'Elowen, love. Get some ale. Your friend looks peaky.' Annie's voice was gentle, with a hint of amusement at its edge.

Elowen nodded, went to a sideboard and poured some liquid from a brown pottery jug into two roughly made pottery cups and handed one to me, setting the other one on the table for her mother. She retreated to sit on a stool to the other side of the fireplace.

'Thank you.' I drank some of the ale gratefully, feeling its warmth help focus me in the moment a bit more.

It was heartbreaking, being in Aunt Bill's cottage without her there. I missed her so badly that it hurt, and now, some kind of invisible force seemed to be taunting me, holding her memory in front of my face, as if to say, *Look how close you can come, and she's still not here. You'll never get back to her.*

I couldn't help but think about the weird time slippage that seemed to happen around Trevarron House and St Nantes; the griffins, the time portal, and now this strange coincidence. Aunt Bill and I had both visited Trevarron House in the past; we'd both slept in the same bedroom, or at least been in it. And now, this.

If there was a ley line running through the village and the

manor house, there was a chance that it lay under Aunt Bill's cottage too. The fact that, of all people, it had been me who had ended up travelling back in time to 1755, made me wonder if there was some kind of energy that I'd absorbed by living in Aunt Bill's cottage in the holidays that made me somehow more drawn to the time portal.

I didn't know. But there were more synchronicities than were really likely. How likely was it that I would travel through time almost three hundred years, only to be taken back to my aunt's house? There was also the curious coincidence that Annie Willcock had passed the journal belonging to her ancestor Evelyn to me, knowing somehow that I would need it. Was I destined to be here, connected to the cottage and whoever lived in it in all times, all realities? There must be a reason I was here. I couldn't help feeling as though Aunt Bill was somewhere behind the scenes, and that feeling was almost worse than anything. The sense, a little like she had died, and as much as I might reach out for her, I'd never see her again.

My throat choked up; I felt as though Aunt Bill might walk through the door at any moment, but there was a terrible grief in knowing that she couldn't.

'Are you all right, my love?' Annie Willcock asked, kindly, and it was all I could do not to burst into tears.

THIRTY-EIGHT

'Betty... Elowen said you are a pellar,' I began, clearing my throat.

'Indeed. Been in the family many years, the knowledge.' Annie nodded. I noticed that she wore a necklace of shells, knotted on a piece of brown leather. She also wore a silk ribbon around her neck, like a choker, which lent her an air of mystery. I knew that the ribbon worn as a choker was in fashion, inspired by Marie Antoinette and the French noblewomen of the day. I was slightly surprised to see a Cornish countrywoman wearing one, but it did suit her.

'Thank you for the book that you sent,' I began. 'It is... intriguing. And beautiful,' I added. 'It must have been in your family a long time.'

'That it be.' Annie nodded. 'Old. Older than myself, but not as old as the hills.' She gave a brief chuckle. 'I trust it has been 'elpful, miss,'

'It's certainly been interesting,' I admitted. 'But what I want to know is how you knew I'd need it.'

'Hmm. A pellar knows things.' Annie shrugged, and lit a fire under the kettle. She set a teapot on the table, took the lid off, and reached into a nearby jar of dried herbs, crumbling them into the pot. 'Elowen said that there was a new lady's maid at the 'ouse, an' that you were different. There was a strange air about you. I consulted the cards, an' they said you needed my 'elp. I rely on my instincts, my bab. My instincts told me you would need to see that book.' She looked up at me with a penetrating gaze. I suddenly felt as though there was nothing I could hide from Annie Willcock.

'I did. Thank you.' I reached into my pocket and pulled out the book. I laid it on the table. 'Here. I brought it back.' I was sad to let go of it, but I knew that the book belonged to Annie and her family. It was an heirloom, a beautiful, personal thing, handmade long ago. I couldn't keep it, and I'd copied out the most important bits of information in it.

'Thankee, miss.' Annie put her hand on the book briefly and smiled. 'I 'ope it was useful.'

'I think so,' I said, wondering how much Annie knew about Trevarron House and the mysteries it contained.

'Hmm,' Annie said, noncommittally, giving me another sharp glance. She went to the kettle and poured the hot water into the teapot. 'I 'spect you'll tell me why you're 'ere in a minute. I be on the edge of my seat.' She raised a sardonic eyebrow. I was reminded again of Aunt Bill, and the familiarity cut into my heart.

'Yes. I wondered if you can help me with something else,' I started, choking back the grief that I couldn't get away from, being here and remembering my aunt. 'I am wondering if you have access to another book, or knowledge of some kind, about when the next lunar or solar eclipses will be. When a shadow passes over the sun or moon, or the sun or moon appears to be aflame,' I clarified, not knowing if Annie would understand what an eclipse was.

'I know what an eclipse is,' Annie replied, slowly. 'What be the reason that you want to know?'

'It's complicated to explain. But if you have an almanac, or something like that, I would be eternally grateful to look at it,' I said. She gave me a long look, and then smiled.

'I 'ave one,' she said, after a pause.

'I'll pay you to look at it!' I exclaimed, suddenly realising that I'd brought coins with me. Mrs Cottingley had brought up my first month's wages in an envelope and I'd stuck it in my pocket without even looking at it. I took it out of the pocket in my cape now and set it on the table. 'Here.'

Annie reached for the envelope and opened it, peering inside. She looked up at me, frowning.

'Miss. This is far too much.' She pushed the envelope back towards me, across the table.

'It's all right. I don't need it,' I said, hurriedly. 'I just need to see the almanac.'

She gave me another long, searching look.

'Lady's maids don't need almanacs, as a rule,' she said, dryly. 'Seems that there's lists in those society papers of all the costume balls an' whatnot, nowadays.'

'It's not for my mistress. Or a costume ball. It's personal,' I replied.

'Personal, she says.' Annie raised an eyebrow. 'If I was a minister, likely I'd be very suspicious of any young woman 'oo 'as *personal* business with an eclipse. But, as I say, I saw in the cards already that you're not a normal young woman, and neither am I. Not as young as you, mind.' She sighed briefly. 'Times're changin', maid. Women like us got to be careful,' she cautioned me. 'Still, if you do really want to give me everythin' that's in that envelope, 'oo am I to argue? 'Tis six months of pellar's earnin's.' She shrugged, and pocketed it.

'Wait there.' She got up and went through a door into another room, returning in a few minutes with a thin pamphlet-type book, and handed it to me. 'There y'are.'

'Thank you, Mrs Willcock.' I took it gratefully. Annie nodded, and watched me as I turned the pages, looking for the astronomical information. Midway through the book, I found what I was looking for.

Even though I was hundreds of years distanced from what the astrologer on my social media had been talking about, I saw that the late summer and early autumn in 1755 also contained a number of eclipses. She'd been right: it was 'eclipse season', and, when I looked along the page, I saw the solar eclipse that had brought me here, and the one that had happened coincidentally when I was in the rose garden. That one had been a lunar eclipse.

Cum luna eclipsatur, chaos regnat. When the moon is eclipsed, chaos reigns.

I shivered. I still didn't know what that meant. But the time slippage had still happened. I didn't know what the chaos the book referred to meant, but if there was even a small chance that the lunar eclipse could somehow facilitate me getting back to my own time, I had to try.

There was another lunar eclipse quite soon: on the coming Saturday. And, after that, there wasn't another for months.

And, then I realised: we had all been invited over to Penlivet, the house belonging to Simon Favisham, that day for dinner.

I swore under my breath.

I'd have to get out of it. There was no way that I could let my one opportunity pass – but I knew what was at stake at that visit. Lord Favisham would demand an answer from Edith, and I knew that she would be all but committing suicide if she said yes. I had to be there to make sure Edith was protected; I cared about her too much to let Simon Favisham have her. I'd failed her once before, at the ball. I couldn't do it again.

This put me in a very difficult position. I had to choose between my loyalty to Edith and my feelings for William, or going home to Aunt Bill and everything that had always been my life.

And I found that I couldn't choose.

'Thank you.' I stood up, passing the book back to Annie. 'I appreciate it very much.'

'Welcome, maid.' Annie gave me a curious look. ''Ere. Pick three cards from the deck. Since you was so generous, like.' She tapped her fingers on a greasy pile of cards next to her. I noticed that the skin on her hands was unusually smooth, like her complexion; I wondered if she had concocted some kind of miracle skin cream, all the way back in 1755.

'Oh, no. Thank you. You've been so kind already,' I demurred, but Annie fixed me with a stern look.

'Three cards,' she said, a little teasingly. 'Din't anyone ever tell ye not to argue wi' a pellar?'

Fine. It would be easier to just do what I was told.

Obediently, I picked up the pack.

'Shuffle it,' Annie ordered. I complied. 'Now' – she took the pack from me and fanned them out on the table in front of her – 'choose three. For your general fortune.'

I did as I was told and chose three cards at random, pulling them out of the deck and putting them to one side.

'Good. Now, turn 'em over.' Annie nodded at the cards. I turned them.

She raised her eyebrows. The cards were what looked like a normal deck of playing cards, but a little bigger, rough-cut around the edges. The colours were different, some of the figures were unusual.

'Hm. 'Tis as I thought' – she pointed to the first card – 'you are from a long way away.'

I nodded.

Further than you know, I thought. *But I am also sitting in my aunt's house. Just, it won't be her house for a long time yet.*

'You're lost. Sad. You want to return.' Annie frowned, tapping the cards. 'But there's an obstacle. Not physical. Somethin' else.' She looked at the final card, and made a face. 'There's a man. He keeps you 'ere... not imprisoned... somethin' else. But—' She pulled two more cards, and laid them over the top of the three.

'Hm. There's danger 'ere, miss. Great danger. You're both in a... It's like a prison, but not... An' you can't get out, except for an act of God.' She shook her head, tapping the last card. 'I never seen such a readin'. It's like...' She took in a deep breath and let it out again. 'All's I can say is, you're both lost, lookin' for each other, always lookin'.'

She looked up at me.

'Do we ever find each other?' I asked. I knew that she was

talking about William and me. We had found each other, and it had felt like we'd done so across time. 'Do we ever stop being lost?'

'Depends, maid' – Annie shook her head – 'depends on you. Not him.'

'What does that mean?' I demanded.

'Dunno. That's what it says. You lead, 'ee follows. Now you found 'im, it's up to you to 'old on.' She picked up the cards and slotted them back in the deck. 'Good luck, is all I can say.'

THIRTY-NINE

We sat in the carriage, bumping along the uneven country lanes to Penlivet House, the Favisham residence. I wondered if I'd ever get used to the sheer bone-juddering discomfort of riding in carriages with no suspension and wooden wheels.

The physical juddering wasn't the only discomfort I was feeling.

Since things had developed with William, life had been very awkward. We had only slept together twice; on paper, it was far too soon for anyone to have caught feelings, but somehow I knew that he *had* – and, my own feelings were much deeper than I wanted to admit. There had been a few occasions in the week since we'd been together at the pub when he had caught my eye, around the house. It had just been moments when we passed on the stairs or in corridors, and I'd curtseyed and let him pass, but the tension between us was palpable.

If he spoke to me at all in public, he was his usual gruff self. He was always grumpy, though never rude with the staff. He spoke to everyone politely, but never with any friendliness. The servants often rolled their eyes behind his back: *Milord is as 'appy as ever,* they'd say. *'Appen that 'is face would never know if 'is heart was happy.* However, they also liked William because he was fair and never asked for anything that he could do himself. Charles, by contrast, they hated, because he was unreasonable and often rang for maids and footmen in the middle of the night to light his fire when it had gone out, or get him more wine.

I was sure that nobody would have been able to tell, from the outside, that anything was going on between us at all. If William spoke to me, he addressed me formally as Miss Penrose, enquired politely yet distantly after my health and, if he needed to, gave me a message for Edith. That was all.

But it was breaking my heart, not being able to go to him. He hadn't summoned me in the past week, and he'd been away for a few days, seeing to business, Mrs Cottingley said. I didn't know what that meant. I hadn't had the chance to question him about the smuggling, if that was indeed what he was doing. He had slipped a note under my door, but it had been brief. *I miss you. I long to have you in my arms again.* But there had been no specific invitation; no more indication that William wanted more secret, private time together.

Yet I felt untethered, unreal, being here, as much as my feelings for William were deepening. And, as nice as the note had been, it had made me see clearly that William called the shots in our relationship. William held all the power about how and when we saw each other, and he always would.

As the carriage bounced along, I realised that my bond to him was as much a prison as a delight. If I stayed here, in 1755, as a lady's maid, William and I could never truly be together. It would always be illicit between us. At best, I would be his secret live-in mistress. At worst, he would discard me when he was tired of what we had, and I'd be cast out of Trevarron House and left to fend for myself. That was unthinkable.

There was also my worry about Edith. I didn't want to leave her in the hands of Simon Favisham.

Edith's face was white. We'd been invited to Penlivet for dinner, but we all knew what the subtext was. Simon Favisham wanted an answer to his proposal.

I knew that Edith and William had spoken privately about it. He had come into her quarters a couple of days after I had told him about the proposal and Edith had asked me to leave. I didn't know exactly what was said, but there were raised voices and when William left, Edith looked like she had been crying.

I didn't want to go. This was the one chance I had to go back through the time portal.

I'd considered pretending to be ill, but in my heart of hearts I couldn't stand the thought of letting Edith go to Penlivet without me. I wouldn't let her walk into an ambush. I had to protect her.

Still, visiting Annie Willcock had put me in a state of shock. It had been so disorienting, being back in Aunt Bill's cottage and yet without her being there, I'd spent every night crying in bed, desperate to go home. I'd dreamed of my aunt walking into the cottage, carrying a basket of fruit from the garden. *Oh. Fancy seein' you here, my pet*, she said, in my dream. *I've missed you.*

I'd wake up from the dream with tears streaming down my face. Being trapped here was taking a toll on my mental health, and I was getting desperate.

William sat on top of the carriage once again; I wondered if he would do it in rainy weather. I guessed that he didn't want to be inside the carriage with me and not know where to look.

I couldn't stop thinking about what Annie had read in my cards.

I *was* lost here. I was more lost than anyone could be: adrift in another timeline where I didn't fit in. But it was what Annie had said about William and I that affected me most. That we had been looking for each other, and now I'd found him, that it would be up to me to hold on to him.

I wondered what that meant, and what danger we were in. I knew that my own misery was getting worse; perhaps that was the danger. That was a bad enough thing.

I also wasn't happy being imprisoned in a small space with Charles again. However, I needn't have worried. He refused to acknowledge me at all, and as soon as the carriage set off, he began lecturing Edith.

'Edith. I cannot defend the fact that you resist accepting Lord Favisham's kind offer of betrothal,' he began as we clattered up the drive. I glared at him, but bit my tongue for the moment. I was a maid, and I was supposed to know my place. Still, Charles made it difficult.

'I am within my rights to consider the offer fully,' Edith demurred, smoothing her skirt nervously. 'William said that I do not need to say yes.'

'William is a fool, then,' Charles scoffed. 'We need the money, Edith. And you are already past marriageable age. Who else will take you?'

'I don't have to get married at all,' Edith argued. 'You don't understand because Simon is your friend. But he is a brute.'

'Brute, indeed,' Charles snorted. 'You women do not know the meaning of the word. Why, when I was in Italy...'

'Was that when you were apprenticed to the first Great Master to take your money, or the second?' I interjected. I couldn't listen to any more of Charles's hateful words. I knew, from what William had told me, that he too had suffered brutality at their father's hands and I felt sympathy for him because of that. It was something that no child should ever experience.

But the fact that he must have known what had happened to Edith, and yet he was still willing to give his sister into Simon Favisham's disgusting, vile hands, filled me with horror. Whatever had happened to Charles had turned him into a cruel man too.

Charles stared at me as if I was something he had just found on the bottom of his shoe.

'Miss Penrose. Perhaps you would remember that you are a lady's maid, and leash that tongue of yours accordingly. And you will call me Lord Charles. Another word out of you and I will have you whipped.' His mean little eyes glinted at me.

'Charles!' Edith cried. 'You cannot be so harsh to Tegan. She is my friend.'

'No, Edith. She is your servant.' Charles looked me up and down cruelly. 'Clara is your friend, and soon to be your sister-in-law. Kindly separate the two in your head. Though' – he grimaced – 'Miss Penrose is an excellent example of how poisonous a spinster can become. See how she speaks to me, a lord, her superior. With no shame.'

'I permit Tegan to speak her mind. Just because we are the fairer sex does not mean that we are mindless, regardless of our age,' Edith argued.

'I advise you not to speak to your new husband in this manner, Edith. It will go badly for you,' Charles replied, looking out of the window.

We drove on in silence. I dearly wanted to tell Charles exactly what I thought of him, but I bit the inside of my cheek. I had to appear as though I understood rank and responsibility, even though the whole concept of being subservient to Charles Trevarron was anathema to me. He was in no way my superior, and it made me furious to think that he thought he was.

'Welcome, welcome, dear ones.' Simon Favisham stood at the doorway of Penlivet House, his arms wide, a delighted smile on his face. He looked for all the world like a genial, pleasant host. I knew that he wasn't, and it was scary how convincing someone like that could be. He'd fooled me, at first; I'd thought he was a friendly, pleasant man, and Edith had thought so too.

Penlivet House was built of weathered granite with slate roofing. It exuded a stern elegance, but where Trevarron had an elegant beauty, Penlivet seemed austere and harsh. I had never visited it in the twenty-first century, but I knew of it. Unlike Trevarron House, it was intact and had become a visitor attraction.

We had followed a long, gravelled drive through windswept moorland and hedgerows of gorse and hawthorn before arriving at the house. The landscape here was similarly more bleak than the land around Trevarron; it was as if all the colour had been drained from the land. I shivered and pulled my shawl around me.

Charles greeted his friend, slapping him on the back, and William followed, helping Edith and then me from the carriage. When he reached out his hand for mine, our eyes met, and it took all of my self-control not to lean forward and kiss him. I could see from his eyes that he too wanted nothing more.

'Lady Trevarron.' Simon bowed deeply as Edith and I followed her brothers into the entrance hall. 'I am so very pleased to see you again. May I say that you are looking remarkably beautiful this evening. As ever.' He kissed her hand.

'Lord Favisham, it is a pleasure,' Edith replied, politely. There was no warmth in her voice, but Simon didn't seem to notice or care.

The entrance hall was dominated by a cavernous hearth, crackling with driftwood and peat, its smoke curling up into an arched chimney. Mullioned windows let in a cold, silver light, and the scent of beeswax and damp stone clung to the walls.

'Dear Clara, come and say hello to our guests.' Clara was dressed in a beautiful blue silk gown with her hair done in ringlet curls, but I felt as though a slight breeze might have knocked her over, she was so slight and wan. Edith hugged her, and I could see relief in her face, presumably because there was at least one friendly presence in the room. Even though she'd insisted that I come, in this setting, I didn't count.

We went into a drawing room where a maid served us wine. I took a glass; if I was expected to tolerate Simon and Charles for an evening, I was going to need something. I looked up to see William watching me from across the room. He nodded politely at me, and then looked away.

He looked very handsome, like he always did. He was dressed in cream breeches, a white shirt and a matching waistcoat and doublet-style jacket in a deep wine red. His black hair was tied back as usual. I wanted to go over to him; to talk to him, touch him, kiss him, but that was very far outside of the bounds of propriety. I was in the dark about what was going to happen tonight. However, I hoped with everything I had that William was going to step in and forbid the wedding.

The room was oak-panelled and hung with faded tapestries and oil portraits of stern-looking men. I wondered if any men in the Favisham family had ever been kind.

'Lady Trevarron.' Simon handed Edith a glass of wine, and smiled charmingly at her. 'I am so happy to see you at Penlivet, but I fear that you have been most cruel over the past weeks. I am heartbroken, and I wish you would put me out of my misery,' he began. I exchanged a look with Edith. I could see that she was growing flushed with anxiety.

It wasn't fair of Simon to put her on the spot as soon as she had entered the house, but I expected nothing less from him. Consent and consideration were just vague ideas to him. In fact, I doubted that consent was a much-talked-about idea at all at this point in time. And to try and make out that Edith was the cruel one and not him, after what he'd done, was awful.

'I don't know what you mean, Lord Favisham,' Edith replied, stalling for time.

'Simon, please. We have known each other long enough, dear Edith. And, as your husband, you do not have to be so formal with me.'

'I have not yet accepted your proposal,' Edith said, quietly. 'You are incorrect to call yourself my husband.'

'Indeed. You make me wait, like a vixen,' Simon continued. 'But you will accept. It is in your interests to do so, and if you do not understand that already, then Charles will explain it to you.' He looked over at Charles for approval. William stood in the corner, silently, his face a mask.

I wanted to say that *vixen* was an insult, but I knew that I couldn't.

'Please be reassured that my sister will accept, Simon,' Charles drawled, drinking his wine in three long gulps. 'It is a formality.'

'I will not accept something I do not want,' Edith said, her voice small. I wanted to hold her hand and tell her that it was all right, that no one was going to hurt her, ever again, but I knew that I couldn't. I could see tears forming in her eyes.

'You will do what I tell you, Edith!' Charles shouted suddenly and threw his wine glass into the fireplace. Clara, Edith and I jumped. 'How dare you defy me!'

Things were getting out of hand and I stared meaningfully at William so that he would intervene. He cleared his throat.

'Perhaps we should let the ladies enjoy the gardens for a moment, Lord Favisham,' he said, his voice gravelly. 'It is such a pleasant afternoon. In the meantime, we can discuss the proposal.'

William didn't make eye contact with me, but walked over to Edith and took her arm.

'My dear,' he said, firmly, with no hint of a smile, 'why don't you and Clara take the air in the gardens with Miss Penrose, and we will see you shortly?' He gave Edith a meaningful look, and Edith took the hint. She nodded, and we left the room.

'I am so very sorry for my brother,' Edith said to Clara as soon as we were in the hallway. She enveloped her friend in a hug, and they stood together for a few moments, holding on to each other as if they were each other's raft.

'I am sorry for mine,' Clara sighed as they parted. 'Miss Penrose, will you join us for a walk? I wish to get away from our brothers for as long as we can.'

I pitied them both: Clara for having to live alongside Simon, and Edith alongside Charles. I wondered what awfulness Clara had had to endure, living with Simon and goodness knows what other male relations. Edith too had certainly suffered deeply and I wished more than anything for her to be safe and protected for the rest of her life. I didn't know if that was likely, however.

Neither of them had any power; both of them were at the mercy of the men around them. I wished that I could transport them both back through time so that they could live lives as modern women and have the choices that they were denied in their own time.

But I couldn't.

FORTY

We walked out into the gardens of Penlivet House.

'This is beautiful, Lady Favisham,' I said as we strolled along a winding path which took us into an artfully tended flower garden. Hollyhocks, foxgloves and daisies swayed in the light breeze between immaculately kept hedges, arranged in concentric square borders. To the right was what looked like a walled garden, and as we walked through its tall wooden door, I gasped as a large courtyard opened around us.

On three sides, wooden arches led off to a different part of the garden. Through one gate I could see fruit trees; through the other, a lawn.

'Thank you. It has been in my family for many generations. Shall we find the fountains?' Clara asked Edith, who smiled warmly.

'Please. Tegan will love to see them.'

Clara took Edith's arm and they walked through the middle archway. I followed, smiling to myself at their obvious fondness for each other. At least there was Clara, in this world of toxic men that Edith had to navigate. At this very moment, I could only assume that William and Charles were making a deal with Simon, and Edith's body was the bargaining tool. I hated the thought.

We had barely begun to talk – Clara and Edith had begun discussing a new book of poetry they had both read and loved – when William strode out of the house, calling out to us. His expression was stormy, and I felt the anxiety that had been roiling in my stomach rise into my throat.

'Edith. Tegan. It is time to leave,' he barked; his tone brooked no disagreement.

'What is it, William?' Edith called out, her brow furrowing. 'We have just arrived! Why would we leave so suddenly?'

'It is time to go,' he replied, holding out his hand to us. His tone was a command. 'Lady Favisham, please accept my apologies for our untimely return to Trevarron House. I trust that you will not think badly of us.'

I desperately wanted to ask what was wrong, but I knew that it would be out of turn to do so. Even though William and I had been so intimate together, in the daytimes, we had to abide by the rules, and that meant that I wasn't expected to address him directly.

However, at that moment, the door that led to the gardens banged open, and Simon Favisham emerged, followed by Charles.

'Trevarron!' Simon bellowed, making Edith, Clara and I jump.

William looked around, scowling. I noticed that his hands curled into fists, and my eyes widened.

'You have made your wishes quite clear, Lord Favisham,' William replied, clearly, but there was fury in his voice. 'As have I. I bid you to allow us to take your leave.'

'I do not allow it. Charles has assured me of a betrothal, and I will take what has been promised!' Simon roared, striding towards where we were standing. Edith and Clara took a few steps backwards. I stood my ground.

'There is no betrothal. Charles spoke in error.' William met Simon's furious glare levelly. 'I advise you to get out of our way, Simon. Charles, we are leaving.'

'We are not! I am staying, and planning to toast our good fortune at uniting our two families!' Charles had followed Simon out and stood to his left like a loyal dog. He looked and sounded just as furious that William was apparently not playing ball with his plan.

Good, I thought, relieved. Whatever had transpired inside the drawing room whilst we'd been outside, it was clear that William had refused the marriage proposal. And, as head of the family, his word was final. For once, I was grateful for the archaic rules that centred all of the family's power in William's hands. Without his approval, there was no way that Edith could be married to Simon Favisham.

'Charles. I am in charge here. I refuse to let this brute take ownership of our sister, and so should you,' William said in a low, furious tone. 'Edith told me that he assaulted her at the ball, and I have made some enquiries as to his good character. It seems that Lord Favisham enjoys hurting women.' He squared up to Simon, who was standing aggressively close to him.

'I see that I am being lectured by the champion of the alehouses.' Simon nodded, smiling, his tone derisive. 'Please do not think that I too do not have my sources of information, Lord Trevarron. Perhaps we both enjoy the company of sluts.' His eyes flickered to me.

'What do you mean by that?' William retorted, following Simon's gaze. I could see that he knew exactly what Simon was suggesting, and that he was deeply offended by it. I also knew that William had kept the secret of his fighting from Edith, and he didn't want her to know. However, I could see from Charles's face that he knew.

'I do not wish to sully the ears of the ladies with your wrongdoing, Lord Trevarron,' Simon replied smoothly. I wanted to punch him in the face. 'I am, at least, a gentleman.'

'You are no such thing!' I cried out, unable to stay silent anymore. 'You attacked Edith at the ball, and I know that you've done much worse! You're a predator and you shouldn't be allowed anywhere near women!'

There was a brief silence while Simon looked me up and down

in surprise. Clearly, he wasn't used to being called out, especially by a woman.

'Kindly muzzle your bitch, Trevarron,' Simon snarled, after a moment. 'I will not be spoken to in such a way by a servant.'

'Tegan. Please.' William shot me a frown, though his voice was even. 'Take Edith to the carriage. I will join you shortly.'

'No!' Edith exclaimed. 'I want to hear this. Lord Favisham, I do not wish to marry you, and I believe that my brother has made my position clear. I wish to know what you meant by calling him a champion of the alehouses. He is no drunk.' Edith looked up at William in consternation. 'William. Is there something that I should know?'

'No, Edith.' William took her hand in both of his and pressed it briefly. 'All is well. Go with Tegan and I will finish up here.'

'No, William.' Edith shook her head. He knew how stubborn she could be; Edith was no walkover, and neither was I. Neither of us had any inclination to get out of the way like good little girls. 'I want to know what's happening here.'

'Ah, my dear Lady Trevarron,' Simon smiled wolfishly. 'Has your brother not told you of his exploits in the alehouses and slums of Cornwall? Why, he is a champion, you should be proud of him.' He brayed an unpleasant laugh as Edith looked in confusion from him to William.

'A champion of what?' Edith asked, confused. 'Alehouses? I don't understand, William.'

'Edith. I didn't want you to think badly of me,' William began, haltingly. 'I... When I was in the Navy, I began to box. After Elspeth died...' He broke off.

'What?' she asked, her eyes wide. 'What did you do, William?'

'I... began competing. Bare-knuckle fighting,' he confessed. 'I did it once and won, and was asked to do it again. I... found solace in it. It is a way for me to cope.'

'Fighting?' Edith's voice wavered.

'He beats other men until they are bloody, Edith,' Charles said, his voice hard and cruel. 'Is this your beloved brother? The great

Lord William De Vere Trevarron? The gentleman you have adored so?'

I could hear the jealousy and peevishness in Charles's voice. How he hated William. I could see that now.

'William... it can't be so. Please tell them they are mistaken,' Edith pleaded with him. Tears started rolling down her cheeks. 'I thought... you were the only one I could trust.'

'You can trust me, Edith.' William took her hands in his; I could see the desperation in his face. This was breaking his heart as much as it was breaking hers. 'It was just a thing I did to help me cope with my grief. I am not a violent man. You know that I would never hurt you,'

I could see how difficult for him this confession was. He had tried hard to keep it from her, but he must have known that it would come out one day.

'Oh, William,' Edith began to cry. 'How could you?' Her shoulders crumpled and I reached for her, enveloping her in a hug. 'I trusted you.'

'You can still trust me, Edith,' William pleaded with her. 'Please.'

'I confess that there were times I wondered where you were going at night – I saw you leave in the carriage more often than I would ever have mentioned – but I assumed it was the work of the estate that took you away. How wrong I was.' Edith wiped her eyes with her sleeve.

'Did you not see his fists, Edith?' Charles sighed loudly. 'Are you so stupid to assume that he wounded himself on a horse, or whatever other unlikely reason he gave you? I have known for a long time that our brother is not the powerful lord he pretends to be. He is little more than a common brawler, and worse. Which is why I deserve to take the lordship of the family over him.' He crossed his arms over his chest defiantly. 'He left us to go to the Navy. He left us with Father. Do you think he deserves your loyalty and love now?'

Edith shook her head. I could see that she didn't know what to think; she was processing everything she had just learned, and it was hard for her.

'How do you think lordship works, Charles?' William snorted. 'You do not just decide that you will take it. I am the older brother. The lordship is mine until I die, when it comes to you. That is the way it has always been. That is the way it will always be. Your dissatisfaction at my decisions have no bearing on the reality.'

'That is as may be, my dear brother' – Charles smiled smugly – 'but if my older brother is convicted of a crime, then I take the lordship.'

'Of what crime?' William scoffed. 'Fighting, even for a prize of money – which I always give away to the poor, incidentally – is not enough of an issue to land me in prison. The magistrate will not be interested in that, believe me.'

'Perhaps you are correct, brother.' Charles nodded. 'But smuggling might. And murder most definitely would.' He raised an eyebrow. 'What do you have to say to that?'

FORTY-ONE

'What?' William spat. 'How dare you utter such an infamous allegation?'

'Easily. Because it is true,' Charles replied, smoothly. 'We all know that, William. Well' – his eyes travelled to me – 'perhaps not all of us.'

I realised suddenly that Charles and Simon both knew about William and my relationship. My stomach lurched.

'Your whore may not be aware of your crimes, brother,' Charles continued, giving me a poisonous glare. 'Though, indeed, she is hardly a rule follower herself. Always slipping out of the house at night for all kinds of lustful, devious errands.'

Edith looked at me warily.

'How dare you. How dare you speak to Tegan in such a manner? And to accuse me of Elspeth's murder?' William raised his voice. His fists clenched tighter in anger. 'You are beyond the pale, sir!'

As I held Charles's hateful gaze, I realised that it was he who had lurked outside my room that night.

'Tegan, is it? Hm. Perhaps I should have been enjoying Tegan's delights all this time, as you were,' he addressed William. 'A whore such as she surely will give away her dubious virtue for mere pennies.'

I shivered. If it had been Charles outside my door that night, then he had come with evil intent and I'd been lucky that he'd walked away when I surprised him by opening the door. I don't know what exactly he intended, but I knew that he perceived me as a threat, and he wanted to hurt me. That was more than enough. I shivered.

William swore, and balled his hands into fists.

'He dares say it because it is the truth, William,' Simon repeated. 'And if you do not allow the marriage between Edith and I, I will be making sure that the magistrate you so confidently believe you have in your pocket, knows about both misdemeanours. Clearly, as my brother-in-law, I would prefer to keep that information to myself and not to trouble him.' He raised an eyebrow. 'It is an open secret both about your fighting and your smuggling ring. The death of your wife was also, as you know, fervently gossiped about at the time.'

William strode toward Simon, but I caught his hand and looked deeply into his eyes as he turned to me.

'William. I know that you didn't hurt Elspeth. You are incapable of it, surely,' I beseeched him, begging him to confirm, once and for all, that he wasn't the monster Simon was trying to paint him as. He wasn't what the rumours said. I knew that he was a good, caring man, even though it was hidden under his natural gruffness.

'Of course I didn't.' His tone softened, briefly, as I touched him. 'My darling. I would never have hurt Elspeth. Just as I would never hurt you.'

I knew, then, that he was telling the truth. I knew it in my heart and my body, just like I had known it was William that I'd dreamed of, all the years before I met him.

'See how he speaks to his whore,' Simon jeered, behind William. William released my hands, pressed them gently, and leaned forward, whispering in my ear. 'Go, please. I would not see you hurt nor hear any more of this filth.'

He turned back to his opponent.

'You have no evidence.' William advanced on Simon, slowly, his tone menacing. 'You cannot blackmail me. I will not allow you to take my sister and abuse her as you have abused others before her. Edith's body and soul are not available for barter, and neither is Trevarron House. I will die before I let you have either.' He delivered it all in a low, careful tone, but every word was heavy with threat. 'I failed to protect her once. Not again,' he added. I felt Edith sob in my arms, and held her tighter.

'Then you will die, or rot in prison. It depends on whether the judge and jury decide on hanging. Surely, they would, for such a heinous crime as murder, even if they overlook the smuggling.' Simon got up close in William's face. 'Such a beautiful young thing. Such a waste. I would have enjoyed sampling her myself, if she was still alive,' he murmured, and William's face twisted in rage.

'William, no!' Edith cried, but it was too late. William couldn't control himself any further, and he lashed out.

William's cravat was loosened, his breath sharp and uneven, eyes alight with a fury that refused to be masked by civility. I knew that there was violence in him. I'd known it since I'd first seen him standing over his opponent, blood dripping from his fists and a look of savage triumph on his face.

He didn't need a weapon to hurt anyone. His fists were more than enough to grind Simon Favisham into a bloody pulp. I wanted him to. For Edith and for all womankind.

His blow met Simon's jaw; I heard the impact as bone met bone, like a scream of a boat's rudder against intractable rock, coming in to shore. Simon recoiled, his eyes watering, but he stayed on his feet.

He unbuttoned his waistcoat and threw it to the ground. He smiled as if nothing were amiss, though his eyes, those pale, calculating orbs, gleamed with something darker.

'So, this is how it must be, Trevarron. A common brawl,' he said, voice languid. 'No great surprise. I always took you for a thug. Your wife knew it.' He wiped blood from his lip.

William moved before the words had finished leaving Simon's mouth. He charged at Simon, shoulder low, slamming him into a nearby tree. He grabbed his fellow lord by the collar and drove his fist into Simon's gut – once, twice, and then again.

'Your mouth will never utter my wife's name again, and I will not stand for you insulting Tegan, either. And you touched Edith when you were not welcome to. I saw her tears. I saw her fear of you. The bruises on her wrist where you forced her. You are the brute, not I,' William growled, his voice ragged. 'And I will see you ruined for it, not the other way around.'

Simon snarled and retaliated, elbowing William hard across the temple and forcing them apart. He grabbed a nearby fallen branch and swung it wide. William ducked, the thick branch smashing into the tree. He tackled Simon once more, and they fell to the ground.

'Misunderstandings are so common, especially with women of her... delicate temperament.' Simon panted, a nasty grin on his face. 'I assure you that I did nothing unusual. Nothing that she should not come to expect as a married woman.'

'You are a beast. You should not be allowed near women at all,' William roared, and wrestled Simon to the ground. 'I have seen plenty of men like you in my years on this earth. You treat women like cattle. You hate them. You never learned how to be a man, and honour a woman as a queen.'

'I bow to no woman. You make yourself a beggar to do so, Trevarron. It's perhaps why you have ended up fucking the servants, like the powerless cuckold you are,' Simon grunted as William struck him in the mouth and crushed his windpipe with the full weight of his forearm.

They fought like animals now – civilised men stripped of everything but rage. Simon was a better fighter than I would have expected, but William was stronger. I could see the heft of his muscle under his jacket and the sheer hard thickness of his thighs as he straddled Simon, pinned him to the ground and started raining blows on him.

'William! No!' Edith cried, and ran over to them. She caught at William's arm as it raised up to strike Simon again. 'Stop it! This isn't the way!'

'Edith. Get away from here,' William growled. 'This isn't for your eyes.'

'Oh, William. How naïve you are.' Simon coughed, his voice reedy from where William had all but choked him. His face was already swollen and bruised, and blood was smeared across his brow and his cheek. 'Thinking you are such a gentleman to shelter your sister from me. When we both know what the realities of the world are. Edith is a spoiled brat. The sooner she weds me, the sooner I can educate her in the ways of the world. Just like you did with Elspeth.'

'I told you not to utter my wife's name,' William said, his voice low and full of hate.

'I will utter exactly what I wish, in my own home,' Simon replied. 'And I will disclose to your whore' – his eyes flickered to me again, and he smiled nastily – 'exactly how Elspeth died, so that she will not make the same mistake of trusting you.'

'You know nothing!' William roared and drove his fist into Simon's face. This time, I heard Simon's nose break. I winced. It was dehumanising to watch, whether Simon deserved the violence or not.

'I know that Elspeth was running to the cove, through the woods, to warn you that the customs men were coming,' Simon said, sounding as if he was choking. He spat out a mouthful of blood. 'She was a good wife, wasn't she? A loyal, sweet girl, and she knew that if customs found out what you were doing, they'd have arrested you. Because you're deep in, up to your neck in backhand deals, aren't you, Trevarron?'

I stared in disbelief at William, but as his eyes met mine, I could see that Simon was right. I saw the naked truth in his shameful gaze. It was true. William hadn't murdered Elspeth, but she had died because of him, nonetheless.

'We all know that you control all of the smuggling business on the north Cornwall coast. It was too big for them to look the other way, and she knew it. She was running to warn you they were coming, and she tripped and fell and hit her head. She'd still be alive if it wasn't for you. And you have to live with that, every single day,' Simon Favisham spluttered. 'See what a man he is, Edith. See what the great William Trevarron really is: a criminal. A brawler. A thief and fraudster.'

I noticed that Charles had stood back from the fight; I wasn't surprised that he was refusing to get involved. He was a coward and a bully. However, I watched as he ran inside the house and returned after a few moments with two of the groomsmen: heavyset men who followed him back to where Simon and William were still fighting.

William yelled out suddenly, sounding like he was in great pain. I ran towards them, but Charles had run back to the fight and was screaming at the groomsmen.

'Pull them apart!' he yelled, in a panic; they looked at each other doubtfully, but then strode in, both of them grabbing William and, with some effort, pulling him off Simon Favisham. It was then that I saw a dagger in Simon's hand. It looked for all the world like something a pirate would use – medium length, with a blade that curved at the end and an elaborate gold handle. The blade wasn't thick, but it looked very sharp. He held it out, as if to threaten William.

William groaned in pain, his hands on his side. His hair had come undone from its neat ponytail and his black curls spilled over his collar.

'You had better leave, Trevarron.' Simon snarled, panting, and wiped his hand over his sweaty brow.

'Take your bitch sister and your whore of a servant and go. And please be sure that I will not forget what has happened here today.' He grimaced, and spat out a tooth.

I was shocked at the obvious change in Simon Favisham. I'd always known – especially from what Edith had told me – that he was an abusive, horrible man, but to see the mask of civility slip so totally, and to watch him and William fight like dogs was upsetting and unnerving. It was so far beyond what I ever expected to see in normal life, and somehow, in this timeline, I expected it even less. I had bought into the illusion, because of the formal speech and the customs and etiquette of the upper classes in the eighteenth century, that life was more genteel here. When in fact it was far more brutal, and now I'd seen exactly how brutal it was.

I led Edith away. She was crying; I pried her away gently from Clara, who held on to her like a raft.

'Please, Clara. Come with us,' Edith whispered. I knew that she feared for the safety of her friend, being left here with Simon and Charles, but Clara shook her head, her eyes wide with fear.

'I must stay,' she murmured. 'Go, quickly.'

I helped Edith to the carriage and helped her inside it, and then, when we were inside and William had jumped up on the roof again, I held her in my arms as we rode back to Trevarron House.

Cum luna eclipsatur, chaos regnat. When the moon is eclipsed, chaos reigns.

Evelyn Willcock's words came back to haunt me as we rode along. It was the day of the lunar eclipse, and she had been right. I thought about her other warning: *Tread carefully if you are gifted, for the lines of power lead to heaven and hell.*

I was, by virtue of my bloodline or my connection to Aunt Bill's cottage, gifted with the power of time travel. I believed that was what Evelyn had meant. Aunt Bill had done it, and so had Evelyn Willcock. I suspected that Annie Willcock may have too.

I had found heaven in William's arms at Trevarron House, but Trevarron also sat on a perilous abyss.

When we reached the end of the gravel drive, a group of armed men was waiting for us.

FORTY-TWO

As soon as I saw the men waiting for William, I knew there was only one way to save him.

'What is the meaning of this?' I heard him cry out as he jumped down from the top of the carriage. But we all knew. Simon Favisham had engineered this whole drama to get what he wanted, and now the constables were going to arrest William and take him away unless I could create a distraction and take him with me back through the time portal.

As far as I knew, it might already have happened. The eclipse was today, but I didn't know if there was a particular time of day the time portal opened. There was still a considerable chance that it wouldn't happen, but I had to try.

And now, it was my only chance to save William. Annie Willcock's words came back to me: *You lead, 'ee follows. Now you found 'im, it's up to you to 'old on.*

I wondered what would have happened if William had assented to the marriage between Edith and Simon. Presumably, Simon and Charles had sent a message to the closest constabulary at the same time as we had left Penlivet to race to Trevarron and arrest William. I knew that a lord's say-so would be enough to arrest anyone in this day and age. I knew from my studies that policing was different in England in the 1700s; Sir Robert Peel would not establish what became the modern police force until 1829, and even then, that had only applied to London until, slowly, different regional police forces had joined up to one national force in the 1850s.

In 1755 there were still informal arrangements, especially in more rural areas like Cornwall, and I'd understood from Betty that there were four local constables that covered quite a large area. There was no standardised training and there was certainly no opportunity for feedback or anything like quality assurance, which basically meant that the local constabulary could do more or less whatever they wanted, without much comeback.

I had to think fast. I had to take charge of this situation, otherwise William would be lost.

'Edith. These men have come to arrest William.' I looked her in the eyes, keeping my voice level. 'We can help him, but you have to follow my lead. All right?'

She nodded, looking frightened, but I knew she was with me.

'All right. We're going to pretend that you're hurt, and that Simon Favisham attacked you.' I reached out for her hair and mussed it. 'You have to look dishevelled,' I explained, and she nodded.

'Rip my dress,' she whispered. 'Here. I'll help you.'

I was taken aback by Edith's fortitude. She had been through so much that it would have been completely reasonable of her to have zoned out, dissociated or had a huge tantrum right then, but, despite it all, she was with me. I loved her already, but I loved her even more for that.

Together, we ripped Edith's bodice and a little of her skirt. I nodded.

'All right. And if you have to, faint,' I said. 'I'm sorry. I'm so sorry for everything, Edith, but this is what we have to do.'

'It's all right. I trust you, Tegan,' she whispered, and my heart went out to her.

She nodded grimly. We could both hear the voices of the men outside rising and getting more agitated.

I got out of the carriage.

'My lord,' I said, clearly and calmly. 'Please assist me. Your sister is most unwell.' I gestured at the carriage where Edith sprawled on the seat.

'What?' William looked at me quizzically. I shot him a meaningful glance.

'Your sister, Lady Trevarron, needs medical attention,' I said, clearly. 'Lord Favisham's blows must have been harder than we thought, for she is faint and I fear she may be losing blood.'

'I see.' I saw from William's eyes that he understood. He was standing a little uncomfortably, but I assumed that he was sore from his fight. 'Please, sirs, assist me in taking my sister to her room. We are returning from Penlivet House where Lady Trevarron was brutally assaulted by Lord Favisham when she refused his advances.'

William leaned into the carriage and picked Edith up in his arms, grunting with the effort. She drooped in them admirably. I would have smiled if the situation wasn't so perilous.

'But Lord Favisham instructed us to come here to arrest you for assault,' the sergeant said, confused. 'It does look as though you have been in a fight, my lord.'

I could see that the constables were unsure about the situation, and that they were uncomfortable with having to arrest William. It wasn't usual for local law enforcement to do anything but defer to lords and ladies, here; in this time, I knew that the gentry could all but do whatever they wanted without fear of reproach or punishment. It was unfair and it was crappy, because it meant that men like Simon Favisham had carte blanche to do whatever they wanted.

But it also meant that these local constables didn't feel right about arresting William, and we could make that work to our benefit.

I knew that I had to play on their insecurities and the lack of information as effectively as I could, and that the best way to do this would be to awaken their deference to class, and their protective instinct as men.

'Lord Trevarron was engaged in a fight, sir.' I nodded deferentially. 'But he was merely protecting his sister, Lady Trevarron's honour.' I looked down meekly for a moment. 'Please excuse my indelicate comments. It is very upsetting for all of us, and Lady Trevarron being such a frail creature. As her lady's maid I am deeply concerned for her wellbeing.'

'Ah. Right y'are.' The older constable nodded. 'Let me get the doors for you, Lord Trevarron, while you take your sister to her quarters. Perhaps you would like to send for a doctor, miss.' He nodded, and I curtseyed thankfully.

'Yes, of course, sir. Thank you for your kindness,' I gushed, and ran inside. William followed me, carrying Edith.

'If you would like to wait in the drawing room, officers, I will return directly, and we can discuss the matter at hand,' William said, his tone businesslike and in control. I thanked God silently for his life of being lord of the manor and bossing people around like he owned them – and the way that they accepted it.

They nodded and sat down. I supposed that there was no thought in their heads that he would run away.

But that was exactly what I was going to tell him to do.

FORTY-THREE

'Don't say anything. Just listen to me,' I said to him as soon as the three of us were alone and up the back stairs to Edith's quarters.

'What on earth is going on?' William hissed. Edith opened her eyes and sat up in his arms.

'William. You can let me go now,' she said in a low voice. 'Tegan engineered all of this. I'm perfectly fine.'

He set her carefully on the floor at the top of the stairs and leaned against the wall for a moment with his hand on his side. Suddenly, I realised that he looked uncharacteristically pale.

'William. Are you all right?' I asked, but he waved away my concerns impatiently.

'I am well. What was this pretence for?' he hissed.

'Listen. You need to get away. Fast,' I whispered. 'We don't have much time. The constables are going to take you otherwise.'

'They would not dare!' William began, but I shushed him.

'William. Don't be so naïve. You are in danger.' I took both of his hands in mine. 'Simon Favisham has played you.' William looked askance at me. 'He has deceived you and lied to the constables,' I explained, remembering to use phrases he would understand. 'You can't just bluster your way out of this.'

'Tegan is right,' Edith whispered. 'Simon is furious. There is no knowing what he will do.'

'I didn't kill Elspeth, Edith. You have to believe me,' he took his sister's hand, but she nodded, quickly.

'I do. And I know that you would never hurt anyone unless they deserved it, or, presumably, as in the case of your boxing matches, agreed to be there.' She gave her brother a sad smile that tugged at my heart. 'I know you did your best, when we were young. There is nobody to blame for what happened except Father. And he is dead.'

William nodded. He reached for her and enveloped her in a hug.

They stood together for a moment, their foreheads touching. William was bent forwards, his arms around her. Edith was so petite, compared to him.

'I'll have to send for the doctor for you, Edith.' I didn't want to interrupt them, but I knew that we had no time. 'Get into bed and I'll get Betty to come and wait on you. Complain of a headache, and show the doctor your bruises.' I raised my eyebrow at her. 'It's not like Simon Favisham didn't give you those.'

She looked unsure. 'But I have had them since the ball.'

'Doctors are men: make him feel sorry for you. Play up the vulnerable woman card. Tell him the truth; that Simon assaulted you at the ball and he went for you again today. He can have hit you and it won't show for a few days. Act faint and dizzy,' I instructed her. She nodded.

'What will you do? They cannot arrest William.' She looked at us both, wide-eyed.

'I'm afraid that they can.' I frowned. 'William, I believe that you didn't murder Elspeth. But I know that you are involved in smuggling. And the bare-knuckle fighting won't help you to look innocent. Simon Favisham is an evil bastard. But he knows that he can have you up on charges just on his say-so, and circumstantial evidence. The rumours are there. And if people know that you have this... violence in you, they'll make assumptions about you. It could go very wrong for you.'

I knew that would happen if William didn't leave now. Aunt Bill had told me the story. The police had come to arrest Lord Trevarron after he was accused of murder, but he disappeared.

'They will arrest you,' I said, calm and clear so that he would hear me. 'I know that they will. And I know that you have to leave...' I held him to me briefly in a tight embrace and then released him. 'Now.'

After all my sneaking around the grounds at nighttime, I had come across a few different ways in and out of Trevarron House, and, after scrawling a note for Betty and leaving it with Edith, telling her to ring for a servant in ten minutes, I led William down the back stairs from Edith's quarters and out of a narrow door onto the side of the house. He raised an eyebrow at our route, but said nothing. I assumed that he must have known all the secret ways in and out of the house; he had lived in it most of his life.

Once we were outside, I clung to him for a moment. It was too hard to say goodbye; I felt very deeply that we were supposed to be together. Our souls had called to each other across time. We had dreamed of each other. For some reason, we had been brought here, at Trevarron House, together, even though we were born three hundred years apart from each other.

But I had to let him go.

William pulled me to him and kissed me hard, fiercely, passionately. I kissed him back just as feverishly. I couldn't believe that this was the last time I would see him, but it couldn't be any other way.

'Come with me,' he panted, breaking off the kiss. 'We can go somewhere for a while, then come back... put things to rights. I have a good family lawyer. I'm sure that some sense can come of all of this.'

'I can't go with you. You have to leave,' I repeated.

'Why can't you come with me?' He frowned. 'Please, Tegan. I can't lose you.' He reached for me again and held me tight.

I couldn't explain it to him. I couldn't explain that I had one chance to get back to my own time, and every second that I'd spent away from Trevarron House and the rose garden today had endangered my chances of getting back.

There was no time to explain. He had to go now, and so did I.

I could hear voices coming around the side of the house; the sound of running feet.

'I'll find you,' I murmured in his ear. 'Go to the gatehouse. I'll find you.'

It was a lie, but it was the only way that I could get him to go. He nodded, and started to run. I noticed that he was clutching at his side, but he made it to the trees and under cover, and I hid behind a row of rose bushes just as the constables ran by.

When I was sure that there was no one else coming, I ran to the rose garden.

The almanac had said that the moment of the lunar eclipse was actually 6.47 p.m., though it would be visible for hours. I guessed that it was a process that lasted a while. I'd been nervous about going to Penlivet that day in case we couldn't get back in time, but I'd had to go; Edith had needed me, and I was glad I had.

I knew that the time was almost right, and if I missed the moment that our two timelines aligned, I would be stuck in the eighteenth century. I knew that a lunar eclipse opened the portal, but I wasn't sure that it would return me to the twenty-first century. Maybe it would, and the chaos that Evelyn Willcock had referred to had already happened that day. Or maybe the nature of the time portal under a lunar eclipse meant that its results were chaotic, and the timelines could go anywhere.

It was a huge risk, but I didn't have another choice.

I also knew from Aunt Bill that William — because he had to be the lord she had been talking about — had disappeared mysteriously after being accused of murder, and had never been brought to trial. Hopefully, that meant he would get away safely.

The rose garden was deserted. It usually was, but I lived in fear of going one day and finding some of the maids there. I looked up fearfully at the grand clock that sat atop the tower on top of Trevarron House. It was almost time.

It was coming. I could sense the slowing of the moments around us. The leaves of the rose bushes stopped their gentle movement. It grew darker around us, and the sounds of the house, in the background, began to dampen.

The view through the gateway dimmed, and I saw the slip happen. For one moment, Trevarron House was there: complete and undamaged. Then, the blurring of images, which made me feel as though I had to rub my eyes. For a few brief moments, both houses existed. Trevarron was as it had been in William's time, and as it was in my time, at once.

I had walked into the rose garden through the far gate, and was standing at the centre, by the water fountain. I remembered how the water had slowed, before.

'Tegan!'

I turned around in alarm, only to find William limping into the rose garden.

'William! What are you doing?' I ran to him. The whole side of his shirt was soaked in blood.

'I... I couldn't lose... you,' he panted. His face was deathly white.

'I told you I'd meet you at the gatehouse,' I said, but he shook his head, smiling.

'I... knew... you wouldn't. I had a... premonition...' He coughed, and his shirt darkened further. I opened it and saw a terrible gash on his abdomen. 'I knew you would be here.'

'Oh, no.' I swore under my breath as I peeled back his waist-coat to see a larger bloodstain spreading on his white shirt.

'It's nothing,' William muttered, but I ignored him.

'It's not nothing.' I'd seen Simon holding the dagger, but assumed that he hadn't actually used it. And, since William had ridden on top of the carriage as he usually did on the way back, I hadn't seen how bad it was. He'd run away from the constables.

I had assumed he would be all right, because William fought all the time and he was always all right.

Until now.

'William. This is bad. You need to get it seen to.'

'I ... am ... fine.' He could barely speak.

'You have to listen to me. We don't have much time.' I could hear loud voices approaching. 'When we first met in the rose garden, I hadn't been set upon by highwaymen,' I began, as clearly as I could. 'I wasn't sent here as Edith's new lady's maid. I'm not who you think I am.'

'Then who are you?' William panted. 'Why should I believe you?' He was struggling to stand.

'There's no time to explain.' I couldn't tell him now that I was from another time, that time travel was possible, that, in the twenty-first century, Trevarron House had been a burnt-out ruin for a long time. That I was a modern woman, educated, vaccinated, independent, able to vote and work and have relationships with whoever I wanted, whenever I wanted, without being married.

I remembered Annie Willcock's words to me. *There's danger 'ere, miss. Great danger. You're both in a... It's like a prison, but not... An' you can't get out, except for an act of God. You're both lost, lookin' for each other.*

'Because you know it's true,' I said. I looked him squarely in the eyes. 'You dreamed of me for years, and then I appeared one day, out of the blue. I dreamed of you too. I never told you that. But I did. I dreamed of that exact spot at the edge of the gardens, on top of the cliffs, looking down to the sea. It was sunset. And you were in silhouette, always. And it wasn't until I stood there with you and I saw your profile... and I *felt* you. And I knew you were the one I had been dreaming about, all of my life,' I finished, breathlessly.

'I didn't know that you dreamed of me too,' he said in a low voice; he held on to the gatepost of the rose garden to help him stand. I knew that the moment was almost here; it was less than a minute before the time slippage would occur.

I took his hand in mine.

'Please, William. Please trust me,' I pleaded. 'I know it's a lot to take in. But you have to believe me.'

'No,' he whispered. 'I can't trust you. Not after you lied to me, all this time. You betrayed me.'

'What do you mean?' I asked, aghast.

'We were so intimate. I shared things with you I would never have shared with anyone else. There are things you know about me that no one else has ever known.' He coughed, and wiped a smear of blood from the side of his mouth. 'I trusted you, Tegan. But it seems that you didn't trust me. This whole time, you weren't who I thought you were.'

'William. Please. Come with me.' I held out my hand to him. Time was slowing all around us. William stared in confusion at the changing vision through the gate.

'What? I don't understand,' he murmured.

'William! You have to come with me now! It's your only chance!' I cried, and wrenched his arm, pulling him with me towards the gate. I couldn't miss it this time. This time, I had to go back, and he had to come with me.

'No!' he cried out, pulling away. 'I don't know what this is, Tegan. What is happening?'

'You have to come with me, William. Trust me! Please! You won't be safe, otherwise!'

'I won't! I can't!' He shook his head and stepped backwards. I watched, in slow motion, as the constables ran into the rose garden and took hold of him. I could see that they were shouting at him, but I couldn't hear their voices anymore. Everything was slow and nightmarish.

'William, please!' I cried out, as I stepped into the gateway.

I felt the energy of being between times take me. It was like being ripped in two. I felt nauseous, dizzy, discombobulated. I tried to keep my eyes open, to reach out for William, to call to him, but a sudden light blinded me: it was like trying to look into the sun.

I shielded my eyes against the light. I had a sudden vision of my dream: of standing on the rock on the cliff, looking out over the sea as the sun set in hues of deep pink and orange. Of William, next to me.

But the last thing I saw was William's tortured face as he was pulled away.

Cum luna eclipsatur, chaos regnat. When the moon is eclipsed, chaos reigns.

I felt myself losing consciousness. I felt the touch of his fingers on mine, and then there was nothing.

A LETTER FROM THE AUTHOR

Dear reader,

Huge thanks for reading *An Ocean of Time*! I hope you were hooked by Tegan and William's story.

If you want to join other readers in hearing all about my new releases and bonus content, you can sign up here:

www.stormpublishing.co/kennedy-kerr

If you enjoyed this book and could spare a few moments to leave a review, that would be hugely appreciated. Even a short review can make all the difference in encouraging a reader to discover my books for the first time. Thank you so much!

I am a huge fan of time slip romances and I thoroughly enjoyed creating Trevarron House and all its characters. I wanted to write a lush, romantic story about two people who are fated to be together, their destiny linked through time. I love north Cornwall and, having grown up in the West Country, have always found it to be a truly special and magical area, full of breathtaking landscapes, high black cliffs and dramatic, crashing waves. Cornwall's beautiful old manor houses, the mythical tales of King Arthur at Tintagel and the region's history of smuggling all came together to make a backdrop of intrigue, romance and mystery for this story to evolve inside.

I also wanted to write about women in history, and think about how women like Edith Trevarron might have lived, and the challenges they faced. As much as *An Ocean of Time* is about Tegan and William and their unshakeable bond, it is also a story about Edith and the choices – or, lack of choices – she faced, but also the resilience that she shows, and the efforts she makes to be a part of the world around her through being an avid reader and thinker, even though men like Charles and Simon try to make her stay small. Sadly, even now, women often face the same kind of brutality that Edith is forced to endure.

However, I also wanted to present an alternative experience: Aunt Bill and the Willcock women are all strong and independent – unmarried, living alone, helping their community, having knowledge of the secret magic of the time portal and coming and going into the past at will. Tegan's initiation into this group of women is empowering, as is the flowering of her sensual nature with William. I think it's possible (and indeed preferable) to write a romance that empowers women. Tegan never loses herself with William, but she enjoys him, enjoys their lovemaking and experiences the overpowering feeling of meeting her soulmate, across time.

Thanks again for being part of this amazing journey with me and I hope you'll stay in touch – I have so many more stories and ideas to entertain you with!

Kennedy Kerr

www.kennedykerr.com

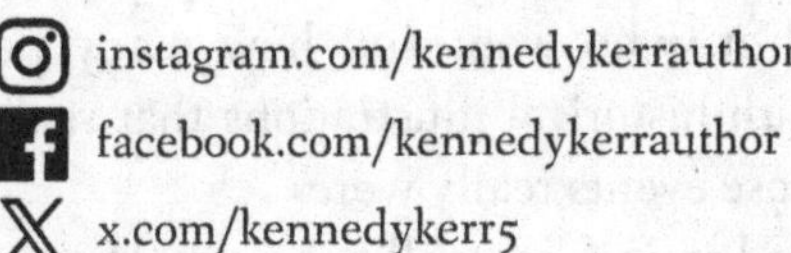

instagram.com/kennedykerrauthor
facebook.com/kennedykerrauthor
x.com/kennedykerr5

AUTHOR'S NOTE

My vision for Trevarron House was based on Polesden Lacey, a National Trust property in Surrey in the UK, and Pencarrow House in Cornwall, though I was also inspired by the beautiful gardens and interiors of Arundel Castle. Polesden Lacey was in fact only built in 1824 and was owned from 1906 by Margaret Greville, a socialite who was friends with King Edward and Queen Elizabeth. However, it has a sense of the grandeur I needed for Trevarron House, and I based Trevarron's gardens almost exactly on Polesden, particularly its stunning rose garden.

I am indebted to Geri Walton's brilliant online resource regarding masquerade balls in the eighteenth century, which details the types of costumes that were popular, the venues the balls were held at, who went and how many people tended to attend, along with historical illustrations that really give a flavour of how lavish those events really were.

The Jamaica Inn in Cornwall has a whole museum devoted to the subject of smuggling which is well worth a visit (as is their Daphne du Maurier museum, as well as restaurant, tea room and gift shop!) and in which I learned about the extent of smuggling in Cornwall in the eighteenth century, the reasons for it (high taxes on essentials) as well as the important takeaway that most Cornish smugglers were considered gentlemanly.

Elizabeth Boyd was a real person. Born in 1710 and died in 1745, she was an English writer and poet who supported her family by writing novels, poetry, a play, and a periodical. Boyd is one of three known members of the Shakespeare Ladies' Club, a group that campaigned to have more Shakespeare plays presented in London theatres. *The Snail: Or the Lady's Lucubrations* (1745), which Edith reads in this book, was an ambitious project to produce a regular periodical aimed at aristocratic ladies. Only one volume was produced and there is an indication in her writing that her health was failing. Elizabeth represented the kind of 'literary lady' of the time that I felt someone like Edith Trevarron would have known about and emulated.

Edith herself I based somewhat on the poet Dame Edith Sitwell, who belonged to an aristocratic family and had two brothers, Osbert and Sacheverell, who were also writers. However, to my knowledge, Edith was not restrained in any way as Edith Trevarron is, and, living at a different time period to my Edith (1887–1964) and in different circumstances, enjoyed a successful literary career and independent life. The Sitwells were also close as siblings.

Edith Sitwell, like Edith Trevarron, had a largely unhappy early childhood and love life, but remained a larger-than-life character, dressing flamboyantly and keeping a literary circle. The Sitwells' family residence is Renishaw Hall in Sheffield, England.

On the subject of ley lines – the concept of mystical lines that run through the earth – this only became popular in the late nineteenth and early twentieth centuries. However, it is predated by an ancient feng shui concept of 'dragon lines' – the idea that certain parts of China are rich in 'qi' or life force, and that these areas – usually mountains – are lined by lines, like pathways or veins. I wanted Trevarron House to be sited on the crossing of two mystical ley lines, as legend says exists under places such as Glastonbury

Tor in the UK. I thought that this would provide Trevarron with its special time-bending capabilities and mark it out as a special place.

As such, though it would be slightly unlikely that anyone in 1600s or 1700s Cornwall would have been aware of the idea, it could possibly have been the case that a keen reader might have been privy to some archaic documents, folios or knowledge of this kind. They might also have had even had a mystical reveal of that knowledge from a supernatural or angelic force, as has been documented in many lives of saints and other mystics, such as Mikao Usui, the founder of the Japanese healing method of Reiki, who reportedly 'received' Reiki as a technology and an energy on a twenty-one-day meditation on Mount Kurama. I thought that it might be possible that Evelyn Willcock and her family, as pellars – practitioners of the Cornish tradition of folk magic, herbalism and fortune telling – would know of the idea of ley lines through their own mystical experiences and perhaps some research from arcane sources. However, on this subject, I beg the reader's discretion and slight suspension of disbelief.